Dark Water

Dark Ship

Dark Horse

Dark Shadows

Dark Paradise

Dark Fury

Dark Hunt

Dark Path

Dark Prey

Dark Prey

© 2021 Evan Graver

www.evangraver.com

All rights reserved. No part of this publication may be reproduced, distributed, or transmitted in any forms or by any means, including photocopying, recording, or other electronic, or mechanical methods, without the prior written permission of the publisher, except in the case of brief quotations embodied in critical reviews and certain noncommercial uses permitted by copyright law.

ISBN-13: 978-1-7365521-0-0

Cover: Wicked Good Book Covers

Editing: Novel Approach Manuscript Services

This is a work of fiction. Any resemblance to any person, living or dead, business, companies, institutions, events, or locales is entirely coincidental.

Printed and bound in the United States of America

First Printed February 2021

Published by Third Reef Publishing, LLC

Hollywood, Florida

www.thirdreefpublishing.com

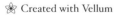 Created with Vellum

DARK PREY

A Ryan Weller Thriller

EVAN GRAVER

"Water shapes its course according to the nature of the ground over which it flows;
The soldier works out his victory in relation to the foe whom he is facing.
Therefore, just as water retains no constant shape, so in warfare there are no constant conditions.
He who can modify his tactics in relation to his opponent and thereby succeed in winning, may be called a heaven-born captain."

Sun Tzu, The Art of War

CHAPTER ONE

Wrightsville Beach
North Carolina

It was the perfect night for thievery.

With no moon, the night was darker than most as the fifteen-foot inflatable boat coasted through the water. Tim Davis sat on the port tube by the transom, one hand on the thirty-horsepower Mercury outboard. It was overkill for this little boat, but when they had to run, it was best to have too much than not enough.

For now, Tim held the throttle just above idle as the boat cut almost noiselessly through the marsh just off the Intracoastal Waterway, what many referred to as the ICW or 'The Ditch.' Their target was Motts Channel Marina, where Tim and the two young men with him would steal electronics, outboards, cash, and other items as they vandalized the sportfishers, sailboats, and runabouts tied to the docks.

"Ready, boys?" Tim hissed, just loud enough for the two men to hear over the burbling motor.

John and Patrick Jefferies—otherwise known as John Jeff and P.J.—both nodded. The two looked more like twins than brothers born two years apart. They were both wiry, with long limbs and shoulder-length blond hair. Tonight, they wore black hoodies and cargo pants stuffed with tools to aid in their plundering.

Tim guided the boat into the marina and circled around, dropping John Jeff at the dock closest to shore. P.J. hopped out onto the middle dock, and Tim tied the inflatable to the concrete pier that formed the protective seawall. His first target was a massive Billy Holton Custom Carolina sportfisher.

Tim was up the bridge ladder in a matter of seconds. Using a screwdriver, he made quick work of prying the instruments from the console and overhead mounts then used side-cutting pliers to slash through the wires. Tim piled the depth sounder, chart plotter, GPS, and radar screens into the inflatable, then returned for the VHF, the satellite radio, and the speakers.

It didn't take long for the inflatable to fill with gear after Tim hit two more boats. He checked his watch and motored into the marina. Holding the boat in place at the end of the middle dock, Tim watched P.J. pile his own assortment of stolen objects in the inflatable.

As they pushed off to collect John Jeff, a spotlight snapped on, centering Tim and his accomplice in its beam, and a voice boomed over a loudspeaker, "Stop! You are under arrest."

Tim blinked multiple times, looking at John Jeff, silhouetted in the light. A long time ago, the boys had decided that if one of them got caught, the others would run. There was no sense in all of them being swept up by the pigs. Without another thought for his companion, Tim spun the tiny boat around and rolled the throttle open to the stop. The front end leaped up, and P.J. scrambled forward to act as a counterweight. Waves slapped the boat's hard-plastic bottom as it zipped across the water.

There were only so many places they could hide. Every water channel led back to the Intracoastal, and Tim figured marine units were converging on their position if the cops were already at the docks. His only choice was to hide in the shallow channels that cut through the marsh islands between the mainland and the outer barrier island. The lights of Wrightsville Beach provided scant illumination on the black water.

Cutting the engine as they rounded a spit of land and entered a small tidal creek, Tim hunched low in the boat. P.J. lay on the nose of the inflatable, giving directions. A police boat raced past them, blue and red lights flashing in the light bar mounted on the T-top of the center console. Tim knew they liked to hunt in pairs. Somewhere out there was another patrol boat, searching for them.

Tim craned his neck to see around P.J. and gauge their position in the tidal river. Fortunately, the tide was coming in, providing more clearance between the bottom of the inflatable and the sticky mud and sand. He was thankful they had added a hard-plastic bottom to the boat, otherwise the razor-like oyster shells could slice the PVC hull open like a fat chick opening a bag of potato chips.

Suddenly, P.J. held up a hand in a fist, and Tim jerked the motor's lanyard, killing it. They drifted forward, the marine patrols racing all around them. Tim felt his heart thundering in his chest, and his hands were damp with sweat despite the cool November air.

From the moment he'd started this venture, Tim had known that he'd get caught. It was just a matter of time.

He considered dumping the electronics overboard and hauling ass south to where they'd left his pickup truck. *Screw the duck*! He couldn't get caught now. Not with everything on board. It would mean a long stint in Bertie Correctional Institution up in Windsor. *Two strikes*. Tim cursed under his breath.

"I think we're good," P.J. whispered.

Tim nodded and fitted the lanyard in the outboard and jerked the starter rope. The motor purred in the darkness, but to Tim's ears, it sounded like a locomotive screaming through the night. He eased the throttle forward. As they approached the mouth of the tidal creek, P.J. stood and looked in both directions, then signaled Tim to go right.

"What the hell?" Tim muttered. His truck was south, not north. Then he saw the fast-approaching patrol boat. He rolled the throttle open and the inflatable jumped forward, knocking P.J. off balance and dumping him on top of the electronics.

They shot north along the ICW, heading toward the C. Heide Trask Bridge and the cop cars lying in wait on it. Tim's heart sank, knowing they were being boxed in by the police.

He had to fight. He wasn't going back to jail.

With the marine patrol gaining on him from behind, his hand involuntarily tried to open the throttle farther, but it was already at its stop. The extra weight of the stolen goods helped keep the boat stable, but it was still a choppy ride as the PVC tubes flexed under speed.

The bridge was just ahead. If he could get under it, maybe he could disappear into the islands again. If he stayed on the main channel, it was a run of over four miles to the Mason Inlet and the Middle Sound marsh. His optimistic side loved a good chase, but in his heart, Tim knew they would never make it.

"P.J.," Tim called over the rush of wind. "Get ready to roll off."

From the bow, P.J. gave a thumbs-up, then spread himself out along the port side tube. Tim fought to bleed the last few horsepower from the outboard as he maneuvered toward the left side of the channel, closer to the docks and marinas that lined the Intracoastal Waterway just south of the bridge. He chopped the throttle, and P.J. rolled off, his arms crossed over his chest and his back absorbing the shock caused by hitting the cold, black water at speed.

Tim didn't hang around to see if his friend surfaced. He immediately twisted the throttle to its stop.

He raced under the Heide Trask Bridge, made a hard left into a narrow creek, and roared through the twisting channel. The boat barely fit under the bridge on Summer Rest Road as he entered a shallow slough. Keeping the power at maximum, he zoomed through the dark until he could go no farther, and the boat beached itself on a mudflat.

Tim jumped out of the boat and ran.

With each step, he sank ankle-deep into the sticky, foul-smelling mud. Splashing water had soaked his pant legs, and he'd lost a shoe by the time he made it to a stand of trees. He was on foot, in a residential neighborhood, and could flee in any direction. The police boats couldn't follow him past Summer Rest Road, and the cop cars would have to spread out to search the winding streets.

Tim flipped the hood of his black jacket over his head, shoved his hands into his pockets, and started walking.

A smile crept across his face. He'd escaped again.

CHAPTER TWO

Wrightsville Beach Marina

Ryan Weller awoke with a start as his Fountaine Pajot Saba 50 catamaran, *Huntress*, rocked in the wake left by the speeding boats. He jumped out of bed, stepped to the rectangular window, and saw the receding marine patrol boats silhouetted against the flashing lights of the police cars on the Heide Trask Bridge.

Pulling on shorts and a T-shirt, Ryan ran up to the salon and stepped onto the aft deck. He'd forgotten how chilly an early November night could get in North Carolina. Goose pimples rippled across his flesh and he shivered. He retreated to the salon and watched through the wide windows as the police cars sped across the bridge toward Wilmington and the patrol boats congregated on what he knew to be a small channel, heading inland.

"What's going on?"

Ryan turned to see his fiancée, Emily Hunt, coming up the steps, wrapping a robe around her waist. She looked beautiful, even with her tousled blonde hair. "The police are chasing a boater," he said.

"What time is it?"

Glancing at his Citizen dive watch, he said, "It's four a.m."

Emily yawned. "It's too early to be up. Let's go back to bed."

Ryan followed her to their stateroom and stretched out on the bed beside her. Emily nestled into the crook of his arm and laid her head on his chest. He smoothed her hair down so it wasn't in his mouth, closed his eyes, and forced himself to relax.

Try as he might, he couldn't slip off to sleep. His mind zeroed in on the same two questions: why were there cops everywhere, and who were they chasing? His adrenaline had spiked, and his need-to-know instincts had kicked in, making him restless as more questions bubbled to the surface.

The questions led his thoughts to a familiar place: examining faces from the past. Ryan opened his eyes and stared at the ceiling, willing them to go away. There were only two things in life he hated more than dreams of the dead men that haunted his sleep: snakes and self-doubt.

Self-doubt was far from a new entry, but, more recently, it had never felt more prevalent. Asking Emily to marry him had been the best move he could have ever made—in his and many others' opinions—and there was no doubt of their future together. What plagued him was the thought of what to do next with his life.

He had come full circle.

Ryan had grown up in Wrightsville Beach, learning the construction trade at his father's firm before taking a job at Wrightsville Beach Marina, where he worked with the owner,

Henry O'Shannassy. Instead of going to college, Ryan had refurbished an old Sabre 36 sailboat and left home the day after high school graduation for a trip around the world. He'd spent time in the Caribbean and crossed the Panama Canal before diving into the Pacific. There were so many places to see and so many reefs to dive that Ryan felt like he'd barely scratched the surface during his two years under sail.

While he loved diving and exploring, Ryan had always felt there was more to life than just whiling away his days at sea, drifting from one tropical paradise to another. Partway through his voyage, he'd put in at Darwin on the northern coast of Australia. While waiting on a spare part for the Sabre's engine, he happened upon a bar crowded with personnel from the Royal Australian Army Ordnance Corps, who were making the most of their downtime after completing a day of training exercises at the air force base. Ryan had started chatting with one of the blokes about scuba diving, and soon he was being regaled with drunken stories of disarming ordnance and blowing up IEDs in Iraq.

After returning home, Ryan had joined the U.S. Navy and made it through the Explosive Ordnance Disposal, or EOD, school on the first try, then spent the next ten years working all over the globe, serving multiple tours in Iraq and Afghanistan, and deploying on both aircraft carriers and amphibious ships. On his last trip to Afghanistan, a group of Taliban had attacked the convoy of EOD vehicles Ryan had been traveling in as they headed out to dispose of a large cache of confiscated weapons. During the ambush, Ryan had dragged his injured lieutenant from the lead Humvee and helped stabilize his spinal cord injuries before leading a counter assault.

With two Purple Hearts pinned to his chest, the Navy had sent Ryan home to recuperate. It wasn't long after his return to active duty that he found he no longer had a passion for being a cog in the military industrial machine, and he had gotten out.

Since then, he'd drifted between jobs as a carpenter for his father and as a commercial diver for Dark Water Research, one of the largest commercial diving and salvage concerns in the world, with whom he'd helped stop terror attacks and raised sunken gold. Now no longer officially affiliated with DWR, he was struggling to build a life with Emily and move forward, but the siren song of the deep was tugging him back in, and he had promised himself that he would no longer put his body in harm's way.

But it was a promise that he knew he would break.

Tucking one hand behind his head, Ryan ran the other along Emily's side, treasuring the feeling of her body against his. When he was a young man, his father had given him some advice. He'd said that life had an order to it, and while Ryan was single, that order should be: God, his job, and then himself. The Navy had clarified it with: God, country, service, self. They left no room for family, and the old joke was that if the Navy wanted you to have a wife, they would have issued her with your seabag.

His father had also said that when Ryan got married, the order would change, becoming: God, family, job, self. With that in mind, Ryan now had to figure out how to reorder his priorities, because for the last twenty-plus years, it had always been job and self.

Emily rolled away and snuggled under the blankets. Ryan slipped out of bed and pulled on his shorts and T-shirt again, this time remembering to add a layer of hooded sweatshirt to ward off the chill. In the galley, he started a pot of coffee before stepping off the boat and going for a run in the predawn.

He remembered traveling this same route on the evening that Greg Olsen's grandfather had offered him a job as a liaison between Dark Water Research and Homeland Security, working cases the government wanted handled with discretion. He had craved the action then, just as he craved it now.

Yep, his life had come full circle. Or maybe it was a figure eight, with the center being Wrightsville Beach. All his new ventures seemed to emanate from there.

Sprinting along the beach toward Johnnie Mercer's Fishing Pier, he knew he had to tamp down those cravings and concentrate on his future. How long would it be before Emily started talking about children? Had he thought this through? Was getting married the right thing to do?

Emily was the right woman, of that he was certain, and now that he had her in his life again, he wasn't letting go. He had put a ring on her finger and committed himself to something that was far greater than anything else he had done in his brief life.

The sun was just rising above the ocean when he reached the pier, and Ryan stopped to watch the day arrive in shades of orange and yellow. Gradually, the ocean lightened and took on its glossy blue hue. Waves rushed from thousands of miles away to wash onto the sandy beach. The waves rolled in, dragged the sand out, and rolled in again. It was always the same water that ran up on the beach and back out. He tried to find a metaphor for life in those waves—but it was lost on him.

After watching the sun clear the horizon, he turned and ran along the street back to the marina.

When he arrived at *Huntress*, Emily was sitting on the aft deck, her knees pulled up to her chest and tucked under an oversized sweatshirt as she sipped coffee from her mug.

Ryan kissed her on the forehead and slid open the salon door.

"I would have gone with you," she said.

"I didn't want to wake you."

She followed him down to the bedroom and stepped into the shower with him. With a grin, she said, "I guess I'll get my exercise another way."

An hour later, they emerged from the bedroom. Ryan wasn't sure how clean he'd gotten in the shower because the stall was a tight fit with two bodies in it, but at least there had been lots of soap suds. When the hot water gave out, they'd moved to the bed. Now, dressed in cargo pants and a sweatshirt, he poured himself a coffee and stepped outside.

Ryan had just sat down when Henry O'Shannassy came strolling down the dock. Despite there being three generations between Henry and his relatives who had immigrated from Ireland, the old man still liked to talk with a brogue, although he generally let it fade when discussing important topics. "Hey, laddie. You hear all that commotion last night?"

"Yeah. The marine patrol was chasing someone."

"Aye. It was another bloody thief. They struck over at Motts Channel Marina and took a bunch of electronics. The cops caught one of them, but the other two escaped."

Ryan nodded and Henry continued. "Them boys left their boat over in the slough behind the Grand View Apartments. The kid they caught's name is John Jefferies. John Jeff, they call him. If he was there, so was his brother P.J. and that no-good Tim Davis."

"Did the police recover any of the stolen gear?" Ryan asked.

"Some."

"Good for them. You want a cup of coffee?"

Henry grinned. "Black like my soul, laddie."

"Aye, and black it is," Ryan replied.

They stepped inside and Ryan poured the older man a fresh cup of Black Rifle Coffee Company's Silencer Smooth blend, a favorite of Ryan's. He had picked up the 'black like my soul' line from Henry and used it often, and, sometimes, his soul felt as black as the coffee he liked to drink.

Emily came up the steps from the stateroom and refreshed her own cup before sitting with the men at the table. Ryan filled her in on the previous night's events.

"The thieves have been hittin' marinas up and down the Carolina coasts," Henry said. "I think it's a ring of 'em workin' together."

"What makes you say that?" Emily asked.

"They all operate in much the same way, usin' a small boat or comin' in with scuba gear. All they take are electronics or loose valuables that haven't been locked up."

"No motors or whole vessels?" Ryan asked.

"Oh, they take them, too," Henry said.

"Have they stolen from here?" Emily asked.

Henry nodded solemnly before sipping his coffee. "Twice. I've put up video cameras and alarms, but many of the boats don't have any security measures other than a lock on the door, an' you know how flimsy they are."

Ryan nodded, remembering all the times that thieves had broken into his sailboats over the years.

"Your buddy Chad Yeager had his place broken into. He lost ten outboards in one night."

"What place does Chad have?" Ryan asked, perplexed that he hadn't heard of this before.

"He's got a boat repair and sales facility off Oleander Drive. Yeager Marine. Started it about the time you left to work for DWR."

"Who's Chad Yeager?" Emily asked.

"He and Ryan used to be runnin' mates in high school," Henry said. "Them boys was inseparable. Thick as thieves, with nothing on their minds but wine, women, and song." Henry's face reddened slightly as he remembered who he was talking to. "Forgive me, Miss Emily."

She smiled and glanced at Ryan. "He's still that way."

"Well, if he be chasin' any women around but you, ya let me know an' I'll straighten him out." Henry slid his sleeves up like he was about to box with Ryan.

"Thanks, Henry," Emily said, "but I'll keep him too busy to worry about other women."

Henry raised a thick eyebrow. "A man might take that as a threat."

She winked at Henry. "It's more of a promise."

"Uh ... About Chad," Ryan broke in. "You said he had some stuff stolen?"

"Yeah. They hit him good. The second time they came through, they took a boat. Police found it half-sunk up by Ocracoke."

"That's a shame," Emily said.

"Yeah. Some people say it was an inside job, but I don't know." Henry shrugged. "Chad was always a decent enough lad."

"Why do they think it was an inside job?" Ryan asked, intrigued that his old friend might be into something shady.

"You know how it is. There's always scuttlebutt about the docks." Henry took a sip of coffee and changed the subject. "How's your one-legged friend?"

"Mango? He's good," Ryan said. "He and his wife are running a sailboat charter business in the British Virgin Islands."

"Is that where you're headed?" Henry asked.

"We haven't decided," Ryan replied with a glance at Emily. "I think the plan is to stick around here until Christmas, then head south."

"I know you'll figure it out, laddie. Ya always have." Henry stood. "Thank you for the coffee. I could spin yarns with ya all day, but I need to be gettin' back to work."

Ryan walked Henry out to the dock. When Ryan stepped

back into the salon, Emily said, "I know that look. This doesn't have to do with your friend Chad does it?"

She'd pegged him dead to rights because he had to know whether his old friend was involved in something shady. And if he was? Well, Ryan would be there to lend a helping hand to get him out of trouble, just like old times.

CHAPTER THREE

Sliding out of the Jeep Wrangler Unlimited, Ryan stood beside his father's pickup truck and inhaled the scent of freshly cut wood. Weller Construction had started in David Weller's garage when he and Kathleen had lived in Wilmington. Gradually, the business grew, and the couple had moved both the business and their young family to the beach. Now the construction company had a large shop situated in the airport business park where they made cabinets and other custom carpentry items to meet a customer's needs while they did remodels and flipped houses.

Even though the shop had enormous dust collectors, sawdust still floated on the breeze, and it smelled like home to Ryan. Before leaving to join Dark Water Research, Ryan had run his own remodeling crew and had been a partner in the flipping business. His brother still hadn't forgiven him for leaving him with a partially completed house when Ryan had changed jobs.

David got up from his desk and stepped to the counter when Ryan and Emily entered the office. "To what do I owe this pleasure?" he asked. "Do you want me to put him to work, Emily?"

"Why does *everyone* think I need a job?" Ryan lamented.

"We're created for work, son. I taught you that."

"Thanks, but I've got plenty of work lined up. Besides, Emily is keeping me busy as her chauffeur and wedding planning assistant."

"Your mother would love for you to have the wedding here, you know," David said.

Ryan held up his hands in defense.

"I wasn't talking to you, son. I was talking to my new daughter-in-law."

"Thanks, David," Emily said. "I'm sure my mom would like me to get married in Fort Lauderdale, so she doesn't have to travel."

"Well, wherever you two decide to tie the knot, just know that Kathleen and I will be there."

"Thanks, Dad. Anyway, the reason for our visit—what do you know about Chad Yeager and his boat repair business?" Ryan asked.

David cocked his head. "I heard he opened a shop, but that's about it. I haven't talked to him in years."

"You haven't heard about him being in trouble or anything like that?" Ryan asked.

"Well, I heard he had a minor dust-up with the law shortly after you left for Texas, but I think it was something like a DWI. Maybe resisting arrest, too. If you wanted to be sure, you should talk to Kyle. I'm sure he'd be happy to hear from you."

"I didn't think about that," Ryan mussed.

David pulled a business card from an ancient Rolodex. "Here's his number."

Ryan typed the number for Kyle Fowler into his cell

phone and saved it before he handed back the card for the New Hanover County sheriff's deputy.

"Why the sudden interest in Chad?" David asked.

"Henry told me he had some boats and motors stolen from his place. I was just interested in what was going on."

David nodded thoughtfully. "You know how Chad is. I wish he'd gone around the world with you, but he stayed here, and he got into trouble. He's been straight since then, as far as I know. Other than the DWI."

"Thanks, Dad." Ryan rapped the counter and stepped toward the door.

"I know you and Chad used to be friends, Ryan, but be careful."

Ryan paused, his hand on the doorknob. He looked back at his father and nodded. "I will be."

He held the door for Emily, and they stepped outside. The temperature had risen to the low sixties. Ryan took off his sweatshirt and tossed it into the back seat of the Jeep.

"Who's Kyle?" Emily asked after Ryan started the engine.

"He's another guy that Chad and I were friends with. He's a detective at the New Hanover Sheriff's Department nowadays."

"You joined the Navy, Kyle became a sheriff's deputy, so how did Chad go off the rails?"

"Chad always did his own thing. He was the guy you could count on in a fight, to score free beer, and to get us into trouble. Kyle was the strait-laced goody-two-shoes, and I was in the middle."

Emily smiled. "I think you lean more toward Chad than you want to admit. So, how about you score me some of that free beer, sailor."

He patted her on the knee. "Why don't we forget about the beer and skip straight to the scoring part?"

Raising her eyebrows, Emily said, "See what I mean? You're trouble."

Ryan turned out of the airport business park and drove across town. Fifteen minutes later, he pulled into the lot of what had once been a large retail store that Chad had repurposed for his repair shop. Inside a fenced-off section of the old parking lot were bass boats with massive outboards, center console fishing vessels, and sailboats with stepped masts.

Ryan held the door for Emily as they walked into a small showroom that housed a modest assortment of spare parts and accessories, along with a selection of new Mercury and Yamaha outboards. They approached a service desk and Ryan asked to speak to Chad Yeager.

"He's out back," the man said.

"Which way?" Ryan asked.

"Through the door." The guy pointed over his shoulder and went back to looking at parts on the computer.

Ryan and Emily followed the vague directions and entered a massive shop that took up most of the building's interior. Fiberglass dust had settled on every surface, and the smell of chemicals hung heavy in the air, mingling with the scent of freshly cut lumber.

In a far corner, a man was using a grinder on the side of a sailboat to prepare a hole in the fiberglass for repair. Ryan was about to walk over and ask him where Chad was when he glimpsed a lean, bald man in the storage yard having an argument with a man in a business suit. The suit was taller and heavier-set than Chad, with slicked-back black hair and a diamond ring on his pinky.

Something about Chad's customer raised Ryan's hackles.

"Stay here," Ryan said to Emily. "I want to see if I can eavesdrop on what they're saying."

She nodded as he strolled toward the open garage doors.

He slid his hands into his pockets to look less threatening and smiled.

"It's over," Chad said with a sweep of both hands away from his body.

"You owe me," the suit said menacingly.

"I did what you asked and now I'm done, just like we said," Chad replied.

"Hey, Chad," Ryan called, wanting to break up the confrontation. "Long time no see, buddy. The service guy said you were out here."

Both Chad and the suit looked puzzled at the interruption, but Chad quickly recovered his composure and, with a wide grin, walked over to shake Ryan's hand. "What are you doing here, bro? I heard you were in Texas."

"I'm just visiting family," Ryan said. "Henry said you had a place over here, and I figured I'd check it out."

"Chad," the suit called out.

When Chad turned to look, the man gestured with his hand to symbolize making a phone call and said, "Tomorrow."

Chad shook his head and gritted his teeth, his jaw muscles flexing as he clenched his fists.

"Easy," Ryan said as the suit walked away. "What's the deal with that guy?"

"Nothin', man," Chad snapped. Then his smile returned as his gaze fell on Emily. "Is she with you?"

"Yeah. That's my fiancée."

"You *lucky* bastard."

Ryan paused for a moment to look at Emily. He *was* lucky. Her layered blonde hair, the color of harvest wheat, fell just past her shoulders, and her eyes were cornflower blue. Even in her oversized sweatshirt and with no make-up on, she was stunning.

Chad stepped over to her and extended his hand. At five-feet-ten, Emily was several inches taller than Ryan's friend.

Ryan knew it wouldn't dissuade Chad because he was a first-class dog.

He let go of Emily's hand and slapped Ryan on the back. "You remember that summer our junior year when I stole that cooler of beer and you snagged Henry's runabout? We went up to ... Oh, shit. I can't tell that story." Chad rubbed his head as he laughed. "What about that time we went over to Mason Inlet and we ... Nope. Can't tell that one, either."

Emily looked pointedly at Ryan. "Do all your stories include chasing women?"

"They used to," Chad said. "Then Ryan fell head over heels for Sara and I got stuck with Kyle as a wingman. And boy, did he *suck*."

"Have you seen much of Kyle recently?" Ryan asked.

"He made detective over at the sheriff's department. Come over to the office. I could use a drink."

They followed Chad to his office and stepped inside. Chad grabbed a beer from the fridge. "You want one?"

"It's a little early for me," Ryan said, and Emily agreed. Chad popped the top off a Budweiser and sat down behind his desk.

Chad and Ryan spent several minutes reminiscing about their youth before Ryan asked, "Who was that guy you were arguing with?"

"Just an unhappy customer. We fixed his boat, and I've been doing bullshit repairs for him for free ever since. I was just telling him he wasn't welcome here anymore. I hate to do it, but sometimes you gotta cut the strings. Sometimes, the customer is *not* always right."

Ryan's phone pinged, and he held it up to see the screen. "We gotta get out of here, Chad, but we're staying at Henry's marina. Come by and I'll buy you another beer."

He wrote his cell number on a scrap of paper, and Chad slipped it into his pocket.

"Sounds like fun," Chad said. "Good to see you, man. I hope you stick around for a while."

"I'm glad you're doing good here," Ryan said. The two men shook hands, and Ryan and Emily walked back to the Jeep.

As they settled into their seats, she asked, "How can you be friends with a guy like him? He gives me the creeps."

Ryan laughed. "He can come across like that, but I assure you, he's a good guy."

Emily frowned. "Why didn't you ask him about the outboards?"

"Because he wouldn't have told me the truth." Ryan started the Jeep and drove out of the parking lot. He turned toward the marina and *Huntress*. As he drove, he thumbed the button on his phone to call Kyle Fowler.

Kyle answered with a wary hello.

"Hey, Kyle, it's Ryan Weller. How are you?"

"Good." Kyle's voice lightened at hearing his old friend. "I heard you were back in town."

"Bad news travels fast," Ryan said.

"I think there's a warrant out for your arrest, Weller," Kyle said jokingly. "Something about being a lady-killer."

Emily turned to Ryan with her eyebrows raised. He shrugged and apologized with contorted facial expressions and hand gestures.

"You busy?" Ryan asked. "We can get some barbeque."

"Sounds good," Kyle replied. "I'm at the courthouse for a trial. Meet me at Parchies at noon, if that works for you?"

"Roger that. See you in a few."

They took a circuitous route across town and pulled to a stop beside a tiny block building. The restaurant on Princess Street had been there for years, and Ryan had eaten there many times.

Kyle Fowler was a few inches taller than Ryan's six foot

and had brown hair cut into a fade and styled with gel to make the front spiky. He wore a pressed uniform and took off his wide-brimmed hat as he entered. He shook Ryan's hand, then Emily's, after Ryan introduced her.

"Glad to meet the woman who finally captured this guy's heart," Kyle said. Turning to Ryan, he added, "I didn't think I'd see you again after you ran off to Texas. How's the job?"

"It was good," Ryan said. "Now I'm a consultant."

Kyle shook his head and smiled. "You always were a dreamer." To Emily, he said, "You better be careful with this one."

"So I've heard," she said with her own coy grin.

They ordered barbeque platters with sandwiches topped with coleslaw. Ryan and Kyle gave theirs a liberal dosing of Tabasco before digging in.

After they finished eating, Kyle said, "Thanks for lunch, but I can tell you didn't come here to reminisce. What's on your mind?"

"What do you know about the break-in at Chad's place?"

"Oh, that." Kyle's mouth tightened. "He lost some outboards, and they stole a boat and trailer."

"I heard it was an inside job."

"I can't comment on an ongoing investigation," Kyle said.

"I understand that, but this is Chad we're talking about," Ryan urged.

Kyle cleared his throat and glanced around the crowded room before saying, "Not here."

CHAPTER FOUR

By the time Ryan and Emily returned to the marina, it was mid-afternoon. Ryan went to find Henry, who always had odd jobs for him to do. The former commercial diver turned salvage consultant helped the marina owner refuel boats, repair engines, and perform maintenance on customer's boats. Ryan needed something to occupy his time as he and Emily whiled away the days, waiting for Thanksgiving and Christmas.

Ryan had already planned their route south, using charts of the Intracoastal Waterway and the Atlantic Ocean between Wrightsville Beach and Fort Lauderdale, where they planned to visit Emily's mother and older brother. From living in the area, Ryan practically knew the North Carolina section of the Intracoastal by heart, having traveled the length of it from Virginia Beach to Cape Fear multiple times.

Kyle arrived at six p.m. as promised. He had traded his uniform for jeans, a dress shirt, and a light jacket. Ryan handed him a beer, and they settled onto a sofa in *Huntress'* salon.

"This boat is nicer than anything we ever thought about

owning as kids," Kyle said. "You must be rolling in the dough as a consultant."

"Thanks. Being my own boss has its benefits," Ryan replied.

"I know you don't want me prying into your work, so I'll get right to why I came." Kyle leaned forward, placing his elbows on his knees.

He told Ryan and Emily about how Chad had stolen a car after high school graduation. The court had charged him with a Class H felony for larceny, and he'd spent six months in jail. When he got out, Chad started working at a local marina as part of his probation and learned how to fix motors. The owner sent him to school in Orlando for watercraft repair. Chad had gotten the DWI down there, and the guy who'd paid for the school fired him for misconduct.

After Chad returned to Wilmington, he worked for various marinas and repair shops before branching out on his own, slowly building his business to what Ryan and Emily had seen on Oleander.

"Supposedly," Kyle continued, "Chad borrowed money from a loan shark to expand his business because he couldn't get financing from a bank. The guy he's in business with isn't someone who takes no for an answer when he doesn't get his money back."

Ryan described the man he and Emily had seen arguing with Chad.

"That's Rocky Bianchi," Kyle said.

"He's the guy Chad owes money to?" Emily asked.

"Sure is," Kyle said.

"Chad was telling Bianchi that he'd done what had been asked of him and told Bianchi that he wanted out," Ryan said.

"I don't know what the deal is between them," Kyle said. "What I can tell you is that the guys who broke into Chad's business were thorough. They cut a hole in the back fence to get in, and I think to escape through if the police showed up. They used bolt cutters to snip all the hoses and cables to the engines, and my guess is they had a lift in the back of a truck to get the motors off the boats. You know how heavy they are."

Ryan nodded.

"Anyway, about two weeks after all the motors disappeared, someone stole a cabin cruiser from Chad's lot. The marine patrol found it lodged on Howard Reef off Ocracoke. The serial numbers had been ground off the hull, the engine, and the stern drive. The cops were only able to identify the boat's owner because he'd registered the dash-mounted Garmin GPS. Those units have a serial number inside the housing."

Both Ryan and Emily nodded because they knew about the hidden serial numbers.

"It turns out the guy who'd registered the GPS had sold the boat to Chad two days before Chad reported it missing."

"Did Chad receive insurance payouts?" Emily asked.

"I don't know," Kyle said. "Wilmington P.D. is handling the case. I sniffed around to see what was happening, but since Chad and I are old friends, the only thing they would tell me is what I've already told you."

"Don't worry about it, man. Thanks for coming over and telling us what you know. How have *you* been?" Ryan asked, changing the subject. "How's the family?"

"Good. Cheryl and I just celebrated fifteen years together last July." Kyle pulled out his phone and opened a picture of his wife and kids. "John is thirteen going on twenty-one, Mary is ten, and little Stevie is eight."

"Oh, how cute," Emily said.

"Only when they're sleeping." Kyle grinned.

Ryan laughed. "You wouldn't change a thing, would you?"

"Not one," Kyle replied.

"We should get together for dinner," Emily said.

"That would be great," Kyle beamed. "Speaking of dinner, I need to get going. Thanks for the beer."

Emily walked Kyle out onto the aft deck as Ryan picked up the empty beer bottles. In a hushed voice, Kyle said to her, "Ryan has a soft spot for Chad. He always has, and it's gotten him in a lot of trouble. Keep a close eye on him, okay? Chad's up to no good, and I don't want to see you guys sucked in by him."

"Are you hitting on my fiancée, Kyle?" Ryan asked.

"Nope. I'll call you about dinner after I talk to Cheryl."

"Sounds good," Ryan said, slipping his hands into his pockets and watching his friend walk up the dock. Once Kyle was no longer in earshot, he asked Emily, "What did he say to you?"

"He was telling me about his kids. He's a nice guy."

"Yeah, he is," Ryan said thoughtfully. "What do you think about having kids?"

"I enjoy sending them back to their parents."

"Do you want to have kids?" he asked.

"Maybe. I mean, I didn't have my life planned out, and I figured if I met the right person, it might happen."

He spread his hands and grinned. "Well, here I am."

"Yes, you *are*." Her voice was husky as she kissed him. "Close the door and let's get some dinner."

Ryan hadn't known what she would say about having kids, but he hadn't expected her to deflect the question. Maybe she didn't want to have them? He had never planned to have a family, either, but now that he'd found the love of his life, it was time to think about leaving a legacy beyond a fat bank account.

Ryan ran a hand through his hair and sighed. There was plenty of time to worry about kids later. They hadn't even said their vows yet.

"Do you want me to check into Chad's insurance carrier?" Emily asked.

"Nah. It's probably nothing more than a coincidence."

"Are you sure?"

"Yeah. Come on, let's get something to eat. I need to think about something else. Chad always was the center of attention."

Ryan stopped on his way to the fridge to watch out the window as a trawler came alongside the dock in front of them. He ran outside and caught the stern line that a short, older woman with long brown hair tossed to him. Pulling on the line, he helped snug the big boat to the dock as the woman jumped down with the bow line and wrapped it around the dock cleat.

She tossed her hair back and extended her hand. "Thanks for your help. I'm Andrea. My husband, Gary, and I are traveling the Great Loop."

Ryan shook her hand as Gary appeared at the rail, wearing a Columbia fishing shirt and khaki shorts. "You look like you need a beer," he said to Ryan. "'Cause I sure need one."

"Always," Ryan said.

Andrea climbed back aboard the trawler as Gary shut down the engine. A moment later, Andrea appeared on deck again with three beers. Gary took his, and she handed the third to Ryan, who tilted it toward them in a toast. "Welcome to Wrightsville Beach Marina. You did an excellent job docking the boat. The currents can be strong here on an incoming tide."

"This ain't my first rodeo," Gary said with a grin.

"My fiancée and I were about to grab some dinner," Ryan said. "Would you like to join us?"

"That would be lovely," Andrea said. "But we need to get the boat straightened up. We've been traveling all day. Perhaps tomorrow?"

"Certainly," Ryan replied. "We're on *Huntress* right there. Holler if you need anything."

"Thank you," Gary said.

Ryan walked back to his catamaran and climbed aboard. Emily had a plate of leftovers warmed up and waiting for him on the table. He sat down beside her, and he told her about their new neighbors as they ate.

Eventually, their topic of conversation came back around to Chad and his boat shop.

"What's going on?" Emily asked. "You haven't seen him in years. Why are you so interested in what he's doing?"

Ryan shrugged. "I don't know, but I can't stop worrying about him."

CHAPTER FIVE

The old outboard coughed in the early morning darkness as Tim Davis applied power. He wasn't happy about the latest incarnation of a workboat. It was a dinged and battered aluminum skiff with an Evinrude that was so old it probably had grandchildren. Despite Chad Yeager's assurances, Tim had his doubts about the health of the motor.

He let off the throttle, and the engine popped. How was he supposed to make a clean getaway when the cops or the people he was robbing could hear him coming from a mile away?

That's probably what Chad wants, the bald bastard.

"Whaddaya think, P.J.?"

"I say we go home. That motor will give out on us and we'll have to paddle back to the truck."

Tim turned the skiff and chopped the throttle, the engine popping again as he let the current carry them through the dark marsh, following the blinking navigational lights along the Intracoastal Waterway.

"Let's hit that boat up ahead," P.J. said.

Tim steered the outboard in the direction P.J. was

pointing and goosed the throttle to carry them across the channel. One of the good things about living along this stretch of the ICW was that the docks projected hundreds of feet out from the mainland. The boats tied to them were easily accessible, and the owners wouldn't know there was a problem until they checked on the boat long after the thieves had made their escape.

While Tim didn't want to rip off a boat so close to where they'd put the skiff in the water, P.J. was right. They needed a win after losing all their gear from the last heist, and they needed bail money for John Jeff.

The skiff coasted to a stop alongside the bigger boat. P.J. climbed on board and handed the electronics to Tim as he ripped them out of the sportfisher's console. A few minutes later, they were coasting downstream again, this time with a tarp covering the stolen items. They hit two more boats on the way back to the truck.

Unfortunately, the outboard stopped working as they approached the dock. Tim hopped overboard into the chilly, chest-deep water. He grabbed the painter and started hauling the boat toward shore.

When Tim reached the dock, he tied off the boat and stomped to his old truck, water squishing from his shoes. His anger at the outboard and at Chad Yeager for giving them such a piece of shit helped to take his mind off the fact that he was soaking wet and cold.

Tim backed the trailer into the water, and the two men horsed the skiff onto it. After pulling the rig out of the water, P.J. strapped the back of the boat to the trailer, pulled the drain plug, and jumped into the passenger seat of the truck.

They rode in silence toward Wilmington, each staring at the scenery as it flashed past in the headlights. Their haul wasn't as large as they'd planned, but it would still put food on the table. Tim lit a cigarette and used the hand crank to roll down the window.

Half an hour later, he pulled the truck to a stop beside an isolated, run-down shack on a branch of the Northeast Cape Fear River. The two men carried their loot inside and stacked it on shelves in a bedroom they'd converted into a storage room and office. From their hideout, they sold their stolen items online via sites like eBay and Craigslist. Most people would never know they were purchasing stolen goods, nor did they care as long as they got a good deal. In Tim's experience, everyone had a shady side to them.

"I'm gonna check the websites," P.J. said as Tim headed for the door.

Tim knew P.J. would spend more time looking at porn than doing any work. After changing into dry clothes, Tim walked to the rickety dock at the end of a sandy path. He slipped a canoe into the stained and slow-moving water and paddled upstream in the predawn to where he'd left his trotline strung from the gnarled roots of a bald cypress tree. He pulled in two catfish and reset the line, then let the canoe drift downstream as he flicked a lure toward the bank, hoping to catch a largemouth bass.

As he stepped onto the dock, Tim's cell phone rang. He was slow to answer it, not wanting to come back to reality. If he could pay the rent by fishing and hunting, he could leave the theft ring behind, but Tim hadn't figured out how to do that yet. They were barely scraping by on what they made from stealing electronics and the occasional boat, but it was enough to pay the rent on the shitty river shack they lived in.

"How big was the haul?" Rocky Bianchi asked once Tim finally answered.

"That outboard Chad gave us was a piece of shit. It quit on us, and I had to pull the boat to shore."

"I didn't call to listen to your sob story, Davis. Did you get anything?"

"Yeah. P.J.'s putting it online right now."

"Good. Listen, I've got a Hinckley 40 picnic boat in North Myrtle Beach. I've got a driver to run you down there and you and P.J. bring it back, doing your thing along the Intracoastal."

Tim laid the catfish on the fileting table and sighed. "When do we leave?"

Bianchi didn't hesitate. "Tomorrow night."

CHAPTER SIX

Fall had taken deep root, and the trees were almost bare. Ryan zipped up his light jacket as he stepped off *Huntress* and headed for the marina office. He hadn't missed North Carolina's blustery weather, and he wasn't looking forward to another month of falling temperatures before he and Emily could escape south to the tropical climate that he'd grown accustomed to over the past years of working and sailing in the Caribbean.

He remembered several times during his childhood when it had snowed at the beach, and he was thankful he'd missed the last time in January 2018, when nearly three inches had fallen. Now, he prayed it wouldn't get much colder than it already was, because Fountaine Pajot hadn't designed their catamarans with freezing temperatures in mind. He didn't want to have to winterize the boat and move into his parent's house. That thought sent more of a shiver down his spine than the cold.

Banging through the office door, Ryan headed straight for the coffee pot and poured himself a cup. Henry stood behind the counter with Tom, the marina's tall, red-headed mechanic, going over the work orders for the day. With winter approaching, the workload had slackened, and Tom could handle most of it, but he let Ryan do some, especially if it was a job like the one Henry had just handed him.

Ryan groaned as he read the work order. He would have to wedge himself into an engine compartment on a Hunter 30 sailboat to change the engine oil and filter.

"You wanted to help," Tom smirked.

"Whatever," Ryan muttered and walked out to find the boat and get to work.

As he crossed the yard with his arms full of jugs of motor oil and a siphon pump, Gary joined him. They chatted about various attractions along the ICW and in the Wilmington area before Gary invited Ryan and Emily to dinner at six that evening.

Ryan stepped onto the Hunter sailboat, unlocked the cabin door, and went below to survey the engine room. He was thankful that this was a newer model, with a remote oil filter mounted to the top of the engine where it was easily accessible. After pulling the dipstick and fitting the suction tube into the engine, he pumped the handle and vacuumed the oil from the sump. It took him an hour and a half to complete the job, with plenty of cussing at the engineers who had designed the boat. They always seemed to fit the engine into the hull as an afterthought.

When he got back to the shop, Ryan dropped the old filter into a bucket with several others and poured the used oil into a container for recycling. He didn't think he would miss spending hours working underwater, but after the stress of that oil change, he'd gladly go back to being a commercial diver.

Henry had him perform a few more odd jobs throughout the afternoon, and by the time Ryan finished, it was time for him to get ready for dinner with Gary and Andrea.

When he stepped into their stateroom on the *Huntress,* Emily was in the shower. He thought about joining her, but decided he needed a good scrub to get all the dirt off his skin.

When they were both dressed, they walked to the Blue Water Grill and met Andrea and Gary at the entrance.

The two couples enjoyed a pleasant dinner, sharing stories about traveling along the Intracoastal and the hazards of boating. Once the plates had been cleared, Gary and Andrea invited Ryan and Emily to join them aboard *Due South,* their VDL Pilot 44, for a nightcap.

Following them to the lower salon, Ryan and Emily sat at the dinette while Andrea mixed margaritas.

Halfway through their drinks, Andrea asked, "How did you two meet?"

"I was investigating sailboat thefts, and Emily worked for an insurance agency," Ryan replied. He took a sip of his margarita and glanced around the boat's interior, admiring its layout and the spiral staircase leading down from the pilothouse. "We hit it off, and we've worked several cases together since. What about you?"

"Similar circumstances," Gary said. "We worked together and developed an appreciation for one another. We've been married for almost thirty years. Got five kids, all of them out of the house. Now that it's just the two of us again, we decided we needed to treat ourselves to this boat and this trip."

"I could think of worse ways to spend your freedom," Ryan said amiably.

After another round of drinks, Ryan and Emily walked back to *Huntress* and got ready for bed. As Ryan was pulling the covers over himself, his cell phone rang. He groaned as he reached for it, but he didn't recognize the number on the illuminated screen. Normally, he didn't answer unknown numbers, however he didn't think a telemarketer would be calling about his vehicle's warranty at this time of night.

He held the phone to his ear. "This is Ryan."

A hoarse voice whispered, "Help me."

Adrenaline shot through Ryan's veins as he sat up. "Hello? Who is this?"

The caller drew in a sharp breath. "It's me, Chad."

"Where are you?" Ryan demanded, jumping out of bed and grabbing his clothes.

"At the shop."

Chad's labored breathing wheezed in Ryan's ear. "I'm on my way," Ryan said urgently. "Hang tight."

Ryan pulled on his clothes and saw Emily was doing the same. Chad's painful, ragged gasps made Ryan move as fast as he could.

"Do I need to call an ambulance?" Ryan asked.

There was no response from Chad.

Sensing there might be an element of danger to Chad's situation, Ryan slipped his Walther PPQ M2 nine-millimeter pistol into his inside the waistband holster. He and Emily ran for the Jeep. "Chad! Chad?" Ryan shouted.

Emily jumped into the driver's seat and Ryan climbed into the passenger side, straining to hear his friend.

"Where?" Emily asked.

"Chad's shop."

Ryan pulled the phone away from his ear as Emily sped out of the parking lot. At the stop sign, she looked both ways, then charged left, bumping over the curbs instead of following the normal flow of traffic. Thankfully, at this time of night, there weren't many cars on the street.

He saw the call with Chad had disconnected, but instead of calling Chad back, he dialed 9-1-1 and told the operator to send an ambulance to Yeager Marine on Oleander.

Ryan squeezed his eyes shut as Emily careened around a

corner, blowing through a light just turning red. What had happened to Chad? He'd sounded like he was in serious pain.

Ten minutes later, they screeched to a stop in front of Chad's marine repair shop. Ryan jumped out before Emily had the transmission in park and ran to the front door. He yanked on the handle and found the door locked. Unable to get in that way, Ryan turned and ran along the building toward the chain-link fence, which he rapidly scaled and dropped over the other side. In the distance, he could hear the wail of the ambulance's sirens.

Ryan kept running along the building to the open garage door at the rear. As he approached, he slowed and drew his pistol, holding it at compression ready, elbows tight to his sides and hands at his chest. Ryan didn't know what awaited him inside the building, but he wanted to be cautious and be ready. Turning through the open garage door, he saw the upper half of Chad Yeager's body protruding from beneath a toppled sailboat. It appeared as if the blocks on the twenty-foot craft had given way and the boat had rolled onto Chad.

Still scanning the building's interior, Ryan ran to Chad. The man's face was a mass of blood and bruises. The cell phone he'd used to call Ryan lay by his right hand.

Ryan placed a finger on Chad's neck and found a strong pulse. His phone rang as he holstered his pistol. He saw it was Emily and answered it.

"The ambulance is here. Do you need help?"

"Yeah. I'm coming to the front door right now."

A moment later, the paramedics followed him through the building to where Chad lay unconscious under the boat. The two medics worked in concert to assess Chad's injuries before Emily helped the three men lift the sailboat back onto its keel. While the others held it in place, Ryan jammed some stands under the hull to keep it upright.

"It looks like he blocked it with his hands, so the boat

didn't crush him," the older paramedic said, "but those facial lacerations aren't from this boat falling over. Someone worked him over really good."

Ryan nodded, but kept his thoughts to himself. He had a fairly good idea who had beaten his friend.

The paramedics loaded Chad onto a stretcher and wheeled him to the ambulance. Ryan asked which hospital they were taking him to and said he would meet them there when they told him it would be New Hanover Regional Medical Center. Once the red-and-white emergency vehicle had receded into the night, Ryan and Emily locked the shop using a set of keys Emily had found on Chad's office desk before climbing into the Jeep to follow.

Ryan and Emily arrived at the medical center just in time to see the paramedics loading their empty stretcher back into the ambulance.

"How is he?" Ryan asked.

The older paramedic flicked away a cigarette butt and glanced around. "The docs took him straight into surgery. One of his broken ribs punctured his right lung."

"Damn," Ryan muttered.

"He'll be all right," the medic said, digging in his pocket. He pulled out a piece of paper and handed it to Ryan. "Your friend woke up long enough to tell me his mom's phone number, then he passed out again."

"Thanks, guys," Emily said.

"No problemo, ma'am. Just doin' our job."

Ryan and Emily walked into the hospital. He doubted the nurses would tell him anything, so he dialed the number from the piece of paper the paramedic had handed him. Ryan had been to the house where Chad had grown up more times than he could count, but he hadn't spoken to Janice Yeager in years. When she finally answered, she sounded like he had awakened her from a sound slumber, yet he recognized her voice instantly. It had the same gravelly quality it had always had, and he wondered if she still smoked Pall Malls.

"Mrs. Yeager, this is Ryan Weller."

"A voice from the past. It's good to hear from you." He could hear the smile in her voice. Janice had always treated both him and Kyle as if they were her own sons.

"Same here, Mrs. Yeager," Ryan said.

Janice's voice turned hard. "Why are you calling me, Ryan?"

"It's Chad. He's at New Hanover Regional. He told the paramedics to call you, and they gave me your number."

She sighed. "What's he gotten himself into now, Ryan?"

He heard the wheel of a lighter strike against flint, and he took a deep involuntary breath along with her as she took the first drag on the cigarette. Pall Mall cigarettes were the first brand he'd smoked, stolen from Janice's purse by her wayward son.

"He was working on a sailboat when it fell on him," Ryan informed her. "He's in surgery right now to fix a collapsed lung and a broken rib."

Janice let out another deep sigh. "I'll be right there."

"I'll see you soon," Ryan said before ending the call.

Emily looked at her fiancé curiously.

"What?" He felt uncomfortable under her gaze.

"I've seen you in a lot of situations with your friends, but never one where you had to make a call like that. You handled it well."

Ryan nodded and blew out a breath through puffed-up cheeks. It wasn't the first call he'd made to the family of an injured friend, and he hated doing it. He also didn't want to hang around the hospital because he'd spent more than his fair share of time in them, but he wanted to be there for Chad. Once Janice arrived, he and Emily could leave. In the meantime, they sat in the hard-plastic waiting room chairs, and Ryan thought about Rocky Bianchi, the man he'd seen arguing with Chad. He needed more information about the man other than what he'd gleaned from talking with Henry and Kyle.

Janice Yeager arrived forty minutes later, wearing jeans, a cream blouse, and a light wrap around her shoulders. In her late fifties, she had a mane of strawberry blonde hair and crow's feet around her eyes. Ryan remembered her laughing a lot, despite her being a single mother and taking in two extra hooligans. She'd always made them feel at home and kept her fridge stocked so they had plenty to eat.

Ryan stood and gave her a hug, smelling her familiar scent of cigarette smoke and perfume, then he walked with her to the nurses' station. As Chad's emergency contact, Janice was told that the doctor would be out to talk to her as soon as he finished the surgery.

With nothing else to do but wait, Ryan and Janice stepped outside into the cool night air for her to spark up a cigarette.

"You want one?" she asked.

He shook his head, even though he really wanted to smoke it. Ryan stood beside the older woman and breathed her second-hand smoke, reliving the past.

Two hours later, the doctor came into the waiting room. He guided them into a private corner and, in hushed tones, told them that Chad would make a full recovery. He would need to get plenty of rest, the doctor said, and he asked if Chad had a place to stay while he recuperated. Janice nodded emphatically. Ryan realized he didn't even know where Chad lived, just that he had a business on Oleander.

It was yet another thing to add to his list of things to find out.

"Can I see him?" Janice asked.

"Yes." The doctor nodded. He glanced between the three waiting faces. "He has lacerations to the face and hands that are more consistent with a fist fight than a boat falling on him. Do you know anything about that?"

"No, sir," Ryan answered. "When we found him, he was under the boat."

The doctor pursed his lips and nodded thoughtfully. "Well, however he came by his injuries, he's in expert hands now. I'll check on him later. For now, I'll show you to his room."

They followed the doctor down the corridor, and he motioned for them to go into the room when they reached it. Chad lay under a heavy layer of blankets, his face a mass of bruises and cuts. Beside him, an array of monitors tracked his heart rate, breathing, and blood pressure, while an IV machine dripped fluids into his arm.

Janice turned to Ryan, her face grim and her mouth set hard. "It was that damned Rocky Bianchi. I just know it."

As Ryan stood in the dark room, he clenched his fists and vowed to prove it.

CHAPTER SEVEN

Leaning against the countertop of *Huntress*' central island, Ryan sipped his coffee and thought about Chad and his injuries. While he believed Bianchi had ordered the beating to warn Chad not to back out of whatever business deal the two of them had, Ryan wasn't certain he had the whole picture. Even though he trusted his gut and went with his hunches, this felt different. Warning bells were clashing in his head, and he couldn't figure out why.

After finishing his first cup of coffee and making headway on the next, Ryan dialed Janice Yeager's number. She answered on the third ring, sounding tired.

"Did you get any sleep?" Ryan asked her.

"Some. The chair in Chad's room is damned uncomfortable, and the nurses were in and out all night."

"How's he doing?"

"The doc says things look fine, but I'm still worried."

"About what?"

"Can you come to the hospital?" Janice asked.

"Sure. I'll be there in a half hour." Ryan hung up and swallowed the last of the morning's second cup of coffee, then grabbed his jacket.

"Where are you off to?" Emily asked, emerging from their stateroom.

"The hospital. Mrs. Yeager wants me to come by."

"Do you want me to go with you?"

"Nah." Ryan zipped his jacket and grabbed the Jeep's keys.

"Okay. I have some work to do, anyway."

She ran a hand through her hair, then leaned in and kissed him. He pulled her close and wrapped her in his arms, pressing his lips more firmly to hers.

A moment later, Emily pushed him away. "Get out of here, mister, before you sidetrack me."

"You're the one who kissed me, remember?"

"Oh, I remember." She winked at him and gave him a coquettish smile.

He grinned back and turned toward the door. She followed him across the salon and swatted him on the behind as he stepped outside. He straightened and twisted to see Emily jerk the sliding door closed and lock it. She stuck her tongue out at him as she turned away.

Ryan shook his head with a smile and walked to the Jeep.

Thirty minutes later, he pulled into the hospital's parking lot. He found Janice Yeager feeding quarters into a vending machine to get a cup of coffee. Ryan waited his turn and did the same before they walked to Chad's room, blowing on the steaming cups and sipping carefully from them.

Janice sat down in the chair beside the bed. Ryan took a minute to look at Chad. His face had turned deep shades of purple, black, and yellow. Small bandages held the cuts closed on his face.

"Thanks for coming Ryan. Chad doesn't have many friends, just people that like to hang around, and when the beer runs out, so do they." She cleared her throat and sipped her coffee.

Ryan remained silent, letting her take her time in saying whatever was on her mind.

"Chad doesn't think I know this, but I know he's in neck-deep with a man named Rocky Bianchi."

"I met him yesterday," Ryan stated. "He and Chad were having a heated argument."

"Bianchi's nothing more than a yardbird, strutting around and occasionally spurring the other chickens."

Now that she had gotten to the heart of the matter, Ryan felt it was time to ask questions. He pulled up a chair beside hers. "Tell me why you're so worried."

Janice toyed with her cup. "Chad needed money to open his shop and went to most of the banks in the area to get financing, but they didn't want to loan him any money. We scraped together about twenty thousand dollars, including me cashing out part of my 401K. He rented the building on Oleander, stocked it with his tools, and started advertising, but he needed money for overhead, parts for the showroom, and cash to get the outboard motor dealerships, so he went to Bianchi."

"And Bianchi took a piece of the business and demanded Chad jump through some hoops as he paid the money back," Ryan added.

Janice nodded. "I don't know what Chad was doing for him but knowing Bianchi, I wouldn't doubt he has Chad involved in something illegal."

"Chad didn't think he could get the money another way or purchase additional items as he had spare cash?"

"I tried to talk him into doing just that, but *you* know how he is. He told me he and Bianchi were friends and that Bianchi was going to give him a good deal."

Ryan nodded. Chad was as stubborn as a rock, and when

he made up his mind, he wasn't going to change it. "How did he and Bianchi meet?"

"I don't know, Ryan. But I'm worried about the trouble *that man* has gotten my son into."

Ryan took her trembling hand in his. "It's going to be all right, Mrs. Yeager."

Janice Yeager's gaze moved up to meet Ryan's, and she squeezed his hand. "I've seen that look before. Please don't do anything stupid."

"I promise," Ryan said solemnly.

"You always were a good kid." Janice let go of his hand.

Ryan stood, but before he could open the door to leave, Chad's raspy voice stopped him.

"It's not your problem."

Spinning around, Ryan approached the hospital bed and leaned down to see Chad's eyes behind his swollen lids. "Tell me who did this to you."

Chad licked his thick lips and closed his eyes. When he opened them again, he stared straight at Ryan. "I can take care of myself, but they said they would go after my mom."

Glancing at Janice, Ryan said, "I'll protect her. You just worry about getting well."

A tear rolled out of Chad's eye and ran down his cheek. He shook his head. "It's not that easy."

Janice held a cup with a straw in it out to her son, and Chad took several long swallows of water.

When she withdrew the cup, Chad watched his mother with sorrow in his eyes. Then he turned back to Ryan. "Mom's right. I screwed up by doing business with Rocky. I thought I could outsmart him, but he has a noose around my neck."

"What do you mean?" Ryan asked.

"When I borrowed money from him, he wanted a stake in the shop," Chad said. "I was desperate and signed the papers.

But now that I've paid him off, he refuses to give his share back to me."

"That doesn't give him the right to bully you," Janice said.

Chad motioned for another drink of water. He swallowed and drew in a deep breath.

"I've been selling boats for Rocky, but I found out yesterday that they were stolen, and he's been forging the paperwork for them. That was what you saw us arguing about."

Ryan nodded.

"I'm trying to live a clean life and stay out of trouble, but Rocky knows I've sold his stolen boats and keeps telling me he'll rat me out to the cops if I stop helping him. This beating was a message to me. I need to keep my mouth shut."

"But you can't keep going on like this," Janice said. "I can't keep visiting you in the hospital."

"Then we'd better figure out how to get you out of this mess," Ryan said.

CHAPTER EIGHT

Emily Hunt pressed the *End* button on her cell phone and laid it on the counter. She lifted her cup of tea to her lips and watched out the rear salon windows as a large sportfisher motored past.

Finishing her tea, she went down to the master stateroom. She retrieved a bag from the hanging closet and started packing clothes into it. The phone call she had just ended had been from the company she'd worked for before becoming a private contractor. Ward and Young, one of the nation's leading insurance agencies for private and commercial vessels, had asked her to attend a class in Fort Myers to become a master marine surveyor, specializing in accident and fraud investigations. While she had several certifications in marine surveying, they were for smaller, non-commercial vessels. Passing the proposed course would allow her to inspect ocean-going cargo carriers. She had asked Ward and Young to pay for the class as part of her new contract, and they had readily agreed. She just hadn't expected it to be this soon.

Finished with packing her bags, Emily picked up her phone and dialed the number for Greg Olsen, Ryan's long-time friend and the owner of her fiancé's previous employer, Dark Water Research.

Greg answered on the third ring with, "Do I need to come kick his ass?"

Emily chuckled at the thought of the paraplegic flying across the country to kick Ryan's ass. "No, but I want you to send Rick Hayes."

"What? You don't think I can do the job?" Greg retorted.

"I know you can do the job," Emily replied. "Ryan's been a good boy. Did he tell you that we got engaged?"

"*Congratulations*! He told me he was thinking of proposing, but not when he was going to do it."

She held out her hand and admired the diamond on her finger. "He proposed two weeks ago. I'm surprised he didn't tell you."

"I just got back from Nicaragua. But I'll still come kick his ass for the fun of it. So, tell me why you need Rick's help."

"I have to go to Fort Myers to take a class." She then told Greg about Ryan reconnecting with Chad Yeager, seeing Bianchi and Chad arguing at the repair shop, and how Chad had looked as if someone had beaten him to within an inch of his life. "I think Ryan is going to do whatever he can to help Chad, and I'd like to have someone here watching his back."

"That sounds like Ryan. Always rushing in to help his friends," Greg said. "I have Rick on another job, but I can send Scott Gregory."

Before Greg Olsen had become disabled, he'd been a hard-charging Navy lieutenant, leading an Explosive Ordnance Disposal detachment, with plans to return to DWR to take over the reins from his father. But life had thrown him a curveball when an IED had detonated under his Humvee, leaving him paralyzed from the waist down. Despite his confinement to a wheelchair, he had still become CEO of DWR for a brief time before stepping down to build his private military company, Trident, where he employed a group of former Special Forces operators, including Scott Gregory, an ex-Navy SEAL whom Emily and Ryan had worked with on several occasions.

"Sounds perfect," Emily said.

She knew that not only was Scott a top-notch operator, but he and Ryan also worked well together.

"When does he need to be there?" Greg asked.

"I have to leave in two days."

"I'll have Scott there tomorrow and, in the meantime, try to keep your boyfriend on a short leash."

Emily laughed. "Thanks, Greg, but you know better than that."

"No worries, Em. We gotta watch out for our boy. Call me if you need anything else."

"I will." She ended the call and slipped the phone into the back pocket of her jeans. She could breathe easier knowing that Scott would be there to help Ryan in her absence. And if the look in his eye when he'd left that morning was any indication of how he would proceed, Emily was positive Ryan would need backup.

―――

THREE HOURS LATER, Emily heard a knock on the hull and went topside to find Andrea standing on the dock. Emily grabbed her jacket and stepped outside.

"We're casting off in a few minutes," Andrea said. "I wanted to say thanks for your hospitality and to give you my phone number. Call me if you're in the Florida Keys. We reserved a mooring ball in Boot Key Harbor, and we'll be there all winter."

Emily took the slip of paper Andrea handed to her and

tucked it into her jacket pocket. "I've been to Boot Key several times. You'll love it there."

"Where's your boyfriend?" Gary asked from the deck of *Due South*.

"Visiting a sick friend."

"That's a shame. I hope your friend gets better. Anyway, tell Ryan we said goodbye. We're heading south. This cold weather is for the birds." Gary rubbed his hands and blew on them for effect.

"I agree," Emily said.

Andrea climbed down to get the lines, but Emily told her to go back aboard and she would get them. She cast off the bow line, and Gary swung the bow into the current with the thruster. Once Emily let go of the stern line, he eased the engine power on, smoothly slipping away from the dock.

Emily watched *Due South* motor down the ICW and silently wished her new friends fair winds and following seas. Then she went back onto *Huntress* and warmed up leftover fish tacos. She was just sitting down to eat when Ryan stepped aboard the big catamaran and came inside the salon. He gave her a quick kiss on his way down to their stateroom.

When he came back up, he asked, "What's the suitcase for?"

The knot in Emily's stomach tightened. Telling him she was leaving was harder than she'd thought. She wondered if the knot was from her telling him she was leaving or if it was from having to tell him she'd called Greg. Half of her wanted him to tell her to stay because he needed her help. "Remember that surveyor's school I wanted to attend? Ward and Young found me an open slot."

"*Cool*! When do you leave?"

"The day after tomorrow."

"That was quick." Ryan grabbed a bottle of water from the refrigerator.

"I know. I'll be back before Thanksgiving, and this cert will compliment my International Association of Marine Investigators membership and certifications."

"I'm glad they didn't drag their feet and try to screw you over."

"I *was* their best investigator, *mister*."

"And still are." Ryan reached across her and grabbed a taco.

"Hey! Get your own."

"I just did." He grinned as he took a bite. After chewing and swallowing, he said, "I talked to Chad and his mom. Chad borrowed money from Rocky Bianchi and Bianchi had him selling stolen boats. Now he's squeezing Chad because of it."

"Oh no."

"Yeah. It's not good," Ryan conceded. "Chad said he was being coerced with the threat of violence against his mom and himself."

Emily sighed. While she had suspected Ryan wanted to help his friend, the look of determination on his face now told her she'd made the right decision to call Greg. She hoped he wouldn't see it as a betrayal of his abilities. But she had to tell him. "I called Greg."

"Why?" Ryan took a long drink to wash down the last of his taco.

"He's sending Scott to help you while I'm away."

"You don't think I can handle this on my own?" Ryan asked.

"I think you're more than capable of handling it on your own. I just want you to have help since I won't be here."

"Roger that."

Good. She breathed a sigh of relief, having expected him to argue with her, but he hadn't and that was progress. The knot inside her loosened. Either way, it felt better to communicate with him.

Looking out the sliding glass doors to the empty berth aft of them, Ryan asked, "When did Andrea and Gary leave?"

"Not long before you came back."

"*Bon voyage*." Ryan lifted his water bottle in salute.

"Amen," Emily remarked. "I'm ready to head south myself."

"You and me both," he responded, reaching into the fridge to grab another taco.

When they finished eating, Emily retreated to the stateroom to work on her caseload. She heard Ryan speaking to Barry Thatcher, a computer hacker whose skills they'd enlisted before, asking him to dig into the life of Rocky Bianchi and his business dealings. When the call was over, Ryan came down the steps and nuzzled her neck.

She giggled. "I've got work to do."

"I know, but I won't see you for a while, so I've got to fortify myself until your return."

"You're hopeless," she said, bending her neck so he could nibble on her ear.

Before he could distract her further, his phone rang, and he answered it. She relished the warmth of his hand as he gently massaged the back of her neck, thinking how much she would miss him while she was gone.

When he hung up, he asked, "Want to go for a ride?"

CHAPTER NINE

Ryan drove them to downtown Wilmington and found a parking spot in one of the city garages near the government buildings. They walked into the large brick-and-glass office building on the corner of Chestnut and North Third Street. It housed two banks, several law offices, and their destination, the *Wilmington Star News*. Ryan and Emily took the stairs to the newspaper's office, and at the reception desk, Ryan asked to speak with one of their reporters, Ray McClelland.

According to Barry Thatcher, McClelland had authored several stories about Rocky Bianchi and his nefarious business dealings for the newspaper. While Barry worked his magic from the computer keyboard and could give them the nuts and bolts of Bianchi's operations and a dossier of the man's past, it would be McClelland who could give them immediate details.

"I'm sorry," the receptionist told them. "Mr. McClelland isn't here. He's covering a story for us at the Latimer House."

"I've always wanted to go there," Emily said. "I read they have a lovely tour."

"It's a beautiful place," the receptionist commented. "There's a movie being shot near there, and that's what Mac is covering."

"Mac, huh," Ryan observed.

Emily smiled. "I guess we're going sightseeing."

Ryan had been to the Latimer House many years ago, during a school field trip, and he hadn't enjoyed it one bit. Back then, it had been boring to his young mind to look at clothes, dishes, and tools from the mid-1800s, and he doubted it would be any better now.

The couple walked the four blocks along the tree-lined street, stopping so Emily could read several of the historical plaques along the way.

Latimer House, which housed the Cape Fear Historical Society, had originally been built by local merchant Zebulon Latimer in 1852 in the then popular Italianate style. Designed to be perfectly symmetrical, the home had an identical layout on all four floors, and the same number of windows and doors on each floor. As they entered, Ryan grumbled to himself about forking over the fee, while Emily studied a pamphlet about the Historical Society and their efforts to preserve downtown Wilmington.

"They host weddings here," she announced.

"I thought we were going with a beach theme," Ryan said.

"Oh, we are, but it never hurts to have a contingency plan. I believe *you* taught me that."

"I knew that would bite me in the ass," he grumbled. "Let's just go across the street to the Justice of the Peace and get it over with."

"Get it over with?" Emily said dubiously.

"You know what I mean."

"I most certainly do not *know* what you mean."

"I mean that it would be easier to not make a big production out of it."

"So now I'm making a *production* out of getting married? I suppose you'd like me to just stay home barefoot and pregnant, too?"

Ryan took a deep breath and glanced around the foyer. Fortunately, the only people within earshot were the old ladies behind the ticket window, and they seemed to relish the scene before them. He took Emily by the elbow and led her deeper into the ornately furnished home. "What I want is for you to be happy. I'm not backing out of this, but we're living together. A marriage certificate is just a piece of paper that says we can do what we're already doing. It's just the government enforcing rules and collecting money."

"Is that *all* it is?" she asked, eyebrows raised.

"What difference does it make whether we go across the street and see a judge or get married in front of a large group?"

"You're not helping your case," Emily warned.

"Can we drop it?" Ryan asked.

"For now," she said frostily.

Closing his eyes, Ryan took another deep breath and blew it out through puffed-up cheeks, picturing himself as a dragon breathing his irritation out as fire. When he opened his eyes, Emily had left him in the hallway and was meandering around the rooms, looking at the exhibits.

He deserved her ire. Why was he so irritated about the thought of getting married in a lovely garden behind an old home? Was it because Wilmington held nothing for him anymore? His family was there, but his life was elsewhere, preferably somewhere he didn't have to put on a jacket to stay warm when he left his boat.

As he followed Emily from room to room, examining the relics of a bygone era, Ryan thought about why he had stuck his foot in his mouth. The only family that mattered was the woman he had annoyed. Was it his way of dealing with the feelings he had about her getting hurt because of one of his missions? It was easier to be single, and he had stayed that way for his own selfish reasons. He knew in his heart that if he abandoned this relationship now, he would die a lonely old man, full of regret. No one made him happier than Emily, so why was he constantly trying to give her a reason to leave?

They found Ray McClelland on the second floor. Ryan recognized him from his byline picture in that morning's paper. The reporter was a short, thin man with even thinner brown hair, despite being in his mid-twenties. He was speaking with two other people. One was an older man, and the other was a woman about Ryan's age, with chestnut hair pulled into a ponytail.

The woman smiled when she saw Ryan. "Hey, stranger."

"Hi," Ryan replied cautiously, unsure who she was.

She saw the confusion on his face and stuck out her bottom lip. "You don't remember me?"

"No. I'm sorry. I don't," Ryan replied.

McClelland tried to excuse himself from the awkward exchange, but Ryan stopped him by saying, "I'm here to talk to you, Ray."

"Okay," McClelland said hesitantly.

The woman, looking rebuffed because Ryan had ignored her to speak to the reporter, interrupted them with, "My name is Nicky Pence. You probably remember me as Nicky Bigelow."

Ryan had a sudden vision of her in a blue-and-white cheerleading outfit, the colors of their Hoggard High Vikings. She had briefly dated Chad and had been their senior class president. "*Now* I remember. Nice to see you again." He smiled, although he wasn't sure how convincing he was being. "I don't mean to be rude, Nicky, but we're a little pressed for time, and I need to talk to Mr. McClelland." Turning to the reporter, Ryan asked, "Can we go outside?"

"Sure." McClelland nodded.

"Nice to see you again, Ryan. Will you be coming to the class reunion?" Nicky called after them as Ryan, Emily, and the reporter descended the stairs.

"Not if I can help it," Ryan muttered.

"She seems *nice*." Emily's words seemed like a wicked barb, pricking his already delicate skin.

Ryan didn't engage her but continued outside with McClelland.

When they were on the sidewalk, the reporter asked, "What's this all about?"

"I'd like to talk to you about Rocky Bianchi," Ryan said.

McClelland blew out a long breath and ran his hand over his face and head, then fiddled with his jacket collar. He glanced around nervously.

"It's just us," Ryan assured him, extending his hand. "My name is Ryan Weller."

McClelland shook his hand. "Everyone calls me Mac. Are you any relation to the owner of Weller Construction?"

"That's my dad's company."

McClelland nodded. "I did a human-interest piece on him. He's a helluva nice guy." He paused and looked Ryan up and down. "If you're a local boy, you should already know all you need to about Rocky Bianchi."

"I haven't lived around here in a long time." Ryan said. "Look, Bianchi has my friend in a bind. All I need is some background information."

"Yeah? And I need a beer. Meet me on the back deck of the Shuckin' Shack in an hour."

"Sounds good." Ryan stuck his hand out again, but the reporter ignored him and walked toward a blue minivan.

Ryan led Emily along Orange Street to the Cape Fear Riverwalk, a plank boardwalk that ran almost two miles along the river's edge. They strolled along, gawking at the old buildings and the people, who, despite the blustery day, were out in force, enjoying the beauty of downtown Wilmington. Across the river, in a specially dug basin, was the battleship USS *North Carolina*. She'd been berthed there since 1962, and Ryan had toured her many times.

He cleared his throat and took Emily's hand. "I'm sorry I made you mad with the wedding comments."

"Do you *want* to get married?"

"Absolutely," he confirmed.

"To *me*?"

"There's no one else, Em. I love *you* and want to keep you safe."

Emily smiled tiredly. "As long as we do the jobs we do, we'll never be safe."

She was right. Both of them liked the rush of danger and the excitement of solving a case, but if he kept butting heads with men like Rocky Bianchi, there was no safety for them. He promised himself that when he'd settled this feud between Rocky and Chad, he'd make a concerted effort to put her first, even if that meant he never picked up a gun again. What good was a blushing bride when her groom was face down in the gutter with a bullet in the back of his head? And all because he'd stepped into the fight one too many times.

"What's this really about? Chad or us getting married, because city hall is right up the street and I'm calling your bluff."

He grinned. "Let's go."

"You're serious?"

"Why not?"

"Because I want a wedding with our friends and family. I don't want some secret squirrel ceremony just to make you feel better. You put a ring on my finger, now you get to live in *my* fantasy world."

He looked out across the river at the old battleship, a relic that had seen action in every major conflict in the Pacific during World War II. If he continued this fight about the wedding, he would need the battleship's armor to protect him. When it came to the wedding, she seemed to have gone a little crazy and spent more hours than Ryan could count on the phone with her friends, planning every detail.

"Okay," he said. "I agreed to it, and I'm a man of my word. Beach wedding it is."

"I want you to know that I'm compromising with you, Ryan. Because my dream wedding would be at Vizcaya Mansion in a full white dress with a train and my groom in a tuxedo." She smiled wistfully. "My mother took me there one time when I was little, and there was a wedding taking place on the breakwater barge. I won't bore you with the details, but that's where I've always wanted to get married."

Wanting to please her and get his foot out of his mouth, Ryan said, "Let's do it."

"Are you serious?" she said.

"If that's what you want, then yes."

She grinned devilishly as she pulled out her phone and opened an Internet browser. "Do you want a daytime or evening reservation?"

"What's the difference?" he asked.

"About ten thousand dollars," she replied.

Ryan gulped. He could afford it, and if it made her happy, then why not? "If that's what you want."

"What I want is to be sure that you truly want to get married."

He cupped her face with both hands. "Emily Renée Hunt, I love you and I want to spend the rest of my life with you. Whether we get married in a courthouse or on the steps of the Vatican, I don't care as long as I'm there with you."

"You say the sweetest things."

Ryan kissed her long and hard, pulling her to him and holding her close. They broke apart when a passerby jokingly told them to get a room, and they continued strolling hand in hand along the Riverwalk toward their rendezvous with McClelland.

Seeing the smile illuminating his fiancée's face, Ryan felt his self-doubt beginning to simmer down. Emily's happiness meant the world to him, and even though he was sure he would miss the lure of excitement that beckoned from beneath the waves, he was certain of one thing.

He was going to miss her while she was in Florida.

CHAPTER TEN

John Watson founded the city of Wilmington in September 1732 on the hills along the confluence of the northeastern and northwestern branches of the Cape Fear River under its former name of New Carthage. Since then, the town had grown from a small frontier outpost into a modern port city and craft beer mecca. The early downtown buildings had been built from locally sourced brick and now qualified for historical status. Like many of the shops close to the water, the front of the Shuckin' Shack Oyster Bar was level with the street, and the rear dropped several stories beyond the hill toward the river. This section of buildings along Front Street had an outdoor patio and walkway which ran along the back to provide more seating and a splendid view of the river.

The brick foundations and the custom metalwork used for the stairs and pillars that held up the modern walkway had always fascinated Ryan. Looking at parts of the old walls was like looking at a time capsule of construction.

Ryan and Emily walked up the steps to the covered seating area and told the hostess there would be three of them. She seated them at a round table in a corner of the patio with a view of the river which was partially blocked by a hotel. To the west was another massive apartment complex under construction. Ryan remembered when the elevated walkway had crossed the street to a parking structure that the construction company had torn down to make way for the apartments.

Unsure what the reporter would drink, Ryan ordered two Stella Artois when the waitress came over, while Emily asked for a hard cider.

Ray McClelland joined them fifteen minutes later, by which time Ryan had already drunk both beers. The reporter ordered a locally brewed stout, and Ryan asked for black coffee and a glass of water.

"So, what did Rocky do to your friend?" McClelland asked.

"He had a couple of goons work him over," Ryan said. "They busted some ribs and punctured his lung."

"That doesn't surprise me. Bianchi's one sadistic asshole," the reporter said.

"I heard you were the man to speak to about Bianchi's business dealings."

The server brought their order, and when she'd left, McClelland said, "Yeah. I've written about them, but the only person who seems to care is me. My editor told me to drop it, and the cops don't want to hear about it."

"Do you know why?" Emily asked.

"Money talks and bullshit walks, honey, and I'm the one doing the walking."

"Are you still pursuing leads on Bianchi?" Ryan asked.

"Nope. This business is rough. If you want to pay your bills, you shut up and do what they tell you. I took this job because it was the only one that I could get. A degree in creative writing is as useless as tits on a boar hog."

"Tell me about Rocky Bianchi?" Ryan asked.

"He laid low when he first came to town and snapped up several apartment complexes. Then he turned into a loan shark and from what I've heard, he specializes in taking equity stakes in businesses when they couldn't afford to pay him back. Once Bianchi has his hooks in, it's tough to get them out," McClelland stated.

"How so?" Emily asked.

"This is just hearsay, but the rumor is he's part of the Mob and if someone defaults ... well, it's not good. I'm sure you've heard what the Mob does to people who don't pay back their loans."

"Are you sure he's with the Mob?" Ryan asked.

"I can't confirm it. It's just a suspicion. Rocky has a bunch of small businesses, and added all up, he does pretty well, but he's definitely got money coming from somewhere else. I just don't know where. What few stories we've run about him in the paper are about the money he donates to the arts or the historical society. He came to Wilmington with money, but, again, I don't know how he got it. Growing up, Rocky didn't have a pot to piss in. Maybe he's just a business genius who is struggling to stay out of poverty." McClelland shrugged and sucked down a big gulp of beer.

"That doesn't sound like the Mob to me," Emily said.

"*That* might not, but there are plenty of stories about broken legs and cement shoes," McClelland retorted.

Ryan shook his head. "Cement shoes, really?"

"That's the rumor. A while back, a fellow named John Parnell owned a piece of property that Bianchi wanted. After six months or so of harassing Parnell, Bianchi suddenly became the owner of the property and Parnell disappeared. He left everything behind: house; vehicles; clothes; all the money in his bank accounts. It's a genuine mystery. I checked with the State Department to see if Parnell had a passport, but they said he hadn't left the country."

"So, the theory is that Bianchi had him sign the property over before he shoved him off a boat?" Ryan asked.

McClelland shrugged. "No one really knows, but it makes for a delightful bedtime story, and I think Bianchi uses it to his advantage."

"I thought you were the resident expert on this guy?" Ryan said, thinking this was a waste of time. "What's Bianchi's background?"

"Charles 'Rocky' Bianchi grew up in Bakersville, N.C., in the Appalachian Mountains. It's a tiny town of less than eight hundred people. His parents were a couple of hippies who rejected normal society and taught weaving and basketry at a nearby craft school. Everyone I talked to who knew the Bianchis said Rocky was a normal kid. He went to college at UNC Chapel Hill and graduated with a degree in Economics. During his time there, he changed into the man we see today, coming into money so he could buy the apartment complexes here in town, and open a pawnshop and a used car dealership."

"You went to Bakersville?" Ryan asked.

McClelland nodded. "I wanted background info. Both his parents are dead. His mother died under mysterious circumstances and the cops blamed Rocky's father, who eventually hung himself."

Emily gasped. "That's horrible."

"Did it connect to Rocky?" Ryan asked.

"The old cop I talked to blamed it all on Rocky's dad. But if Rocky had a hand in it, it would definitely change him."

"Why would he want to kill his parents?" Emily asked.

McClelland shrugged. "I don't even want to speculate. What I do know is that after they died, Rocky basically had a free ride through college because people donated money to him, and he received grants based on his poverty status."

"Maybe he saw firsthand how the system worked, and now he's taking advantage of it," Ryan said. "If the cops don't care about him selling stolen boats or whatever else he's into, he probably thinks he can get away with whatever he wants."

"Wait," McClelland said. "You said he was selling stolen boats?"

Ryan nodded, regretting tipping his hand.

McClelland sipped his beer and stared out at the river. A moment later, he said, "Your friend was part of that?"

Not wanting to give more away, Ryan remained silent.

The reporter smirked. "I'll take that as a yes."

"Take it any way you want," Ryan replied.

"I think you have a line on a story, and I'd like to tag along."

"I'll let you know," Ryan said. He handed the reporter a business card for his fictitious business, Maritime Recovery.

"Whose Bob Parker?" McClelland asked.

"He's my partner," Ryan replied. "Just leave a message and I'll get it."

McClelland flicked the card with his finger. "Okay, but if there's a breaking story that involves anything we've just talked about, will you please call me?" He handed his own business card to Ryan.

"I'll keep you in mind," Ryan said, standing and tossing several twenty-dollar bills on the table. "Thanks for the information."

Ryan and Emily walked along the elevated walkway to the far end, then made their way across the street and down a narrow alley lined with overgrown trees on one side and several microbreweries on the other.

"Where to now?" Emily asked as they approached the Jeep.

"I'm thinking barbeque."

"When aren't you?" she asked teasingly.

"When I'm not thinking about other things." He put his arm around her shoulder and pulled her close. They paused by the passenger door and kissed, but Ryan's ringing cell phone interrupted them.

Emily slid into the passenger seat, and Ryan closed her door while fishing his phone from his pocket. He held it to his ear and said, "What's up, Scott?"

"Just trying to get a handle on what we're dealing with."

Ryan gave him an abbreviated version of events as he got into the driver's seat and started the Jeep.

"I'll bring plenty of gear," Scott said. "I'm hitching a ride on the DWR King Air first thing tomorrow morning. We should get into Wilmington around ten o'clock. I'll need you to pick me up at Cape Fear Regional Jetport."

"Roger that. I'll see you then." Ryan hung up and backed the Jeep out of the parking spot, paid for their time in the garage, and headed toward a barbeque restaurant to pick up dinner on their way home.

As they pulled into the lot at Wrightsville Beach Marina, darkness had settled, and the lights glowed along the docks. Ryan glanced at the marina's security cameras on their way to *Huntress*. Cameras and lights were excellent deterrents for thieves, but darkness, particularly the inky blackness of the marshes along the waterway beyond the clusters of city lights, provided them with plenty of cover. The hairs on the back of Ryan's neck stood up as he had the sudden feeling he was being watched.

When they stopped at the boat, Ryan turned slowly in a circle, scanning the surrounding boats, the docks, parking lots, and nearby buildings. He saw nothing out of the ordinary, but he still couldn't shake the terrible feeling that *something* was about to go horribly wrong.

CHAPTER ELEVEN

The Hinckley 40 Picnic Boat was one of the most beautiful boats Tim Davis had ever seen. It had twin Cummins diesels and waterjet propulsion systems, allowing it to have a two-foot draft, perfect for cruising through the shallow waters along the Intracoastal Waterway. He wasn't sure how it would handle large waves, but he figured that if they got into trouble, they could duck out of an inlet and cross Frying Pan Shoals without worrying about either grounding or having other boats follow them through the shallows known as the Graveyard of the Atlantic.

Tim and P.J. had stolen electronics from two boats since darkness had fallen and they'd passed the Big M Casino ship, meaning they were near the Little River Inlet. They stayed on the ICW rather than going out to the ocean. Even though it was close to midnight, they had to be careful which boats they approached. Some were on lifts, meaning it was harder to access them, while others were well lit, including the dock leading to the house.

After picking the electronics off four more boats, Tim threw the throttle forward and rocketed them past Sunset

Beach and Ocean Isle Beach before turning out of the ICW at Shallot Inlet. They rounded the point where he'd partied with other boaters on the wide sandy beach and headed into the Atlantic. If the going was too rough, they could always duck back in at Lockwoods Folly Inlet or the Cape Fear River, but Tim wanted to get back to Wilmington while it was still dark so they could move their cache to his truck with no one seeing them, and running full speed across Onslow Bay was the quickest way home.

The Hinckley handled the three-footers with ease as they raced along. The boat was capable of thirty-five knots and Tim had pegged her needle on the smooth ICW waters, but here, on the heaving seas, he wasn't able to hold that speed. P.J. held on to the grab rails as they bucked through the waves just as fast as Tim could take them.

As they approached Frying Pan Shoals, Tim slowed and studied the situation. White foaming waves broke over the sandbars and rock piles, marking their locations. He'd cut through here frequently, but always during the day.

"Watch the depth sounder and the chart plotter," Tim said.

P.J. stepped closer and manipulated the zoom on the plotter. He pointed to an area they could squeeze through, and Tim steered for the deeper water around the sandbars. It didn't take long to cross the shoals, and the ocean bottom quickly dropped away on the other side.

"Hey, you see that?" P.J. asked.

"What?"

P.J. pointed to their right, farther out to sea. "I saw a flash of light."

"Probably some fishermen," Tim said.

"There it is again."

Tim turned to look at the dim flashing light. It was yellow, not the normal green, red, or white running lights on a boat.

"Someone might be in trouble," P.J. remarked.

"Maybe, but we're not in the rescue business. Let 'em call Sea Tow."

They watched the light continue to flash as they motored north.

"We should go see if they need help," P.J. said insistently.

"We've got a boatload of stolen electronics, man. We can't go helping people out like Good Samaritans and shit."

"*Come on*, dude," P.J. argued. "Maybe we can get a salvage claim out of it."

Tim shook his head. He knew better than to deviate from their plan, but P.J. was, without a doubt, going to wear him out with the constant blabbering about checking out the source of the light. If the boaters were okay, he and P.J. would go about their business, and if not ... *Shit*, maybe a salvage tow wouldn't be so bad. They could get Yeager to put a claim on the boat.

Tim turned the wheel and pointed the Hinckley at the flashing light, now a more persistent flickering on the horizon.

Five minutes later, he pulled alongside a pilothouse trawler riding low in the water.

"Do you need help?" P.J. called to the couple on the trawler's aft deck.

"Yes," the man replied. "We don't have any power."

"Hold on," P.J. said. He went below and grabbed a jumper pack he'd liberated from a boat earlier that evening. Coming back on deck, he held it up and asked, "Will this help?"

"No. Our batteries are too far gone. I'll toss you my anchor line and you can tow us in," the man in the expensive fishing shirt and pants said.

"Let me check them," P.J. offered.

Tim brought the Hinckley close to the Pilot, and P.J. hopped across the gunwales, then followed the man below while Tim moved the Hinckley away so the two boats wouldn't collide in the rough seas.

P.J. examined the batteries and hooked the charger pack to the starter battery. It showed the battery level was extremely low, but he had the man turn the key anyway. The starter slowly turned the crank and pistons in the engine, but there wasn't enough juice to overcome the friction of the spinning metal parts. P.J. called for him to stop, then checked several things before asking him to try again. The result was the same.

The boat heaved in the waves as they hit it square on the port side. They were drifting toward Frying Pan Shoals, and if they didn't get the engine started or take it under tow, the boat would become nothing more than another statistic of the treacherous waters.

Back on deck, P.J. motioned for Tim to bring the Hinckley in close. When Tim was alongside, P.J. told him the batteries were shot and that they would need to tow the boat back to shore. Tim nodded and told P.J. to get the Pilot's anchor line and rig a tow bridle.

Once they had the tow line connected, P.J. rejoined Tim on the Hinckley. As the line stretchèd taut, Tim added power to enable the Hinckley to pull the heavier steel boat through the waves.

"Plot us a course to Bradley Creek. I want to get this tub off the water as fast as we can," Tim said.

"The woman is kinda hot for an older chick," P.J. replied. "Let's stop and have some fun."

Tim pondered that statement for a moment. No one needed to know if the owners were on the boat when they'd found it. Bianchi could work his magic with the paperwork, and there would be no need to file a claim. They could sell the boat and split the profits with Bianchi. It would be a much bigger payday than just delivering boats or selling stolen electronics. Besides, he could use some relief himself.

Pulling back the throttle, Tim allowed the Hinckley to slow. They put out fenders to keep the boats from rubbing together, then allowed the two crafts to drift close. Tim hopped aboard the Pilot and lashed the Hinckley's lines to the Pilot's cleats.

"What's going on?" the older man asked.

"We needed to make a pit stop, old man," Tim said, distracting the man as P.J. smacked him on the back of the head with an aluminum fish club that he'd taken from a sportfisher. Anglers normally used the short, little billy club to kill pelagic game fish, but tonight, P.J. used it to kill a man.

The woman shrieked at the sight of her husband crumpled on the deck, blood oozing from his head. Tim turned to her, and, as he advanced, she retreated into the cabin. He followed, hollering over his shoulder for P.J. to keep the nose of the Hinckley pointed into the waves. P.J. grumbled but followed his instructions.

Inside the pilothouse, the woman ran down the spiral staircase with Tim right behind her. He caught her in the forward stateroom. When he'd had his way with her, he drank two beers from the fridge and exchanged places with P.J.

After an hour, Tim began to worry that the commercial fishermen and offshore anglers would soon be heading out, and he wanted to have the bodies disposed of by then.

When P.J. came on deck, he had the woman slung over his shoulder. By the looseness of her body, Tim knew she was dead. P.J. dropped her beside her husband, and, together, he and Tim wrapped the anchor chain around the two bodies and clipped the anchor to their feet. Tim took them farther offshore into eighty feet of water according to the depth sounder, and P.J. pushed the bodies overboard before jumping aboard the Hinckley.

"Think we should cut it loose?" P.J. asked.

"No. We need the money," Tim said.

What he didn't tell P.J. was that when he'd been with the woman in the stateroom, he'd stripped off her two rings and her charm bracelet and had them both in his pocket. He'd get his own payday when he sold them at the pawnshop.

The sun was just coming up as they maneuvered the Hinckley and the Pilot into the berths that Chad Yeager kept at the Bradley Creek Marina. Tim backed his truck down to the dock, and the two men moved their stolen merchandise to the bed of the truck with one of the marina's two-wheeled carts.

Tim stepped into the Pilot's stateroom to have one last look for evidence of their activities. The bed was missing its sheets, and the room smelled of disinfectant. P.J. must have disposed of them when they were motoring to deeper water. That was fine with Tim.

They got into the truck and drove across town, heading for their tiny river shack.

But there was still something that gnawed at Tim's gut. This wasn't the first time the two friends had shared a woman or buried a body, but there was something different about this one.

Whatever it was, it wouldn't be good.

CHAPTER TWELVE

It was an hour's drive from Wrightsville Beach Marina to the Cape Fear Regional Jetport in Southport, where the Cape Fear River exited into the frothing Atlantic. Ryan and Emily left extra early so they could stop at the Famous Toastery, one of the best breakfast places in town. He opted for a thick burrito and black coffee, while Emily had a mimosa and avocado toast.

Done eating, they headed through town to pick up Scott from the airport. Ryan turned onto Oleander, and as they passed over Bradley Creek, Emily looked out the window at the marina. One of the boats moored there caught her eye. "That's Andrea and Gary's Pilot," she said. "What's it doing there?"

"I don't know." Ryan shrugged.

Emily dug Andrea's phone number from her jacket pocket and dialed it. The call went straight to voicemail. "Turn around," she ordered Ryan.

"What about Scott?" he asked.

"He can wait. It will only take a minute to make sure that Andrea and Gary are all right."

Ryan swung the Jeep around at the next available place and headed for the marina. He stopped in a parking spot several minutes later. They walked to the boat slip, and Emily called out to Andrea. There was no answer.

Walking around the boat on the narrow finger pier, Ryan saw a red stain on the deck. His heart rate increased as he climbed aboard, hoping against hope that it wasn't what he thought it was. Unfortunately, he confirmed his suspicions when he squatted over the spot.

"What is it?" Emily asked.

"Blood."

Emily climbed over the rail and went into the pilothouse, but nothing seemed amiss there. Both went down the steps to the cabin. In the forward stateroom, they saw someone had stripped the bed, and the air smelled of bleach.

"What happened here?" Emily asked.

"I don't know," Ryan answered. He looked about the cabin and saw the door to the engine bay was open. Inside, a jumper pack sat beside the batteries, its cables still hooked to one. Using the sleeve of his coat, he pushed the pack around and tipped it over, revealing the owner's name, phone number, and the name of a boat etched into the plastic surface.

He took a picture of it and left the charging pack in place. "We need to go."

Emily led the way off the boat and back to the Jeep. She tried Andrea's number again. "Now, I'm really worried. Why was there *blood* on the deck?"

Pulling out of the parking lot, Ryan said, "There could be a simple explanation."

"Which is?"

"They had trouble with their batteries and docked at Bradley Creek to fix the problem. One of them fell or cut themselves, and they went to the hospital."

"I hope it's that simple," she said wistfully.

———

RYAN STOPPED the Jeep Wrangler outside the Cape Fear Regional Jetport's new terminal. He got out and stretched his legs while watching for DWR's white Beechcraft King Air to descend. The wind was from the east, off the ocean, so the plane would approach from the west. It was easier for Scott to fly in the private plane than to worry about declaring his firearms and other toys to the commercial airlines.

Ten minutes later, the twin-turboprop King Air broke through the clouds to land, rolled to a stop, and the pilot shut off the engines. Ryan expected Chuck Newland to come bounding down the steps in his Stetson hat, cowboy boots, and flight suit, but there was a blonde behind the controls. He recognized her as Erica Opsal, the second of DWR's pilots and the girlfriend of his buddy Rick Hayes.

When the airstairs unfolded, a grinning Scott Gregory came down them, followed by Erica. Scott was three inches taller than Ryan's six foot, with thick blond hair and a shaggy mustache. He wore jeans, combat boots, and a T-shirt stretched across his muscular chest and arms. He had the Second Amendment of the U.S. Constitution tattooed on his right forearm in the shape of an AR-15 rifle, and his other arm was a sleeve of colorful tats. Among them was a Navy SEAL trident in front of an American flag.

"Welcome to North Carolina," Ryan said, bumping fists with Scott and then Erica.

"It's not the Caribbean, but it's all right," Scott said, looking around.

"I agree," Ryan replied. "Let's get your gear and get out of here."

"Can you drive your vehicle over here?" Scott asked. "It'll make unloading easier."

Ryan got the gate code from the front office and backed the Jeep up to the plane door. Scott handed down his duffle, followed by three hard-sided Pelican cases. He patted the largest and said, "Greg sent this for you. He said he was tired of storing your commercial gear."

When Ryan had left his old crew to hunt for a hijacked freighter, he had also left his dive gear aboard the salvage vessel *Peggy Lynn*. Greg had shipped it from Nicaragua, where they'd been working, to Texas City, and now it was back in Ryan's hands.

With the gear loaded in the Jeep, Erica made her farewells and took off in the plane, heading back to Texas.

"So, what are we into?" Scott asked from the Jeep's back seat as Ryan navigated them north along the Cape Fear River.

"We're dealing with a couple of things right now." Ryan explained about Chad and his association with Rocky Bianchi, then Emily filled him in on the disappearance of Andrea and Gary.

"Have you called the number on the charger pack?" Scott asked.

Ryan had Emily dial the number from the photo he'd taken of the charger pack, and the call connected to the Jeep's Bluetooth speakers, allowing all three to hear the conversation.

When the man on the other end answered, Ryan asked, "Is this Ed Butler?"

"Yeah. Who's this?" the gruff voice demanded.

Ryan introduced himself, then said, "Do you own something called *Skirt Chaser*?"

"Yeah. She's a Hatteras forty-five flybridge. Why?"

"Have you seen her recently?" Ryan asked.

"Hell's bells, son, you can't miss her. She's sitting at the end of my dock," Butler said with incredulity.

"Can you do me a favor? Take a walk out there and look her over? I found a charging pack with your name on it. I'm trying to figure out how it came to be on a boat in Wilmington."

"Wait a minute." The man stomped down the dock, muttering under his breath. After a few minutes, Butler yelled, "*Son of a bitch*! They took it all. Every mother lovin' piece of electronics on my boat. *Everything*. It's all gone."

"Ed," Ryan said, keeping his voice calm. "You need to call the police and report the theft. I can bring your charger pack back to you."

"Keep the stupid thing," Butler growled. "I'll get another one with the insurance settlement."

"Good luck," said Ryan, before ending the call.

"Where's the charger pack now?" Scott asked.

"It's still on *Due South*," Ryan said.

"Let's stop there and talk to the marina workers," Emily suggested.

"Yeah. Maybe they can shed some light on what's going on," Scott added.

Ryan drove them back to Bradley Creek Marina. The boat was in the same slip as when Ryan and Emily had stopped earlier. Getting out of the Jeep, Scott headed for the *Due South* to have a look around while Ryan and Emily walked toward the office.

On their way, they spotted a teenage boy wearing a polo shirt with the marina's logo on it.

"Hey," Ryan called, waving him over.

The kid came trotting up. "What can I do for you?"

"Do you know who brought that Pilot in?" Ryan pointed across the docks to *Due South*.

"I wasn't here. You should talk to Jim in the office."

The couple stepped inside the marina office and store. Ryan figured that Jim, a man about Ryan's own age, would talk more freely with a beautiful blonde, so he motioned for Emily to talk to him while he perused the ship's store and eavesdropped on the conversation.

"Hi," Emily said in her best 'dumb blonde' voice.

"How can I help?" Jim asked, glancing between Emily and Ryan before refocusing his attention on her.

"Can you tell me who brought in that Pilot yesterday?"

"Yesterday?" Jim echoed. "No, ma'am. It came in this morning. See that Hinckley beside it? That towed your Pilot in."

"The couple who own it ... they're friends of ours. Did they say where they went?"

"There wasn't anyone aboard *Due South*," Jim replied. "It was just the two guys on the Hinckley."

Ryan felt a knot of dread tighten in his gut. Emily's suspicions were correct: something untoward had befallen Andrea and Gary.

"Do you know the two guys on the Hinckley?" she asked.

Jim scratched his chin and studied her.

"The couple who own that Pilot left Wrightsville Beach Marina yesterday afternoon," Emily said. "No one has seen them since. I'd really like to know what's happened to them."

"I don't know," Jim said with a shrug. "All I can tell you is what I already have. Maybe ask Chad Yeager, he rents those slips."

Emily glanced at Ryan, and he rolled his eyes. Of course, Chad was involved.

She nodded and thanked Jim for the information. Ryan purchased two sodas and a bottle of water to show his appreciation.

When Ryan and Emily walked outside, Scott was sitting on the Jeep's front bumper. Ryan handed Scott a cold

Mountain Dew and relayed Emily's conversation with Jim to him.

"Remember those trackers we used on our last mission?" Scott asked. "The ones we put in the prepaid card blister packs?"

"Yeah," Ryan said.

"I put one in the charger pack. I figured whoever stole it from Butler would come looking for it."

"That's good thinking."

"Do you think whoever stole the charger pack had something to do with the disappearance of Andrea and Gary?" Emily asked.

"That's the best theory we have," Scott said.

Ryan leaned against the Jeep's hood, looking at the two boats. He took a sip of soda and tried to fit the pieces of the puzzle together. The Pilot had come in with the Hinckley. There was dried blood on the Pilot's deck, and its owners had disappeared. It was easy to assume that Andrea and Gary had succumbed to the sea or the kids on the Hinckley had done something to them. Why else would they have abandoned their boat?

"What about GPS tracks?" Ryan asked.

"I can download them," Scott said, and he rummaged in his gear, looking for the equipment he would need.

"Let's put trackers on both boats," Ryan said, and Scott dug two from the case. "Make a note of their HINs, too." Knowledge of the vessels' Hull Identification Numbers never hurt, especially if they needed to run histories on them later.

While Emily stood guard, watching for anyone who might arrive and claim both vessels, Scott downloaded the GPS tracks from both boats onto a memory stick, and Ryan planted the trackers and jotted down the HINs for both boats.

Less than ten minutes had elapsed from the time Ryan

and Scott had trotted down the dock until Ryan was back in the Jeep. He let out a sigh. Not only had he made promises to his family and to Chad, but now he also felt responsible for finding Andrea and Gary.

"What are you thinking?" Emily asked.

"That we have two problems to solve."

CHAPTER THIRTEEN

As Scott finished downloading the GPS tracks from the Hinckley, Ryan felt his phone vibrate in his pocket. He pulled it out to see Chad's number on the caller ID screen.

Putting it to his ear, Ryan said, "Hey, bud. How are you feeling?"

"Ryan, it's Janice," she whispered.

"Are you okay?" Ryan asked, instantly alert because of the fear in her voice.

"Rocky is here."

"At the hospital?"

"Yes. Ryan you have to come, *please*!"

"I'm on my way, Janice. Hold on." Ryan ended the call and climbed into the Jeep. He beeped the horn as he started the engine.

Scott came jogging up the dock, his head swiveling around as he scanned the docks and parking lots. Once the ex-SEAL was in the back seat, Ryan pulled away, speeding well above the posted limit in his haste to get to the hospital.

Traffic was heavier than usual on Oleander Drive, and Ryan smacked the steering wheel and yelled at the cars in front of him in a vain attempt to get them moving. He swerved around several and cut across oncoming traffic into the parking lot of the municipal golf course, sped the wrong way down a one-way drive, and swerved around an approaching golf cart before shooting out onto a residential side street. Several turns later, he passed his old high school on Shipyard Boulevard.

Twelve minutes after they'd left the marina, Ryan pulled the Jeep to a stop outside the hospital. As he jumped out of the Jeep, he said, "Scott, stay with the gear."

Ryan took off running, aware that Emily was behind him, but his worry wasn't about her. He had to get to Chad's room.

When he burst through the room door, he was breathing hard from taking the stairs two at a time.

But he was too late.

Rocky Bianchi was nowhere in sight. Janice sat in the chair, her face in her hands, sobbing quietly. Chad turned his head to look at Ryan.

Bending over and putting his hands on his knees, Ryan said, "Tell me what happened."

"He told me to get back to work. That there were things he needed to have done," Chad said. He fell silent for a moment, chewing on his lower lip. "If ... If I don't do what he wants, he's going to turn me into the cops for selling his stolen boats. The bastard threatened ..." Chad's brows furrowed as he scrunched his face up, but he couldn't hold back the tear that slipped out. "He told me he would send some guys to my mom's house. Ryan, he said he would let them do whatever they wanted to do to her if I don't continue to help him or if I demand the shares of my business back. What the hell am I supposed to do?"

Ryan's jaw ached from clenching it. There was no way that bastard was going to touch Janice, and if he did, Ryan would put a bullet in the back of Rocky Bianchi's skull and bury him in the swamp where no one would ever find him.

Janice came around the bed, and Ryan enveloped her in his arms. He held her close as he told her everything would be all right. Feeling a hand on his shoulder, he turned to see Emily.

He mouthed a silent "Can you take her?" and passed Janice into Emily's comforting arms. Emily said, "Let's get something to eat," as she led Janice out to the hallway.

Glancing at the clock, Ryan saw it was almost lunchtime. He leaned on the bed, hands grasping the bedrails so tightly that his knuckles turned white. "How do you want to handle this?"

"I want out, Ryan. I can't have them threatening my mom. Coming after me is one thing, but not my mom."

"I know. I know," Ryan whispered.

"I screwed up by trusting Rocky, and now I'm paying for that, but I don't know what you can do to help me."

Ryan sat in the chair beside the bed. As much as Ryan believed that anyone who broke the law should be held accountable, he had a blind spot when it came to his friends. He knew Chad had been involved in some shady dealings in the past, but the past was just that—the past. Everyone deserved a second chance.

The first time Ryan had given Chad a second chance was the day he'd met Chad in the middle school cafeteria. Chad had tried to cut in the lunch line, and Ryan had told him to get out. A shoving match had become a boxing brawl that had left both boys with black eyes and in the principal's office, serving in-school suspension during their lunch period for the next week. The principal had forced them to sit beside each other, and, after the second day, the two boys had become best friends.

Ryan had gotten his fair share of second chances and guidance over the years, and despite seeing the worst in people while hunting serial killers, terrorists, and thieves across the Caribbean, he believed that people were inherently good. Doing evil was a choice, just like doing the right thing was a choice. It was free will.

But he couldn't leave Chad in the lurch again.

Rubbing his face with his hands, he thought back to the day Chad had told him he wasn't going with him on the sailing trip around the world. They had planned it all out and talked about it often, but when the day came, Chad had stood on the dock and waved to Ryan as he sailed away. *Why didn't I make you come with me? Your life could have been so different. And you wouldn't be in this mess.*

But Ryan also knew that people rarely changed. Their nature was their nature, and if Chad was prone to finding trouble at home, who knew what kind of trouble they might have gotten into overseas?

At least Ryan would have been there for him. Now was his chance to make it up to Chad.

"What else are you helping Bianchi with besides selling boats?" Ryan asked.

"I've been supplying skiffs to his swamp rats."

"What about the outboard theft at your place?"

Chad looked sheepish. "That was me. I needed the money."

Ryan shook his head. "Okay. I'll forget about that. If all you do is sell and provide boats, why is Bianchi so interested in your place?"

"Trust me—once he has his hooks in you, he won't let go. He does this with all the businesses he's a part of."

"How many?"

Chad shrugged, then moaned in pain. His breathing was shallow, compensating for the agony it caused against his broken rib. Ryan could sympathize. He'd badly bruised his ribs on several occasions, and the recovery process was long and painful. It was hard to get comfortable enough to sleep or sit, let alone to breathe.

"Maybe half a dozen," Chad said. "He owns a bunch of places outright; some he just muscled his way into. Hostile takeover, they call it in the financial world."

"Where's his office?" Ryan asked.

Chad grimaced as he adjusted his body. "He has an office above his downtown bar, Foxy Lady, and another one at his car lot out on Market Street, by the middle school."

Ryan nodded as he filed away the information for future use. He was building a mental map of Rocky Bianchi's business empire. With Barry Thatcher's help, he would be able to connect all the dots and have a complete overview. Still unsure of some pieces of the puzzle, he asked Chad for clarification. "Do you know any of his swamp rats?"

"The one I always dealt with was named Tim. I never asked his last name, and I didn't want to know. I just gave them a boat to use, and he dropped off paperwork for the boats he brought to my slip at Bradley Creek."

"Tim Davis?" Ryan asked, recalling the name Henry had told him.

"Could be. I'm telling you, Ryan: I kept my mouth shut and didn't ask questions. That was stupid on my part, but when I finally started asking questions, look where it landed me."

"So, you don't know where Davis lives?"

"No, but that kid is trouble, and so are the two brothers he runs with. I heard one of them got picked up by the cops in the middle of stealing shit from a marina over on Motts Channel, near you. Not much more I can tell you, other than that they look like typical swamp rats. You know what I'm talking about."

The term 'swamp rat,' as they used it, referred to rednecks

from the lower income bracket who lived in the low, marshy areas along the coast or up the rivers.

It seemed Henry had been correct in his assessment of the miscreants. "You mean John Jeff and Patrick Jefferies?" Ryan pressed.

"Jefferies sounds familiar. You sure seem to know a lot of Wilmington's finest hoodlums for saying you've only been back in town a few days."

"Henry keeps his ear to the ground. He mentioned having some problems with these kids over at the marina."

"I think they're connected to a lot of the thefts along the ICW."

"You're probably right," Ryan agreed, thinking about the charger pack on board *Due South*. "Do you think they've killed anyone?"

"Hard to say," Chad replied. "I wouldn't put anything past them. Why?"

"When we passed Bradley Creek Marina this morning, there was a pilothouse trawler in one of your berths that belonged to a couple who left from Wrightsville Beach Marina yesterday afternoon. I found a spot of blood on the deck. The manager at Bradley said the kids on the Hinckley towed the trawler in last night, but he didn't see the couple."

Chad shook his head. "Damn bastards. If the cops find that boat in my slip, they'll come looking for me. It's like I'm a shit magnet."

"Which is why we need to move quickly on this. How does it work between you and Bianchi?"

"He brings me paperwork for the boats, and I get a commission for selling them. I assumed they came from his car lot because he horse-trades all the time."

Ryan nodded and leaned back in the chair, stretching out his legs. After a moment of thought, he said, "You want out of all this, right?"

Chad nodded.

"Any ideas on how to do that?" Ryan asked.

"You need to stay as far away from him as possible," Chad replied. "Let me deal with it."

The problem, as Ryan saw it, was that Chad's way of handling it would get him killed. As sound as Chad's advice was, Ryan knew he wouldn't be taking it.

CHAPTER FOURTEEN

After Emily had calmed Janice Yeager, and Ryan had assured her that both she and her son would be safe from whatever harm Rocky Bianchi promised to rain down on them if Chad didn't cooperate, the couple left the hospital and retreated to the Jeep.

Ryan turned to Emily. "How do you feel about getting out of town early?"

She gave him a quizzical look, then crossed her arms. "Why?"

"I'm going to shake the tree and see what falls out, and if you're in Florida, it would bring me peace of mind."

Emily nodded. "I understand. I'll see if I can change my flight." She pulled out her phone and began pecking at the screen.

Scott, who had stayed with the Jeep while Ryan and Emily were inside, got out and leaned against the front fender. "What do you mean by 'shake the tree?'"

"I'm still working on that," Ryan said. Again, he needed to talk to Barry Thatcher and get more information about

Bianchi and his businesses to determine which direction he should go.

Ryan called Kyle Fowler to ask if he knew of any police officers or sheriff's deputies who wanted to earn some extra money by sitting in Chad's room and explained the reasons why Chad and Janice needed protection.

Kyle said he would love to help but had family and work obligations he could not get out of on short notice, but he promised to get someone over there right away. There were always officers looking to make a few bucks on a side hustle, and with Ryan willing to pay cash, Kyle told him there would be no shortage of volunteers.

"How soon can you get someone to the hospital?" Ryan asked.

"Couple of hours. I gotta put out the word."

Ryan thanked Kyle, ended the call, and put his phone away. "Scott, I want you to stay here until security arrives for Chad. Emily, what did you find out?"

"I changed my ticket. I leave in three hours," she said.

"All right. Let's hustle."

Scott retrieved a bag from the Jeep and headed for the hospital entrance, while Ryan and Emily got in the Jeep and sped away.

They swung by Wrightsville Beach Marina and grabbed her bags from *Huntress*, then raced across town to the airport. Ryan dropped Emily at the curb by the departure gate and gave her a quick hug and a kiss.

"I'd tell you to stay safe, but that isn't in your nature." With a smile, Emily said, "Good luck on your adventure. I wish I could stick around to help."

"You're helping by leaving early. Now, learn lots so you can make more money and keep me in the lifestyle I've become accustomed to."

She giggled and kissed him again.

After another round of *I love you*s, Ryan got in the Jeep and drove away. This was the first time they would be apart in many months, and it felt strange not to have her with him. At the same time, it was nice to have some quiet to recharge his batteries.

He had been alone for most of his life, in and out of relationships that always seemed to have an end date the moment they got started, but being with Emily was different. There was never an end in sight when he was with her, even when they'd first met. He loved her for her body, her mind, her passion, and her commitment to her job and to the hobbies she pursued. They both loved to dive, sail, and chase bad guys, even if they had different methods. She was strong and independent, and she wasn't afraid to speak her mind. And she didn't want to change him. Emily accepted Ryan for who he was, although it had taken nearly two years for her to realize that and for them to get back together. She'd broken up with him after a ruthless international arms dealer had kidnapped her and used her as leverage against Ryan.

The couple had buried the proverbial hatchet after reconnecting during the search for a missing freighter, and they had moved in together on Ryan's old sailboat, *Windseeker*. He loved being back with Emily so much that he had asked her to marry him, and now he couldn't imagine life without her by his side.

Ryan stopped at a barbeque joint and picked up sandwiches for himself, Scott, Chad, and Janice, then drove back to the hospital.

By the time he arrived, there was a barrel-chested man with short hair and a mustache occupying a chair in the corner of the room. From his vantage point, the man could see the television and the door to the room. As Ryan entered, the man dropped his paperback and stood, moving into a combat stance, ready to draw his gun, as he ordered Ryan to stop.

"It's okay, Mike," Scott said. "He's one of the good guys." Then Scott made the introductions. Mike Boostrom was a police officer for the city of Wilmington. He said he needed the extra cash, but Ryan didn't like the menacing glance Boostrom gave to Chad and Janice.

Ryan held up the bag of food. "If I'd known you'd be here, I would have brought more sandwiches."

"Don't worry about it." Boostrom sat down and picked his book up off the floor. Ryan noticed it was Robert Kurson's *Shadow Divers,* documenting John Chatterton and Richie Kohler's journey to identify the sunken wreck of a German U-boat sixty miles off the coast of New Jersey.

"That's an excellent book," Ryan said. "I've read it several times."

"I just started diving," Boostrom explained.

Ryan knew that when the rapture of the deep grabbed a man, he would devour endless books, seminars, and training in a quest to conquer his new Everest. Even after thousands of dives, the ocean and her splendor still kept Ryan locked in her embrace. Like a bolt out of the blue, he remembered a Bible verse from Psalm 107 that Henry O'Shannassy would quote to him:

> *Those who go down to the sea in ships,*
> *Who do business on great waters;*
> *They have seen the works of the Lord,*
> *And His wonders in the deep.*

WHY THE VERSE had popped into his mind, Ryan didn't

know, but it had always been apt for sailors and divers. They, indeed, had seen the mighty works of nature at her best—and her worst.

"Keep at it," Ryan encouraged. "It's a great sport."

"You dive?" Boostrom asked.

"A couple of times," Ryan said, and he shot Scott a look when he snickered. He handed out sandwiches and sat beside Janice to eat.

When he finished his food, Ryan said goodbye to Chad and Janice and motioned for Scott to accompany him out of the room. They walked to the Jeep and climbed in.

"Where to?" Scott asked.

"To shake the tree."

Rocky Bianchi's bar was in an old, whitewashed brick warehouse on Water Street, but the solution of lime and water had worn away over the decades, exposing the brick. Ryan and Scott did a drive-by, scouting the bar and the surrounding area for escape routes and looking for potential threats.

Ryan found a parking spot, and the two men strolled along the River Walk for a block to get back to the bar. A sign for the bar hung on an old crane arm that projected out over the street. They walked up the steps onto a new wooden deck where an enormous black man with a shaved head and wooly beard was checking IDs at the door. He just smiled at Ryan and Scott as they passed, not bothering to look at their driver's licenses.

Inside, country music blared from a sound system, and they could hardly hear the bartender when they ordered draft beers from her. Scott lingered a moment to take in her tight-fitting white tank top and black yoga pants before following

Ryan past the pool tables and dart boards to a narrow booth. They sat and sipped their beers while taking in the atmosphere of old nautical signs and artwork. People had plastered stickers on almost every surface of the place, and the crowd was an eclectic mix of tourists and locals.

As they drank their locally brewed craft beers, Ryan watched a large man sitting on a stool beside a door that, he assumed, led upstairs to Rocky's office. He suspected they would have to go through him to see the bar owner.

The waitress, in a similar outfit to the bartender, appeared as Ryan was finishing his beer, and he asked her if Bianchi was upstairs. She gave him a questioning glance and asked if he wanted a refill. Ryan shook his head and dug a twenty-dollar bill out of his pocket. He held it out to her and again asked if the owner was upstairs. Taking the money, she slipped it into her bra and nodded toward the door beside the big bouncer.

Ryan got up, walked over to Bianchi's guard, and told him he wanted to see Bianchi. The bouncer shook his head. Ryan leaned in close to the man's ear and said, "Tell him I'm here about Chad Yeager."

The bouncer narrowed his dark brows, then stood and motioned for them to wait. He went through the door and up the steps. A minute later, he came down and told the two men to go up.

"What's the plan?" Scott whispered as they ascended the stairs.

"Just follow my lead," Ryan said. "Act as my muscle."

"Copy that."

Stepping into Bianchi's office was like stepping back to the era of *Goodfellas* and gangsters, with its heavy oak desk, overstuffed dark leather couch, and frosted glass on the cabinetry. There was even a fake Tommy gun mounted on a wooden plaque above the liquor cabinet. If this guy wasn't in the Mob, he fancied himself as a mobster.

Ryan walked over to the window and looked down on Henderson Alley, a dark narrow gap between the centuries-old buildings. The sun had almost set on the horizon, spreading a rosy glow of reds and oranges across the city.

"What do you want?" Bianchi snapped, not rising from behind his desk.

"I want you to get off Chad's back," Ryan said to the loan shark.

Bianchi shrugged.

"Your river rats are punks," Ryan said. "But you—you're different. You like to strong-arm people by throwing your money around."

"He's still a punk," Scott muttered.

"Get the hell out of my office," Bianchi ordered. "LeRoy!"

"Calm down," Ryan said. "There's no need for your muscle."

"You brought yours," Bianchi shot back.

"He's just my friend."

Bianchi shook his head and smiled wryly as he leaned back in his chair. "If you want the truth, I enjoy having Chad in my pocket. He's easy to control, and he does what he's told. He's a hothead, just like you."

Ryan clenched his fists, trying to keep himself from leaping across the desk and punching Bianchi in the face. Certain people just set him off, and this asshole was one of them.

"How much?" Scott asked, coming to Ryan's aid.

"How much for what?" Bianchi smirked.

"How much will it take for you to leave Chad alone?" Scott responded.

"I told you, I like having him around," sneered Bianchi.

Scott took a step forward. "How much?"

"Half a mil," Bianchi said as LeRoy, the guard from downstairs, came through the office door. "Get them out of here."

He made a hand gesture to LeRoy like he was sweeping out the trash.

Ryan stepped to the desk and stared Bianchi in the eye. "Get off Chad's back. He wants no part in your illegal shit."

Bianchi's eyebrow twitched as a faint smile lifted his left lip. "I'm not making him do anything. He *chose* to do it. But to answer your demand—no, I won't get off his back."

"Let's go, gentlemen," LeRoy ordered.

"You may have money, but you'll never be more than a two-bit con artist," Scott said to Bianchi.

"I'll pay it," Ryan growled, continuing to stare at Bianchi.

The loan shark laughed. "You want to pay deadbeat Yeager's tab?"

"Yeah. Cash or check?"

Bianchi looked down, as if saddened by the offer, and shook his head. When he looked up, he had a thoughtful expression on his face. "It's tempting. It really is. I don't know you from Adam, and you walk in here, wanting to pay a man's debts for him? That takes balls. *Big* ones. But I'm not stupid. It's a hard pass."

"You're making a mistake," Scott said.

Bianchi smiled tiredly. "Maybe, but I don't think so."

Ryan hated him. The man was smug and overly confident. The tension from squeezing his fist made Ryan's arm ache. He glanced down, taking in the enlarged chart of Onslow Bay spread across the desk. His gaze stopped on the name scrawled in black marker at the top right corner of the map.

Parnell.

The name sparked Ryan's memory, and he recalled McClelland, the reporter, telling him that Bianchi had badgered a guy named Parnell. Why would Bianchi have Parnell's nautical chart if their dispute was over a property deal?

Ryan's attention to the chart caused Bianchi to fold it

over. Ryan's gaze flicked to the yellow legal pad beside it, where Bianchi had written a list of names. He'd crossed off several of them. Ryan tried to read them all. *Mary Russell*, *Star of Sumatra*, *Ariana*, *Torrie Lynn*, and *Carrie Jane* were all he could memorize before Bianchi flipped the pad over.

"Now, run along," Bianchi said. "Tell you what. Have a drink downstairs on me."

"I'm not drinking your beer, asshole," Scott muttered.

"I don't care," Bianchi said, his tone low and threatening. "Just get out of my office before I have you thrown out."

That remark made Scott smirk. "Does LeRoy have friends?"

"I got *fifteen* of 'em," LeRoy said, pulling a pistol from under his shirt.

Ryan shouted, "*Gun!*" and reached for his pistol while Scott moved forward in a blur as the bouncer's gun cleared its holster. A moment later, Scott held the pistol, and LeRoy was cradling his right hand with a broken trigger finger.

Scott shoved the pistol into his back pocket and said, "Thanks for the keepsake."

Ryan turned to Bianchi. "Leave Chad alone," he said. On his way out of the office, he stepped around LeRoy, who had dropped to his knees and was groaning from the pain.

Scott wasn't so kind. He brought his knee up into the bouncer's chin and snapped the man's head back, knocking him unconscious. "At least he's not crying like a little bitch anymore." Pointing at Bianchi, Scott said, "I'll see you later."

Ryan and Scott went down the stairs, exited the bar, and walked back to the Jeep.

As they stood in the parking lot beside the water, Scott glanced around, then pulled the pistol from his pants pocket and threw it as far out into the Cape Fear River as he could. There was no point in holding onto a stolen firearm. If LeRoy had committed crimes with the gun, it was best to dispose of it. Although, Ryan supposed in retrospect, polluting the river wasn't the best way to dispose of it.

"Think he'll back off?" Scott asked.

As Ryan opened the driver's door, he said, "Would you?"

"Not if some guy came into my bar and knocked out my bouncer."

Ryan started the Jeep and grinned. "That's what I'm counting on."

CHAPTER FIFTEEN

Rocky Bianchi stepped over his unconscious security guard and opened his liquor cabinet. After retrieving a bottle of water from the mini fridge, he unscrewed the cap and dumped the icy contents onto the bouncer's face.

LeRoy slowly came around, shaking his head to ward off the falling water, but his boss continued until the bottle was empty.

"Get up," Rocky commanded.

The guard clamored to his feet, careful of his broken finger. He swayed as he stood beside the puddle of water on the polished oak floor.

"You're fired," Bianchi growled. "Get the hell out of my office."

"But boss ..." LeRoy protested.

"*Get. Out.*" Bianchi pointed at the door.

As LeRoy retreated out the door, Bianchi told him to send someone up to clean up the mess. Moments later, a server appeared with several bar towels and quickly mopped the floor dry.

When she finished cleaning, Bianchi built himself a

scotch on the rocks and sat down at his desk. This was *not* what he needed right now. His life was complicated enough without some idiots running around, acting like saviors for their deadbeat friend.

Sipping the Macallan twenty-five-year-old single malt, he spread the map back over his desk. How much had that redneck seen, and how much would he remember? Bianchi hoped not enough to give him more trouble. He studied the lines of the ship's courses on the chart, trying to determine the best place to restart his search for the box of gold nuggets Parnell had been trying to retrieve.

He squeezed his eyes shut and rubbed them with his fingers as he thought, *Damn you, Parnell*.

Bianchi took another sip and savored the scotch as his mind worked over his problems. Years ago, John Parnell, a retired Merchant Marine Officer who then became a local offshore fishing and diving guide, had come to him with an interesting proposition. Parnell had access to a steady supply of unrefined gold nuggets. All Bianchi had to do was fence them through his pawnshop, and both men would profit. Bianchi had laughed until Parnell had dumped out a small bag of what looked like corn kernels on the loan shark's desk. The gold nuggets had shone under the bright office lights.

Parnell had taken the scrap price for them but hinted that he was still making a hefty profit. As Parnell brought him more and more gold, Bianchi had had to find new outlets to sell it. He'd had his artisans at the pawnshop craft high-end jewelry with it, while other shipments he melted into gold bars. There was always someone looking to buy gold to backstop their financial portfolios, so he was able to sell it without the normal chain of provenance. Recently, he'd turned to contacts in the financial services world to help sell it to their clients.

Six months ago, Bianchi had offered Parnell top dollar for

a large parcel of land along the ICW. Bianchi wanted to build houses. Parnell had balked, and the squabble had gotten ugly and, worse, *public*. Not ugly enough for them to stop doing business together, but Bianchi had grown tired of Parnell's secrecy. He sent men to track his movements so Bianchi could discover the source of the gold.

Parnell kept a fishing boat at a dock on his land that allowed him rapid access to the Atlantic. Bianchi's men had rented their own fishing boat and reported seeing Parnell making a dive, from which he'd recovered a box. Not long after that, Parnell had shown up at the pawnshop with the gold. They'd recorded where Parnell recovered the boxes, but they'd never established who dropped them. The monitoring of Parnell's movements had taken too long, and Bianchi had been eager to move forward.

Bianchi had studied where the gold could have come from. The most logical conclusion was South America or Africa, as both continents produced considerable amounts of black-market gold. After months of paying the men to follow Parnell, Bianchi had become fed up. He had earned the nickname "Rocky" during his youth, when he'd boxed at a small gym near his family home. He'd carried the moniker through high school and college because he enjoyed being associated with the famous movies and a major film star, and the name had stuck. Eventually, he had put his boxing skills to the test, battering Parnell until he gave up almost everything.

Parnell had revealed that he was friends with a ship captain who routinely sailed between the United States and Africa. The gold had come from Côte d'Ivoire—the Ivory Coast. *An ironic twist*, Bianchi had thought; they no longer smuggled ivory, but gold. The illicit gold poured into the capital of Abidjan from mines in places like Mali, Burkina Faso, Niger, Ghana, and Liberia. The captain received the box from a band of smugglers, then carried it across the ocean aboard his ship before he dropped it over the side near the coast of North Carolina for Parnell to pick up and sell. Each box contained twelve pounds of the precious metal. Everyone in the chain of custody was making windfall profits, according to Parnell, becoming millionaires on the backs of destitute Africans.

Eager to eliminate the middleman, Bianchi had tasked Tim Davis with following Parnell and had told him that after Parnell picked up the next box, he was to blow up Parnell's boat as a warning. Those stupid kids had gotten too eager and mistook Parnell's sport diving for the gold collection. They'd blasted a hole in Parnell's boat, killing him in the process. That had been two months ago, and it had cost Bianchi dearly.

With Parnell dead, Bianchi had gone to Parnell's niece in Texas and offered to purchase the property on a land contract. With control of Parnell's house, Bianchi had taken his time in searching it and the garage for clues to the box's coordinates. All he'd come away with was the map and a list of ship names, but he had a researcher trying to figure out the connection.

Then he'd let his swamp rats rifle through the dead man's house, carting off anything they could use or sell. Once word of Parnell's disappearance had gotten out, the ship's captain had also turned up dead. The smuggling route was blown, and somewhere out in that vast, rolling blue expanse of Onslow Bay was the gold Bianchi needed to sew up his real estate empire. Parnell's niece had called last week, demanding his missed payment and threatening to sell to someone else if he didn't cough up the money by next week. He'd managed to calm her nerves, but not his own.

Rocky Bianchi shot back the rest of his Macallan and reached for his phone. The gold wasn't going anywhere, and those two thugs that had barged into his office and demanded he ease off Chad Yeager needed to be dealt with. He didn't need this distraction right now. There were too many things at stake.

"Mike, how's Chad doing?" Bianchi asked when Wilmington police officer Mike Boostrom answered his phone.

"He was resting when I left. Those boys he's got coming to visit him are gonna be a problem, though."

"That's what I want you to take care of. Find out who they are and run them out of town."

"Yes, sir," Boostrom replied.

"Oh, and Mike? What do you think about Mrs. Yeager?"

"She looks good for her age."

"I thought you'd say that," Bianchi replied. "You may get to enjoy some quality time with her if things continue to deteriorate."

"It would be my pleasure," the beefy cop replied.

Bianchi set the receiver down in its cradle and poured himself another drink. Relaxing back into his chair, he smiled. It was good to have a cop or two in his pocket. With the law on his side, he wouldn't be forced into direct action against the men protecting Chad Yeager.

He could concentrate on finding the gold.

CHAPTER SIXTEEN

Darkness had descended on the city, and a light rain fell. The headlights of the Jeep shone off the wet pavement as Ryan drove across town after his and Scott's visit to Rocky Bianchi's office. Since getting into the Jeep, Scott had remained silent in the passenger seat.

Ryan mentally worked through the list of names he'd seen on the notepad in Bianchi's office. They were all female names, except for *Star of Sumatra*. Ryan had spent more than enough time on the water to recognize them for what they were—the names of boats—and the map beside it cinched it. He wished he'd been able to see more of the chart and the tracks drawn on it. What was Bianchi searching for?

"I take it we're not going back to the boat?" Scott finally said.

"No. We're checking out a lead."

"What lead?" Scott asked.

Ryan focused on driving and slowed as he turned onto the suburban street where Kyle Fowler lived in the town of Kirkland. The two-story house was a cookie-cutter version of the other houses on the street, except Kyle's was brown in color with white trim and had an American flag hanging from a porch pole. Between Kyle's place and the one to the north was a small pond surrounded by trees.

Pulling in beside the deputy's Ford pickup, Ryan killed the engine and got out. He pulled on his sweatshirt to ward off the evening chill, and Scott donned a tan coat.

Kyle stepped onto the front porch to greet them. "Hey, guys. What's going on?"

"I need to talk to you," Ryan replied.

"Come on in." Kyle held the door open for them.

Ryan and Scott stepped inside the warm, well-lit home. Delicious cooking scents filled the air.

A tired-looking woman with brownish-blonde hair falling out of a loose ponytail, came into the living room, wiping her hands on a towel. She wore an oversized sweatshirt and jeans. The couple's three kids clambered into the room after her.

"You didn't tell me you invited guests for dinner," Cheryl said to her husband. She went over to Ryan and opened her arms for a hug.

"When I first walked in here, I thought Kyle had gotten a maid. You look fantastic," Ryan said.

"Thanks. I've lost fifty pounds. You could learn a thing or two about flattery here, Kyle."

"If you're trying to steal my wife, Ryan, you get the kids, too," Kyle said.

Cheryl stuck her tongue out at her husband. "It's good to see you, Ryan. I heard a rumor that you were in town. Where's this smoking hot girlfriend of yours I've been hearing so much about?"

"She's in Fort Myers, taking a class for her job."

"That's too bad," Cheryl said. "I've been looking forward to meeting the woman that corralled the restless Ryan Weller."

"I talked to Kyle about getting together for dinner. Didn't he tell you?"

"No." She flicked Kyle with the towel. "Jerk. Anyway, I've got plenty for dinner if you want to stay."

"We're not here for dinner," Ryan said. "Though it smells good."

"Please stay, Uncle Ryan!" the kids shouted.

"Sorry, guys. I promise I'll come back soon," Ryan declared.

Cheryl smiled. "You sure? I made beef and gravy over mashed potatoes."

"It smells delicious, ma'am," Scott added.

"At least your friends are polite, *Kyle*," Cheryl said.

Ryan knew that not only was Cheryl a professor of Sociology at UNC Wilmington, but she also ran the house and liked to give her husband grief. Kyle normally gave as much as he got, but tonight he just looked cowed.

"What did you want to talk about?" Kyle asked Ryan.

"Can we go to the garage?" Ryan glanced pointedly at the kids.

Kyle led the way and closed the door behind him. The garage was Kyle's den, and it contained a desk, a sofa, a television, and a fridge. He dug out three cold beers and handed one each to Ryan and Scott before cracking open the third.

As Kyle settled behind his desk, he asked, "What's this about, Ryan?"

"What do you know about the disappearance of a guy named John Parnell?"

"Parnell, huh? Not much, other than they found his boat capsized off the old Frying Pan Shoals Lighthouse. Why?"

"I heard he had a disagreement with Rocky Bianchi," Ryan said, sinking into the overstuffed sofa beside Scott.

"The cement shoes rumor?" Kyle laughed. "Sounds like you've been talking to Ray McClelland. Parnell went out when there was a small craft warning. There's no reason to believe that it was anything other than a boating accident."

"Did anyone do a report?" Ryan asked.

"I think the Coast Guard investigated," Kyle replied.

"But not New Haven's finest?"

"We've got too much of our own work to do than to worry about rumors. Besides, you know anything blue water is the Coast Guard's territory."

"What was Parnell into?" Scott asked.

"I don't know," Kyle admitted. "Why are you asking all these questions about a boating accident?"

"Because I think it's connected to whatever Bianchi and Chad are into."

Kyle rubbed his forehead, then held his hand in front of his eyes, pinching his temples. "Leave it be, Ryan." He dropped his hand. "Chad has to work out his own problems. You don't need to get caught up in his shit like always."

"If you were in trouble, I'd be helping you, too."

Kyle let out a long breath. "Hold on." He pulled his cell phone from his pocket and dialed a number. "Hey, Gene. You got a few minutes to talk to a friend of mine about that capsized boat you found off the Frying Pan a couple of months back?" Kyle nodded several times and said, "Okay. In an hour." He ended the call and set the phone back on the desk.

"Gene Terry is a Coast Guard chief stationed at Wrightsville Beach. He's only been there about eight months. I met him during a cross-training event for our marine units. Anyhow, he's the one who went out on the call. He'll meet you at Bluewater Grill."

"That's nice," Ryan said. "My backyard."

"Yeah, well, you're buying the beer," Kyle added.

"That I can do," Ryan assured him. If it meant learning another piece of the puzzle, then Ryan was more than willing to buy a few beers. It didn't hurt that they could stumble back to *Huntress* at the end of the night. "Are you guys officially investigating Bianchi?"

"We know about some of his nefarious dealings, but if there's an investigation, it would be conducted by Wilmington P.D."

"Yeah, I guessed as much," Ryan said.

"I know you're worried about Chad being swept up in this theft ring business, but if he's a part of it, there isn't anything that either of us can do about it."

"I know," Ryan conceded.

"You're a good friend, Ry. You always looked out for us and you're still doing it, but we're big boys now. We made our decisions, and you made yours. I love you like a brother, but maybe you should take that pretty girlfriend of yours and sail away. Don't get caught up in Chad's problems or mine."

"What problems do you have?"

Kyle sighed and sipped his beer. "None that I can't work out for myself."

"You always were a stubborn mule."

Kyle chuckled. "Takes one to know one, brother."

"Yeah, it does." Ryan finished his beer and stood. "Whatever you do, don't screw it up with that woman you've got in there. You're a lucky man, and she's lucky to have you, too."

The deputy smiled. "Relationship advice from Ryan Weller. Never thought I'd see the day."

"It's sound advice," Scott chimed in. "And she cooks."

Kyle chuckled. "Seriously, she puts up a good front, but things haven't been good for a while." He sighed. "I don't want to burden you with my problems." He stood and extended his hand to Ryan.

"It's not a burden, Kyle. If you need something, I'm there, just like I'm helping Chad. You know that right?"

"Some things can't be fixed, Ry."

The three men shook hands before Ryan and Scott drove to Wrightsville Beach Marina.

"That was a long way to go just to get a contact," Scott stated. "You couldn't have just called him?"

"I could have, but you know it's better to strong-arm someone face to face."

"That was strong-arming?"

"Well, more like using my friend to get what I wanted."

"And what is it you're after?"

"When we were confronting Bianchi, he had a chart of Frying Pan Shoals on his desk that he covered up. There was a name on the chart."

"Parnell's?"

"Yes. The reporter Emily and I talked to said that Bianchi was trying to buy a piece of property that belonged to Parnell. Parnell refused to sell and then he disappeared."

"So, you think Bianchi was after something else Parnell had?"

"I don't know what to think right now. Bianchi also had a list of ship's names written on a notepad. I didn't get to read the whole thing before he flipped it over."

"What's your theory, then?"

"Bianchi killed Parnell for whatever is on that map," Ryan answered.

Scott ticked points off by raising fingers. "Bianchi sells stolen boats, has a crew of thieves working the river to steal electronics, and he might have killed Parnell. Why?"

"Everything boils down to three things," Ryan said. "Love, money, and power."

CHAPTER SEVENTEEN

Angie, the waitress at Bluewater Grill, greeted Ryan like an old friend. He told her they were meeting someone, and she directed them to a table by the large windows that overlooked the ICW and the docks of Wrightsville Beach Marina.

"He said he was waiting for you," Angie said.

"Thanks, Angie," Ryan said.

Scott and Angie shared coquettish smiles as she escorted them to the table where Chief Gene Terry sat. He was a slender man with a hawk nose, brown eyes, and black hair. Ryan wondered if he had a bit of Native American blood in his veins. The Coastie had a tall glass of amber liquid in front of him.

Ryan introduced himself and Scott and established their military bona fides. Gene Terry motioned for a refill, and Scott ordered a Corona.

As Angie walked away, Scott said to Ryan, "She didn't take your order."

"I'm here often enough that she knows what I want."

"Do you live nearby?" Terry asked.

"On the Fountaine Pajot catamaran at the end dock."

"*Huntress*?" Terry said.

"That's her," Ryan replied.

"I thought I'd seen you around. We use the Travelift down there to haul out our boats."

Ryan had seen the Coast Guard working on their forty-five-foot SAFE Boats International Defender-class Rapid Response boat. Back when he was a full-time resident of Wrightsville Beach, he'd known most of the Coasties, but they'd rotated since the last time Ryan had been in town. "My old boss had a twenty-five-foot Defender. That thing hauls ass."

"What's he do?" Terry asked.

"He's the owner of Dark Water Research."

"You mean Greg Olsen?" the chief said.

"Yeah." Ryan nodded.

Angie brought their drinks. She set a mixed drink in front of Ryan and brought beers for Scott and Terry.

"Thanks, Ang," Ryan said.

"No worries." She smiled at Scott again, and the former SEAL grinned back.

Terry took a long sip of beer, then set down his glass. "I met Greg when I was stationed in Galveston."

"He's one of the good guys," Ryan said.

"Kyle said you wanted to talk about John Parnell," Terry said.

Ryan nodded. "He said you were the responding unit when they found his boat."

With a roll of his eyes, Terry said, "We respond to everything."

"Was there anything unusual about the accident?" Ryan asked.

"You mean other than the boat being upside down and the owner missing? No."

"No signs of foul play or indications that it was something other than an accident?"

"Not that I can recall ..." Terry trailed off as he sipped his beer.

Nodding to Ryan's glass, Scott asked, "What kind of foo-foo drink is that?"

"Rum punch." Ryan raised his glass in a toast. "We sailors like our rum."

"I *was* in the Navy," Scott said.

"Then why are you drinking Corona?" Terry asked. "At least man up and get a *real* beer. Not that watered-down, mass-produced piss."

Despite having just met Gene Terry, the man fell right into Ryan and Scott's easy banter. It helped that they'd established a professional rapport early on and that they had a friend in common in Greg Olsen.

"Lay off Puddle Pirate," Scott growled.

"You'd fit right in at the Coast Guard, Scott," Ryan said.

"How's that?" Scott asked testily.

Ryan grinned. "To join the Coast Guard, you have to be over six feet tall. That way when the boat sinks, you can walk back to shore."

Terry laughed. "That one's my favorite. I'm not six foot, but I just tell everyone that they issued me a snorkel."

"I was a *SEAL*," Scott stated, as if being a Special Forces operator placed him above the commoners.

"What are you going to do?" Ryan asked. "Write a book like the rest of them?"

Scott held up his middle finger.

"It's okay, Scott," Terry said. "Not everyone is qualified to join the Coast Guard. We have *high* standards."

"You hear that, Weller? They wouldn't take your sorry ass either."

Ryan chuckled. "This is fun. All we need is a Marine to feed crayons to."

"Drink your rum, Bomb Boy," Scott groused.

At the word 'bomb,' Terry sat upright. "I just thought of something. You said *bomb*,' and that made me think of Parnell's boat. There was a particular odor to the burnt interior, and there was a hole in the hull. At the time, I thought it was just because he ran up on a reef, but maybe it was something else. Come to think of it, I thought it was odd that most of the fiberglass splinters faced outward when they should have gone into the boat if he hit the reef."

"Describe the smell," Ryan encouraged.

Terry shook his head and scrunched up his facial features as he thought. "I can't really put a finger on it, other than burned fiberglass and bleach. It's been a while."

Ryan's eyebrows rose. The bleach smell could have been from the use of impure potassium chlorate. By boiling down bleach to a crystalline form and combining it with white gasoline and wax, a bomb maker would have a malleable plastique.

"Where's the boat at now?" Ryan asked.

Terry shrugged. "We towed it in and turned it over to a salvage company."

"Why not to the family?" Scott asked.

"Standard operating procedure."

"What's the name of the salvage company?" Ryan asked.

"Cape Fear Dive and Salvage off Battleship Road," Terry said. "We use them for just about everything."

There was no point in going there now because it was dark, and the salvage business would be closed. They would have to wait until tomorrow. Ryan signaled Angie, who brought them another round.

Terry spun his empty glass. "It's a good thing I don't have to work tomorrow."

"Drink up, Coastie," Ryan said. "We've got all night."

Scott's phone pinged, and he dug it out of his pocket. "The Pilot and the charger pack are on the move. Looks like they're together."

"We'll worry about it later," Ryan said. "The only place I'm going after I leave here is back to *Huntress*."

Angie brought a fresh round of drinks to the table.

Scott put his phone away and raised his glass. "To the wind that blows, the ship that goes, and the lass that loves a sailor!"

Ryan and Gene raised their glasses in response and took big swallows.

Unbeknownst to Ryan, Scott, and Gene Terry as they poured alcohol down their gullets, several men watched them from the darkness; men with no intention of letting anyone cause trouble for their boss.

CHAPTER EIGHTEEN

The next morning, Ryan groaned as he rolled over in bed and reached for the ringing cell phone. His head ached, his mouth was dry, and his limbs felt heavy and weak. All the rum punches had taken their toll on him. He hadn't drunk that much in a long time, and both Scott and the young Coast Guard chief outpaced him nearly two to one as the evening had progressed and they told stories about their time in service.

Sitting on the edge of the bed, rubbing his face, Ryan held the phone to his ear and grunted.

"Good morning," Barry Thatcher chimed, much louder than Ryan wanted, so he bumped the volume button down a few times.

"What's up?" Ryan croaked.

"You sound like you had a rough night."

"Something like that." Ryan's stomach grumbled. He needed carbs to ward off the hangover, or another drink to replenish the alcohol in his system. "You're up early this morning."

"I haven't been to bed, yet. Besides, it's seven-thirty. I

thought you military guys got up at the butt-crack of dawn."

Ryan stifled a yawn, wishing Barry would get on with it and stop making small talk. Having to concentrate on the conversation was making his head hurt worse. Was this what it was like to get old? If it was, it sucked. Tim McGraw had it right in his song *My Next Thirty Years*. Ryan needed to drink more lemonade and not so many beers. McGraw had also said he was going to settle all the scores, and there was only one thing Barry would call about: helping Ryan settle a score.

"Tell me about Rocky Bianchi," Ryan said.

"He's a real piece of work," Barry said. "He preys on the poor and less fortunate."

"What do you mean?" Ryan asked as he pulled on shorts and a T-shirt.

"His business model centers on those who need money in a hurry. The pawnshop when people have something to sell, for example. His used car business not only sells cars but also gives car title loans at high interest rates. North Carolina state law caps unlicensed lenders at sixteen percent, but this guy is charging one lady almost eighty percent plus fees. And she's not the only one he's gouging. It's larceny."

"Okay. That's something I can work with. What else?" Ryan put the phone on speaker and started making coffee. The smell of coffee and the sounds of Ryan's conversation seemed to rouse Scott Gregory from his slumber, and he joined Ryan in the galley to listen in on the conversation.

"It all works together. His tenants come to him to buy a car and they take out a buy-here-pay-here loan, then he loans against the title when they can't pay their rent. When they miss a payment, his repo agency takes possession of the car and he resells it to another sucker. His towing company contracts with the repo agency and his car lot. They run cars all over the eastern seaboard."

"So, it's all legit, except for the high rates."

"They write contracts to ensure everything is above board," Barry stated. "He's even doing the same thing with boats; that's why he sends Tim Davis to pick them up. Your friend Chad is in on that scheme by being the boat dealer, and, from the financials I've seen, he gets a kickback from Bianchi."

"How long has that been going on?" Ryan asked.

"Something happened in 2018 that caused Chad to need money," Barry said. "He got a cash infusion, but I can't find any records of him repaying a bank or other traditional lender. He has, however, been writing a check to Bianchi for years, so you don't need three guesses to know where the money came from."

"That's about the time he started the repair shop. He said a conventional bank wouldn't touch him, so he went to Bianchi for a loan."

"Makes sense," Barry said. "Interestingly, he stopped the payments about six months ago."

"Chad said he paid off the loan, but because he's been selling the stolen boats, Bianchi has him over a barrel and is forcing him to keep doing it."

"And that's what this is all about? Helping him get out from under Bianchi?" Barry asked.

"That's the size of it. Bianchi sent some thugs to beat up Chad and they put him in the hospital. Then he threatened Chad's mother."

"White knight Ryan to the rescue? Why do you always drag me into this shit?"

"Come on, Bare. You know you love it when I call," Ryan said.

"Ha. Do I love getting my house blown to bits? *No.*"

"To be fair, you blew up your own house," Ryan said.

"That's true, but only because we had to escape from men who followed *you* there. Whenever you call, I know there's danger involved, and I need to protect myself and Carmen. So, I'll be doubling my usual fee."

"You have a *usual* fee?" Ryan asked.

"It's more of a sliding scale—and you're all the way at the top."

"If I remember right, you compensated yourself with some of those illicit funds we found on the last job. Seems like that should count for something."

"Yeah, my house in St. Thomas," Barry said. "I *miss* that place."

Ryan poured hot black coffee into his new favorite mug, the design of which featured a Navy EOD badge, referred to as 'the crab,' and an old brass diving helmet. He'd lost his last favorite mug when his old sailboat had burned to the waterline.

"What about the pawnshop?" Scott asked, steering the conversation back on track as he poured himself a cup of coffee.

"The pawnshop has to report who they buy merchandise from and give the serial numbers of that merchandise to local authorities. That lets police track stolen goods and who sold them. The electronic records I could access from Wilmington Pawn and Gun tell me that everything is kosher. There may be a separate ledger for documenting their stolen merchandise, but I don't see it. My guess is that it's on paper. You'd have to get into the office to look for it. *If* it's even there."

"Oh, trust me," Scott said. "It's there."

"Okay," Ryan said. "So far we have very little to go on."

"Based on what I've told you, yes," Barry replied. "But here's the curious thing."

"Don't hold back, Bare. I'm paying you *a lot* of money for results."

"Okay. This is going to take a bit of explanation, but you'll see it in the end." Barry took a deep breath. "So, Bianchi has this convenience store, right?"

"Right," Ryan agreed.

"The store sells a massive number of cigarettes. By that, I mean *twice* what other retailers in the area are selling." Barry paused, waiting for Ryan or Scott to respond. When they didn't, he plunged on. "So, Bianchi's towing company hauls a car from Wilmington to a car lot in Albany, New York, once a month. My theory is that Bianchi is shipping half of his cigarettes to New York."

"For what?" Scott asked.

"North Carolina has the lowest tax on cigarettes in the country," Ryan said.

"And New York has the highest," Barry added.

"What does that mean?" Scott asked.

"He's smuggling cigarettes from here to New York and making a mint doing it," Ryan said.

"Smuggled cigarettes account for half the cigarettes sold in New York State," Barry said. "What I think Bianchi does is that he packs them into the trunk of a car. Then they put the car on a rollback with a shipping contract to make the transport look legit. Once the cigarettes get to Albany, the guy at the car lot up there sells them, and they split the profit. The rollback comes back to Wilmington with a different car on it for Bianchi's lot. Everything is above board from a legal standpoint, and no one looks twice at a car being towed. I read a story about this guy, Jon Roberts. He used to be one of the largest cocaine traffickers in the world, and he would do the same thing with the rollbacks. He said no one ever looked at them, and he moved tons of coke that way."

"That's good, Barry," Ryan said. "Now we just need to figure out what car the cigarettes are in and get the cops to bust them." Ryan ran a hand through his shaggy brown hair and rubbed his head as he thought. "Do you think they're bringing anything back?"

"I don't know," Barry stated.

Scott's eyes lit up. "There's only one way to find out."

Ryan nodded. "What else do you have, Barry?"

"His bar is doing well," Barry said.

"People like to drink," Scott added.

"Think you can work some magic with that waitress we met the other day?" Ryan asked Scott.

Scott grinned. "That should be an easy task."

"There are lots of complaints about the rental apartments," Barry interjected. "Bianchi doesn't maintain them well, and he charges premium rent to those who aren't on government assistance."

"There's not much we can do about that." Ryan understood why Bianchi let his property maintenance lapse. Rentals could be a money drain, but obviously Bianchi was working the system to his benefit. Ryan's father had kept rental properties for as long as Ryan could remember, and it always seemed to him that the tenants had more rights than the landowner, but his father worked hard to maintain the properties in excellent shape and to keep decent rent-paying tenants in the buildings. But that didn't mean that people didn't destroy the units. Tenants had no equity stake in the apartments. Therefore, they didn't always take care of them. It was hard for a landlord to enforce rules as to proper maintenance and upkeep.

"So, your boy has rentals, a pawnshop, a convenience store and gas station, a used car lot, a towing company, and a repo company," Scott recapped. "That's a lot of ground to cover."

"Don't forget the bar," Barry said.

"Where did he get the money to buy the rentals?" Ryan asked. "The reporter I spoke to mentioned they were the first things Bianchi purchased when he moved to Wilmington, but he had no idea how he funded them."

"Here's the kicker about that," Barry said. "He used low-interest loans from the federal government."

"What about his background?" Scott asked.

Barry recounted what he knew about Bianchi—which matched what Ryan had heard from the reporter, McClelland. Then he added extra information. "After college, he worked for a small financial services firm in Charlottesville. The SEC accused them of embezzlement, but they didn't implicate Bianchi in the scheme. When the firm shut down, he moved to Wilmington, purchased his apartments, and used cash to buy the pawnshop."

"That must be how he got his start-up funds," Ryan said.

"I can't find where he had the money stashed," Barry stated. "Most likely it was in cash somewhere."

"Not offshore shell corporations?" Ryan asked.

"Nothing that flows into or out of his current accounts goes offshore. Everything is in Delaware corps."

"Protecting himself," Ryan suggested. He knew from his research for a previous mission that people set up Delaware corporations to take advantage of Delaware's lax tax laws and to shield themselves from the public's prying eyes.

"That's what I would do if I had that many businesses," Barry said.

"Does he have a criminal record?" Scott asked.

"There's nothing in the federal databases about him. The Wilmington cops arrested him for running an illegal gambling establishment, and he's been under investigation for racketeering and loan sharking, but nothing ever came from them. Bianchi sued the police, claiming that after his arrest for illegal gambling, the cops were harassing him. He won."

"Anything else of interest, Barry?" Ryan asked.

"He's had lots of complaints from his tenants about drug dealers and prostitution in the apartment complexes."

"Sounds like he's the local vice kingpin," Scott stated.

"Oh—and stay out of his reach. He won a few boxing tournaments back in the day."

"Guess that's how Charlie became Rocky," Ryan said. "Can I ask you another favor, Bare?"

"Oh no," the hacker groaned.

Ryan grinned at Scott. "Just put it on my tab."

Ryan's phone chimed, and he looked down at the text message from Barry. "What the heck is Venmo?"

"It's how you're going to pay my bill," Barry said.

"Yeah," Ryan replied dubiously. "Can you get me some information on a John Parnell? He lived in the Wilmington area and had a beef with Bianchi before he went missing. This is all tied into the same case, so just bill me at the end."

Barry laughed. "This isn't a bar, and you can't run a tab. You gotta pay as you go."

Ryan sighed. Before he ended the call, he said, "Just get me the info."

"What's the plan?" Scott asked.

"First, we go look at Parnell's boat, then we gather more intel on Bianchi so we can put the squeeze on him."

"I see where you're going with this," Scott said. "He's into some shady shit, so we round up his minions and make it harder for him to do business."

A man like that had buried skeletons, Ryan reasoned. All they needed to do was dig them up.

CHAPTER NINETEEN

With insulated cups full of black coffee, Ryan and Scott drove across the Cape Fear River on Route 17 and turned off onto Battleship Road, following it south along the river. Cape Fear Dive and Salvage's base of operations was a forty-acre lot with a deep-water dock and a Travelift to move boats in and out of the water. Through the doors of a giant steel building, Ryan could see several boats under repair. There were several other outbuildings that Ryan guessed were more workshops for the salvage gear.

He wove through a small field of pleasure craft on trailers before reaching the office, a double wide house on a block foundation. The two men got out of the Jeep and walked up onto the narrow front deck that held a grill and four chairs around a patio table.

Before Ryan could knock, a voice hollered for them to come in, and Ryan glanced up to see a security camera.

Stepping inside, he saw a portly man with the stub of a cigar in his mouth. He wore a trucker cap advertising the salvage company, a stained T-shirt with the same logo, and shorts, despite the chilly weather. The name on the desk plaque read: Danny Carter.

"Hi there," Ryan said. "I'm looking for a boat you brought in about two months ago. It belonged to John Parnell. Do you still have it?"

Carter pulled his cigar butt from his mouth and picked a piece of tobacco from his tongue. "Who's asking?"

"I'm Bob Parker with Maritime Recovery," Ryan said. He pulled out a business card and handed it to Carter. "I'm here on behalf of Ward and Young."

"Bob Parker, huh?" Carter said as he shoved the card into the breast pocket of his T-shirt. "You here to help me get my claim paid?"

"Something like that," Scott muttered.

Ryan could help him get his claim pushed through if Parnell really was a client of Ward and Young—or, rather, *Emily* could—but he wasn't going to make any more promises than he already had.

The big man behind the counter cocked his head and began shuffling through the paperwork on his desk. He held up a piece of paper and said, "Still here. It's a Judge 34 Express. Nice boat, except for that hole in the hull."

"Mind if we take a look?" Scott asked.

"Who's he?" Carter asked, thrusting his chin at Scott.

"He's an expert on blowing shit up," Ryan replied.

Carter raised his eyebrows, turned down the corners of his mouth, and nodded. "Well, unless you're into underwater demolition, you won't find no work around here."

"That's my specialty," Scott said.

"Maybe you want a job?" Carter asked.

"Nope. I've got one—babysitting this guy." He hooked a thumb toward Ryan.

"Can we see the boat?" Ryan asked.

"Suit yourself." Carter came around the desk and led the

way out the door and down the steps. He waddled as he walked, as if his knees were bad. "Shame about that fella—Parnell, you said his name was? No one can find him."

"We're investigating the incident," Ryan said.

"There she is," Carter said. He paused to light his cigar while Ryan and Scott continued to a boat with the word *Skater* scrawled across the transom.

Skater had a yellow hull, a white windscreen with a fiberglass hardtop over the helm, and an open cockpit that ran nearly half the length of the boat. Ryan liked the look of her. The boat was basically a sportfisher without the tuna tower and outriggers. Parnell had fitted the Judge with an extra-wide swim platform and a large aluminum folding ladder for divers to exit the water. Inside the cockpit, a row of tank holders lined the starboard gunwale. Forward, under the hardtop, were two pedal seats, and short, padded benches on both sides of the boat. She was a no-frills fisher with plenty of room to work.

She rested on her starboard chine, revealing the gaping hole in the port side bow below the waterline. Ryan and Scott both gravitated toward the hole and peered inside. Chief Terry had been right: the fiberglass and wood had bowed outward.

"Looks like something blew a hole from the inside as the boat was cruising along," Ryan stated. "The rushing water broke off many of these shards along the leading edge. It also folded back and splintered off these pieces along the trailing edge, taking these large chunks out of the fiberglass. If Parnell had hit a rock or coral, it would have directed the damage inward."

Danny Carter shifted his cigar to the other corner of his mouth as he listened.

Ryan climbed into the cabin. It was functional but sparse compared to other sportfishers he'd been on, namely Greg

Olsen's Hatteras GT63. That boat had an interior like a luxury hotel. The Judge had just enough room to turn around at the base of the cabin steps. To his right was a small galley, and to the left, a head. Forward was the V-berth bunk with a table in the center that the owner could raise to eat off or lower to make the bunk larger. The bunk cushions were missing. When asked, Carter said they'd disposed of them because the saltwater had ruined them, and they were full of mold. In fact, the salvage workers had stripped anything made of cloth from the interior.

The explosion had ripped apart the V-berth bunk, shattering the locker's door in the blast's resultant pressure wave. Ryan guessed that the rushing water had scoured the interior of the locker, removing any parts of the detonator or residue left by the explosives. The only clues were the outward bend to the hull splinters, the shattered V-berth area, and the charred fiberglass where a fire had raged before the water had extinguished it.

As he backed out of the cabin, Ryan shined his flashlight along the bulkheads, hatches, and overheads, looking for more evidence of the explosion. There were indications of the overpressure wave throughout the interior, and Ryan suspected that a combination of things had conspired to kill John Parnell. First, the boat would have stopped dead as the hull blew out and the water rushed in, throwing Parnell from his perch on the captain's seat behind the wheel. Then the blast wave would have blown him backward. If he'd hit his head, Parnell would likely have been unconscious as the boat slowly rolled over, and he would have succumbed to the water. Or a blow to the head had killed him outright, and his body had drifted off with the waves.

The last thing Ryan looked at was the GPS unit. Being underwater had probably killed its circuit boards, but he asked Carter if he could take it for their investigation. Carter said it was basically a paperweight and Ryan was welcome to have it.

Walking to the Jeep, Ryan explained his theory to Scott, who listened without question. When Ryan finished, Scott said, "There's a third option."

"Which is?"

"Someone killed Parnell elsewhere, dumped the body, set the autopilot on Parnell's boat, and got onto a waiting boat. Once the Judge was far enough away, our killer blew the bomb."

"That's as good a theory as any," Ryan said. "But why kill Parnell?"

Scott shrugged. "Maybe Bianchi couldn't get what he wanted any other way." Then he shook his head. "All this over a piece of land."

"I've been thinking about that," Ryan said. "I think the land was secondary. This has to do with whatever is on that chart in his office and the names on that list he had."

Scott fell silent as he pulled out his phone and began typing on the screen.

Ryan fired up the Jeep and navigated them back to the highway. "What's going on with our trackers?"

"The Hinckley is still in the slip at Bradley Creek Marina."

"What about the Pilot and the charger pack?"

"The Pilot is up at some old boatyard on the Northeast Cape Fear River."

Ryan furrowed his eyebrows.

"It's just north of Castle Hayne Boat Ramp."

"Oh, yeah." Ryan grinned. "There's a little marina and boat junkyard out there." He scratched his head, searching his memory for the name. "It's been a long time since I've been out there, but I think it's called 117 Marine."

"The charger pack is farther upriver." Scott pinched and

scrolled on his phone screen. "Looks like an old shack, according to Google Earth."

"Call Chief Terry and see if he can run the Hinckley's HIN and engine serial numbers."

"Roger that." Scott took the business card for the Coast Guardsman from his pocket and dialed Terry's number. Terry sounded groggy when he answered the phone, but he quickly came around when Scott asked him to run a check on a Hinckley to see if the boat was stolen and gave him the serial numbers. He promised to get back to Scott as soon as he ran the report.

While Scott had been talking with Chief Terry, Ryan had pointed the Jeep toward 117 Marine.

"Do a search and see who owns that property," Ryan said. "A dollar says it belongs to one of Bianchi's companies."

"What are they doing with the Pilot up there?" Scott picked up his phone and began typing.

"They're either stashing it until the heat is off or chopping it up, which is a shame because that's a nice boat."

"You owe me a buck. The property belongs to one Keith Covington."

"Another dollar says Bianchi is involved somehow."

"That's a bet I'm not willing to take, but you still owe me."

Just before they came to the Northeast Cape Fear River, Ryan turned off onto Old Bridgesite Road. The pavement ended at a barrier at the edge of the river where, years ago, the old bridge had been before they'd torn it down. Ryan got out with a pair of binoculars and walked down the sandy beach to the water. He scanned the far riverbank for the Pilot.

"What is this place?" Scott asked.

"*This* is Redneck Beach," Ryan said. He brought the binoculars down but continued to look downriver to where the water swirled around an old bridge piling on the opposite bank which had a powerboat moored to it. The black tannic water hid a multitude of snags, stumps, sandbars, and alligators. Farther down, a catamaran sailboat sat beside a wooden pier.

"I can see you fit right in here," Scott joked.

"I think you look more like a redneck than me, my friend. Now, where's that Pilot?"

"The map shows it's in a little channel, leading inland."

"That's right," Ryan said. "I'd forgotten about that. We'll never see it from here, and if I remember right, there's a giant wooden cabin cruiser on blocks by the main entrance off 117. The rest of the place is a bunch of shitty old boats, motors, trailers, and weeds."

Scott glanced around the sandy parking lot surrounded by a wooden fence that demarcated the gentle slope to the river. There was a wooden T-dock at the south end of the park. "How do you know about this place?"

"My grandfather used to bring me fishing up here. We'd put in at the Castle Hayne Boat Ramp on the other side of the bridge. And me and Chad used to come up here on weekends to drink beer with the other boaters. It's a fifty-mile run down the ICW and up the river from Wrightsville Beach. Takes about eight hours at six knots."

"How many times did you make that trip?"

"Just once. Then we trailered a boat up." Ryan smiled. "We had some good times."

His mind drifted back to that day, when they'd motored upriver in a twenty-foot center console they'd borrowed from Henry. Neither of the boys had planned well for the trip. They'd only brought a cooler with a twelve pack of Budweiser that Chad had stolen from his mom's fridge. By the time they'd stopped for fuel in Wilmington, they were half-drunk and starving. The beer had all but disappeared by the time they'd made it to the beach in the evening, and all the other partygoers had already gone home.

With one can of Bud apiece, they'd beached the center console and toasted their long journey. Tired and sunburned, they had lazed in the evening breeze with their feet in the water. A water moccasin had slid out of the tree roots at the river's edge and swam directly at Chad's leg. As the snake had gotten closer, Ryan had moved toward the center of the boat, ready to climb onto the T-top while Chad laughed at him. Then a gator had suddenly popped up from the depths and snatched the snake from the water's surface. Both boys had screamed in elation and amazement. Moments later, they'd started the motor, passed beneath the bridge to the boat ramp, and called Henry to come pick them up with a truck and trailer.

Seeing the smile on his friend's face, Scott asked, "Is that why you're so hung up on helping this guy? The good times?"

"He's my friend, Scott, and he's in trouble." Ryan turned to face the taller man. "I'd do the same for you."

Scott nodded. "That means a lot."

Ryan slapped his friend on the back. "Let's get some coffee. I think I owe you a dollar's worth."

Ryan drove them to the Luck's Tavern, on the corner of Old Bridgesite and Route 117. The two men ate lunch and drank coffee before heading north again, taking only a cursory glance at 117 Marine as they drove past.

They followed the signal from the charger pack's tracker to a river shack off Shaw Highway, hidden among the dense stands of pines. Neither man saw anything of tactical value, and Ryan turned the Jeep around and headed for *Huntress*.

"Tomorrow, I'll go in on foot to look around and to get some pictures of the place," Ryan said. "When I have what we need, I'll exfil and you can pick me up. Then we let the sheriff handle the arrest."

"Why don't you send them an anonymous tip?"

"Because they need evidence to get a warrant."

"Whatever you get by breaking into the place isn't admissible in court," Scott said.

"That's not *our* problem. We just need to get proof that whoever lives there are the thieves and send it to Kyle."

About a mile down the road, Scott's phone buzzed. He held it up and said, "Pull over. The charger pack is on the move."

Ryan slid into a parking spot of a small tool and die company, slotting the Jeep between two big pickup trucks. Less than five minutes later, a beat-up blue Ford truck sped past them.

"That's them," Scott said, consulting his phone.

Ryan put the Jeep in gear and pulled out of the lot. He stayed behind the decrepit regular cab pickup as it cruised toward Rocky Point.

"Use your Internet and look up Tim Davis' mugshot so we know what this guy looks like."

Scott quickly found the man's photo and held up the phone screen for Ryan to see. If the musician Kid Rock had a redneck North Carolina twin, Tim Davis was it. Except Davis was missing teeth, and his hair was unkempt.

The truck stopped at the Rocky Point Travel Center. Ryan pulled up to the gas pump and filled the Jeep. Tim Davis came out with two cases of beer and two full plastic bags.

"Looks like a party," Scott said.

"Probably just a regular night for those swamp rats," Ryan retorted.

"You would know."

Ryan flipped him the bird as he opened the driver's door and got in.

"Speaking of being in the know," Scott said. "What's up with your girl Angie at the Bluewater Grill?"

"She's a waitress."

"Come on, man. You know what I'm talking about."

"The only woman *I* am knowledgeable about is Emily, and she's taken. *By me*."

"How'd you get so lucky?"

Ryan grinned. "A blind hog finds an acorn every once in a while."

Scott snorted. "What now? I could use a drink."

"Back to the boat," Ryan replied. "We have an op to plan."

CHAPTER TWENTY

It was midmorning by the time Ryan and Scott got onto I-40. In Rocky Point, Scott guided them onto State Route 210. After they crossed the Northeast Cape Fear River, he turned north, heading up Shaw Highway. A mile up the road, Scott slowed and pulled the Jeep into a sandy driveway on the left side of the road that led to a wide-open space where the pines had been cleared.

"Let me put a drone up so I can monitor the situation," Scott said.

Shaking his head, Ryan said, "No." They'd already been over this last night. "That means you'd have to park the Jeep close by, and you'd be conspicuous in such a rural area. I don't know how you grew up, but in areas like this, if someone spots an unfamiliar car parked on the side of the road, they call it in or investigate with a shotgun. We can't take that chance."

"At least take an earpiece so we can stay in contact," Scott insisted.

Ryan climbed out of the Jeep and shouldered the backpack he had packed for the recon mission. He begrudgingly took the Bluetooth earpiece that Scott handed to him and shoved it into his ear, then connected it to his phone. "Happy?"

Scott flashed him a thumbs-up, and Ryan shut the door and ran. Scott was right. They should have put up a drone, but he just wanted to get in and get out.

As he ran, Ryan felt the adrenaline hammering through his veins. He was on a mission, and he had to focus. Putting everything else out of his mind, he sprinted full tilt across the clearing for the woods and the safety they represented.

Once he was under the canopy of the towering pines, Ryan pulled out his GPS unit and checked the direction he needed to head to reach the river shack. According to the small device, he would need to walk just over a half mile, but that could change quickly on account of the several marshy areas between himself and the shack, and he intended to make the walk without getting his feet wet. He was thankful for the cool weather, which meant the snakes would be in hibernation. There were at least six types of venomous snakes in the North Carolina woods, and many more that weren't poisonous. While he knew the snakes with diamond-shaped heads were deadly, his philosophy on snakes was never to get close enough to one to worry about the shape of its skull.

He put the thought of the creepy reptiles out of his mind as he walked through the trees and brush. Halfway through his hike, he had to move slightly northeast to avoid a marshy area, and he eventually came to the sandy two-track lane that connected the cabin to the road.

Ryan stayed in the trees, moving parallel to the track, until the cabin came into view. Crouching down behind an ancient Starcraft runabout boat hull that was missing an engine and sitting on the ground surrounded by weeds, he surveyed his location. Behind the boat was a rusty boat trailer with flat, bald tires and a tree growing through the center of the frame. Closer to the house, Tim's blue Ford pickup sat beside a small aluminum skiff on a trailer near the house's front door.

The house itself was a low rectangle on three-foot-tall stilts. At the back, someone had added a small porch with a tin roof that overlooked the river. A pile of black plastic trash bags sat just off the porch, and more clumps of tall weeds hid a cluster of old, rusty appliances. The whole place looked like a dump. Ryan took out a Pentax camera from his backpack and snapped off a few photos of the truck, its license plate, and the exterior of the ramshackle house.

Staying bent over, Ryan ran across the open yard from the old boat to the side of the house. He stayed clear of the moldy vinyl siding and paused by an open window. It was too high off the ground for him to see through, so he settled for straining his ears to hear whatever was going on inside the house.

After a few minutes of silence, he moved toward the rear of the structure and froze as his foot hit a piece of metal hidden in the tall grass. It smacked the side of an old washer, and the resounding thud seemed to echo around the clearing.

Someone inside the house shouted, "Who's there?"

CHAPTER TWENTY-ONE

The sound of metal thudding against metal beside the house made Tim Davis straighten. He was sitting on the back porch, repairing a trotline, and he pushed it off his lap, careful not to let one of the many hooks imbed itself in his skin or clothing. As he stood, he reached for his Winchester pump-action shotgun and racked a shell into the chamber.

"Who's there?" he shouted.

Making his way down the steps from the porch, he walked among the old appliances, kicking weeds, and searching for whatever had made the noise. It might have been a rabbit or a possum, but Tim was cautious, and he walked the length of the house.

"What are you doing?" P.J. asked, peering through the window screen.

"I thought I heard something," Tim said.

"Ain't nobody snoopin' 'round here. There ain't shit to see. When we goin' to town? I've got a bunch of packages to drop off."

"Tonight. I'm waiting for Rocky to call and tell me where to pick up the next boat."

"How long we got?"

Tim shrugged. "Won't know till he calls." He headed for the back porch again, the shotgun draped over his shoulder.

Halfway there, he stopped and stared at the ground. His head moved from left to right, tracking a trail of crumpled grass across the ground. Tim turned and squatted, cradling the shotgun as he stared through the weeds at the dark underbelly of the house. Was there something—or *someone*—under there? Animals could have made the trail as they came out of the woods and attacked the garbage bags. They had ripped several of them open last night and scattered the contents on the ground. He'd meant to burn them but hadn't gotten around to it.

He crept forward, swinging the shotgun's muzzle toward the house. His eyes tried to discern shapes in the darkness among the stilts, but the bright sunlight made it difficult to see. There *was* something there; he saw a shape move. No—it darted away as he approached. Maybe it was a groundhog or a racoon? Or was some stupid sheriff's deputy sneaking around his property? In that case, he would shoot the asshole in the head and feed him to the alligators.

"Come out, come out, wherever you are," Tim called out, imitating Robert DeNiro's character Max Cady from the movie *Cape Fear*. He fantasized himself in the role of Cady, a man out for justice against a system that had beaten him down.

Tim was almost to where Ryan had scrambled under the house, ready to duck under it and blast the intruder with his gun, when his phone rang. After another long look, he stood and answered it. "Hey, boss." Then, a moment later, he said, "Let me get a piece of paper to write that down."

Walking up the porch steps, Tim forgot about the strange

sound he'd heard, excited about getting back on the water and stealing some useful shit from people who had a lot more money than he did. *Screw 'em*, he thought with a grin as he climbed through the window into the kitchen, where he wrote the address Rocky Bianchi gave him on a notepad. Tim ended the call, tore off the top page, and pocketed the phone and the address. His smile widening, he went to what he and P.J. called the office so he could help P.J. carry packages to the truck.

He opened the door and immediately shut it. "Put your damn pants on, P.J. You gotta stop watching porn."

A moment later, P.J. opened the office door, his pants fastened firmly around his waist. "Yeah. Go screw yourself."

Tim smirked. "Looks like that's what you were doing." He pushed past his friend and picked up a load of parcels. "Wash your freaking hands, and let's get these in the truck."

P.J. went to the bathroom, and Tim carried a load of parcels outside. After three trips, they had them all in the truck. Both men climbed in and headed for town.

Neither of them knew that they would never again return to the river shack.

CHAPTER TWENTY-TWO

Ryan felt Tim Davis staring right at him as he slithered to his right to get behind the washing machine he had so carelessly kicked a minute earlier. He held his breath and tried not to move as Tim squatted in the grass, looking at the trail Ryan must have left as he moved across the yard from the old boat to the house. Tim crept closer; the muzzle of the shotgun aimed straight into the shadows where Ryan hid. Ryan had his Walther clutched in his hand, ready to shoot if the kid so much as touched the scattergun's trigger.

He breathed a sigh of relief when he heard Tim's phone ring and the kid stood to answer it. A moment later, the younger man went into the house, and Ryan tracked Tim's movements via the hollow footsteps on the floorboards above him.

Tim and P.J. soon began moving packages from the shack to the truck. Ryan snapped several photos from his vantage point beneath the house. With the packages loaded, the two swamp rats got in the truck and drove away. Ryan lay under the house, listening to the truck's noisy muffler as Tim added and reduced throttle to negotiate the rutted drive.

When Ryan was sure they weren't coming back, he crawled out from under the house and made his way up the steps to the back porch. A trotline lay stretched across the weathered deck boards, and Ryan stepped gingerly over it to avoid becoming entangled in the large circular hooks.

He removed a pair of latex gloves from his pocket and pulled them on before slowly turning the doorknob. It was unlocked. Ryan's first thought was to barge straight into the house, but then he decided against it as the hairs on the back of his neck rose.

Something wasn't right.

It was a similar feeling to what he would get when he disarmed an IED in the hovels of Iraq.

Why would they have left it unlocked?

While there was still a certain code of conduct in the North Carolina backwoods about leaving the property of others alone, lest they wanted to meet the business end of a gun, Ryan didn't think leaving the doors unlocked was good operational security. And a couple of river rats would know that better than anyone because they'd probably snooped around every property from there to Wilmington.

Stepping back from the door, Ryan scanned the edges of the doorframe, looking for signs of a booby trap or something that would show Tim and PJ that an intruder had tampered with it. He saw nothing to ease the tingling at the base of his spine, and he didn't trust thieves who left their hideout unlocked.

Ryan remembered the old saying that Henry O'Shannassy used to tell him: "A lock keeps a man honest."

To his right was a window. Unlike the rest of the windows he'd seen around the house, this one didn't have a screen. As he examined it more closely, Ryan saw that the paint on the sill had been worn away. The window was open just enough to allow him to get his fingers under the lower sash. Again, he took the time to examine the frame for booby traps before lifting it.

Satisfied there was nothing that would do him harm, he grasped the sash and lifted. The old wooden window rose smoothly in its frame, which was surprising given that the North Carolina humidity usually caused these old windows to swell. Ryan put his head and shoulders through the opening and leaned in to look at the door.

He was glad he hadn't barged straight through. Here, a lock would have kept a man not only honest but alive. Taped into place on the frame opposite the doorknob was a grenade with a piece of fishing line looped around the knob and tied to the grenade pin.

Where had these kids gotten a grenade?

He was glad he'd trusted his gut, and he reexamined the window frame and its surrounding area for similar party favors before climbing through the opening. Once inside, he inspected the grenade and left it in place before looking around the rest of the kitchen. Stacks of dirty dishes and pans lined the counter, and flies buzzed over leftover macaroni and cheese in a saucepan on the stove.

On the counter, beside a hot plate, was a hydrometer which piqued Ryan's interest. He opened the lower cabinets and saw, beside several large glass bowls, numerous bottles of bleach, cans of white gasoline in the form of camp stove fuel, and a box of potassium chloride. In another cabinet, he found blocks of beeswax, det cord, and military-grade remote detonators. All the ingredients to cook up a bleach bomb. Ryan snapped multiple pictures of everything.

Stepping into the adjoining living room, he spotted a massive flatscreen television sitting atop an old tube-type console television. The kids were obviously gamers, given the variety of video game consoles connected to the television. A pyramid of beer cans at least six feet high lined one wall. In an ashtray were endless cigarette butts and marijuana roaches. For the first time, Ryan inhaled deeply, and he realized he'd been holding his breath because the place stank like urine, marijuana, stale beer, and mold.

The next room was a bedroom with a single mattress on the floor, and the kids had converted the second bedroom into a storage room for the electronics. Homemade wooden shelves stretched from floor-to-ceiling and contained electronic gear sorted by similar units. Ryan took pictures of the room and the computer they used for selling the gear, the browser of which they'd left open to eBay. A bidding auction was taking place for several pieces of expensive radar equipment, starting at what Ryan knew to be a third of their retail price. He moved the mouse to the next open tab on the screen and got an eyeful of naked women. That explained the lotion bottle and the empty box of tissues on the desk.

His next stop was the little bedroom. Ryan lifted the mattress, rummaged through the old clothes, and inspected the boxes in the closet. In one, he found two diamond rings strung on a gold charm bracelet. A quick glance at the inscription on a heart-shaped charm made Ryan's heart sink. It read: *To Andrea, love Gary*.

He cursed, and Scott replied through his earpiece, "What's going on?"

"I just found a bracelet that belongs to the owner of the Pilot."

"How much longer will you be? It's been a half hour since the kids left."

"I'm heading out now," Ryan said.

He made his way toward the kitchen to exit the cabin. As he passed the front door, he saw the river rats had installed another grenade booby trap to it, but this one could be disabled by opening the front window and removing the fishing line from the doorknob.

With his camera's memory card full of pictures of the grenades and the electronics, Ryan retreated to the kitchen window and was about to climb through it when he saw a notepad on the counter. Remembering the phone call Tim had received, Ryan picked up the pad and held it to the light. He could see slightly indented writing left by Tim's hasty scribble. Using a pencil from the counter, Ryan gently shaded the paper, letting the impressions show through in faint lines. Only part of the address was visible, but Ryan snapped a picture of it anyway and pocketed the paper before climbing back through the window.

He pulled it closed and went down the porch steps. Forty minutes after entering the house, Ryan stowed the camera in his backpack and began running toward the road.

On his way, he told Scott to pick him up at Location A. They had three prearranged pick-up points, and Ryan was glad he didn't have to swim the river to get to Location C. He sprinted the half-mile along the sandy lane to where it forked, then veered into the trees on the right-hand side of the road. It was a rough slog through the scrub, but he did it to avoid the prying eyes of anyone who might be home at the neighboring house that shared a driveway with the river shack.

Scott was waiting for him when he burst through the tree line. Ryan jumped into the Jeep, and Scott sped away before Ryan had his door closed or his pack situated.

"Well?" Scott asked.

"They have a room full of electronics they're selling on eBay." Ryan fished the piece of notepaper from his pocket. "And I know where they're picking up the next boat."

"That's good. What are we going to do about it?"

"Let someone else handle it." Ryan pulled out a laptop and transferred the pictures from the camera to it.

"Is that a grenade strapped to the door?" Scott asked, looking over.

"Just drive," Ryan ordered. "And, yes, it is."

"Where are we going?"

"Wrightsville Beach Marina." Ryan tapped a button on the Jeep's navigation system and brought up the route for Scott to follow. He then emailed the pictures he'd taken of the river shack to Kyle Fowler. When the email had gone through, Ryan dialed the deputy's number.

Kyle answered with, "Detective Fowler."

"This is Ryan. I just sent you the address and pictures of the hideout being used by Tim Davis. Send a unit out to the shack but be careful. They rigged the doors with grenades. You can disarm the one on the front door by opening the window and removing the fishing line from the doorknob."

"What the hell were you doing there?" Kyle asked incredulously.

"It's a long story."

"One I'd like to hear."

"I also sent you the address in Morehead City where they're picking up a boat," Ryan said. "Send a marine unit in that direction because they're on their way there now. I'm sure they'll help themselves to whatever goodies they can find on the way down the ICW."

"Okay," Kyle replied. "Thanks for the tip."

"These kids are dangerous, Kyle," Ryan said. "I think they cooked the chemicals to make the bomb that blew a hole in John Parnell's boat. And I think they had something to do with the disappearance of an older couple."

"Wait? What are you talking about?" Kyle demanded.

Ryan detailed his talk with Chief Gene Terry, his and Scott's visit to Parnell's boat at Cape Fear Dive and Salvage, and the chemicals he'd seen inside the river shack. "I *guarantee* you'll find an *Anarchist Cookbook* on the computer there." Then he told Kyle about the disappearance of Andrea and Gary and the bracelet and ring he'd seen in the river shack.

"You've *got* to be kidding me," Kyle groaned.

"I wish I was."

"I'll get a team together to go out to the shack. I'll also alert the marine units and the Coast Guard station at Emerald Isle to be on the lookout for Davis and his partner."

"Good," Ryan said. "If you need a bomb tech, let me know."

"If you want in on the bust, you need to apply to be a sheriff's deputy."

"No, thanks."

"This isn't something you should be involved with, anyhow. Let law enforcement handle it, Ryan. Go home and stay there until we get this wrapped up."

"Sure," Ryan said, and he hung up.

"We're not doing that, are we?" Scott asked.

"Of course not. We've got more work to do."

CHAPTER TWENTY-THREE

Instead of heading back to Wrightsville Beach Marina, Ryan directed Scott to the airport and the multitude of car rental agencies there. Ryan and Scott changed places in the Jeep. As Ryan got behind the wheel, he said, "Meet me at The Pit Stop gas station on Market Street. It's beside Bianchi's car lot."

Scott disappeared into the rental office, and Ryan headed for the gas station. On the way, he called Barry Thatcher. When Barry answered, Ryan jumped right to it. "You told me that Bianchi runs a car to Albany every month. Do you know when he does that?"

"It's always around the middle of the month."

"So now," Ryan commented.

"Yep," Barry replied, his mouth full. Barry had clearly put him on speaker, and Ryan could hear him eating. It sounded atrocious.

"How does Carmen put up with you?" Ryan asked.

"She loves me for my money, and my brains."

"I need to have a talk with her."

"It won't do any good, Ryan," Carmen said in the background. "He's brainwashed me."

Ryan rolled his eyes. "Can you give me details about the trips to New York?"

"Last month, they generated the paperwork on the fifteenth and processed the incoming vehicle on the eighteenth," Barry said. "It's like eleven hours one way, according to the map."

"Have they processed the paperwork for this month's run?"

"Not yet. I'll set an alert on it and let you know when they do."

"Thanks, Bare."

"Carmen says to pay the bill. She needs new shoes."

"Is that true, Carmen?"

"I can always use new shoes, Ryan. Did you know I'm also the bill collector?"

"Can you swing by my boat to pick up a check?" Ryan asked.

"A *check?*" Barry laughed. "Cash is king and Venmo is the queen."

The phone went dead in Ryan's hand, and he was glad for it. He slowed as he passed Bianchi's car lot, taking in the variety of used junk and newer cars on the lot. In the back was a fenced-in lot that contained boats, RVs, more cars, and a semi-tractor. Once past the car lot, Ryan sped up and headed for a barbeque joint farther down the road.

By the time he returned to the gas station, Scott had arrived in a white four-door Ram truck. The ex-SEAL was swigging from a can of Red Bull and had the window down. A pair of binoculars sat on the center console.

Ryan climbed into the passenger seat and handed over a bag of food. "Barbeque sandwiches with coleslaw and hot sauce."

"You'll make Emily a nice wife someday."

Ryan snorted and ignored the comment. "Barry said the car lot hasn't generated a manifest for the car going north for this month. Be on the lookout for them hooking one up to a wrecker."

Scott bit into a sandwich and chewed. Around a mouthful of food, he said, "I've seen two wreckers in the past twenty minutes."

"They have to load the car with the cigarettes, too."

"I'd do that in a garage or someplace without prying eyes."

"Same here," Ryan agreed.

"What am I looking for, anyway?"

"Suspicious activity. Bianchi owns this block, from this gas station to the car garage."

"What are the chances?" Scott said sarcastically.

"Just keep an eye out."

Scott grunted and took a swig of sweet tea that Ryan had brought with the sandwiches. "What are *you* going to do?"

"See if I can find someone to repair Parnell's GPS."

"It's a long shot after being submerged in water," Scott said.

Ryan nodded. "Call me if you see anything."

"Will do."

Ryan slid out of the truck and went back to the Jeep. Traffic had picked up since he'd stopped to see Scott, and Ryan switched on the radio. Tapping his fingers on the steering wheel to the beat of the music, he cruised across town to Wrightsville Beach Marina.

It was late afternoon when Ryan stopped the Jeep in a parking spot at the marina. He got out and stood in the chilly air, listening to the wind as it blew past. Somewhere, a metal clip banged against an aluminum sailboat mast, making a hollow *ting* with each hit. The tide was out, and the wind carried the scent of the marsh as it blew over the barrier islands toward the mainland. It was a surreal feeling to be there without Emily by his side. He took out his phone and dialed her as he walked to the marina office.

Emily finally answered with a weary, "Hey, Ryan."

"How are you?" he asked, pausing on the seawall, and staring across the water.

"I'm okay."

"Were you sleeping?"

"No. I'm just tired. This school is intense. There's a lot of information to absorb."

"You can do it," Ryan said. "I'm proud of you."

"Thanks for the vote of confidence. What are you doing?"

"We followed the trackers to a river shack that turned out to be the thieves' base of operations. I sent Kyle up there to raid the place. They're looking for the kids who live there now." He sighed and made a conscious decision not to tell her about finding Andrea's bracelet and rings. Even though he wanted to spare her the burden of knowing they were probably dead, he still felt guilty for leaving her to worry about their safety.

"You don't sound happy about it," Emily said.

"No. I'm happy. I'm ready for a nap myself."

The phone beeped with an incoming call. He took the device away from his ear to look at the caller ID. "Hey, Em, Kyle is calling me. I'll call you back later, okay?"

"Love you," Emily said.

Ryan returned her goodbye and thumbed the button to answer Kyle's incoming call. "What's up, Detective?"

"I'm with the unit at the river shack. They disarmed the two grenades at the door, but there was a third."

Ryan felt his heart sink at the thought of officers dying because of those two little bastards.

"Fortunately," Kyle said, "my EOD techs are thorough. They found it buried in the electronics."

"So, no one got hurt?" Ryan asked.

"Everyone is fine. We're inventorying the cabin's contents now. Thanks again for the tip," Kyle said.

"No problem. What about the kids? Have you picked them up yet?"

"No, but the marine units are out in force. I don't suppose you're out looking for them, are you?"

"Me? No. I'm sitting on my boat, like you told me."

"Somehow, I don't believe you, but if you are there, *stay there*," Kyle reiterated. "We'll get them."

"Roger that," Ryan said, then hit the *End* button and slipped the phone into his pocket.

He opened the door to the marina office and walked in. To help ward off the chill, he poured himself a cup of coffee. As he sipped it, he asked the girl behind the counter if Henry was in his office. She nodded and motioned for him to go in.

Ryan found the older man sitting behind his desk. Henry grinned and leaned back in his chair as Ryan entered.

"What can I do for ya, lad?"

"Do you know anyone who can pull data off this?" Ryan set the water-logged GPS unit on the desk. "It got submerged, but I don't know for how long."

Henry's eyes narrowed. "Where'd you get that?"

"John Parnell's boat."

"Ya canna leave well enough alone, eh?"

"This is important to me," Ryan stated.

Henry sighed, then leaned forward and flipped through his old Rolodex. He pulled a card from the file and flipped it across the desk. Ryan spun it around and searched for Stellar Electronics on his phone. The store was in a small strip mall near the hospital. He could check on Chad while he was over there.

"Thanks, Henry." Ryan slid the card back across the desk.

"I don't know what you're into, Ryan, but be careful."

Ryan stood and picked up the GPS unit. "I will, Henry. Thanks for the info."

As he pulled out of the parking lot, hurrying to get across town before the electronics store closed, Ryan glanced in his rearview mirror when a horn honked behind him. He saw a black sedan had cut off a car and was speeding his way. He slowed to allow the car to pass him, but the sedan slowed to match speed with him.

He narrowed his brows in thought as he turned his attention back to the road ahead. He drove at a normal pace across town, watching his rearview mirror. The black sedan stayed with him.

When he reached the strip mall, he parked and walked into the electronics store, carrying the GPS.

"What can I do for you?" a woman behind the counter asked. She wore a sweatshirt and a pair of jeans, and she'd pulled her dark hair into a ponytail.

"Can you pull information off a GPS unit after it's been underwater?" Ryan asked.

"Possibly. Let me see it."

Ryan handed over the GPS.

The woman rolled it in her hands and examined the plastic casing carefully. Then she grabbed an electric screwdriver and removed the screws that secured the back panel.

"You're lucky," she said. "This unit had a waterproof seal on the cover which kept out most of the water. Some got in, though, as evidenced by these dried salt crystals on the circuit cards and the corrosion on the soldered connections."

"Good," Ryan stated. "Can you pull the information for me?"

"Sure. Give me a few minutes." She took the unit into the back.

"After you download the info, can you wipe the unit's memory for me?"

She cocked her head and narrowed her brows.

With a dash-mounted GPS unit like the one Parnell had owned, there was no chain of custody from one owner to another if sold, as it was up to the owner to register the product with the manufacturer. Ryan never even thought the woman would question him about who owned the unit, as possession was nine-tenths of the law.

To sweeten the pot and keep her from asking any questions, Ryan said, "I'll give you an extra hundred bucks on top of your fee."

The woman shrugged her shoulders. "No problem."

"Be sure to delete the file from your computer if you have to download it there first," he told her.

Ryan walked around the store, looking out the window for the guy from the black sedan. The sedan was nowhere in sight.

Ten minutes later, the woman came out of the back of the shop, laid the GPS on the glass countertop, and held out a memory stick to Ryan. He pocketed it and paid her. She told him to call her if he needed anything else.

"I will," Ryan said. "Have a good one."

Stepping off the sidewalk to cross the street, Ryan saw a bicyclist coming straight at him. He jogged forward a few paces to get out of the way, but the rider veered right into him. Ryan and the cyclist sprawled across the pavement and the latter was up first, snatching the GPS from Ryan's hand and racing away. Ryan rolled into a sitting position and watched as the cyclist jumped into the black sedan and the car pulled out of the parking lot with a squeal of rubber.

The electronic store's door flew open, and the woman rushed out the door. "Are you hurt?" she asked breathlessly.

Ryan stood and brushed off his jeans. "I'm all right."

"What happened?"

"Exactly what I thought would happen. Well, I didn't expect the guy on the bike."

"Is that why you had me wipe the unit?"

"Yep."

"What's on that memory stick?" she asked.

"That's what I need to figure out," Ryan said.

CHAPTER TWENTY-FOUR

Scott Gregory fiddled with the Pentax camera Ryan had left with him. Boredom had set in long ago and he'd grown weary of sitting in the truck, but he was being paid to do a job, and this was far better than anything Greg Olsen had sent him to do lately. His last job with Trident had been executive protection for an English diplomat to Ethiopia, making the rounds to bolster trade in 'the home country,' as the Dip had put it. Scott smiled. While 'Dip' was short for diplomat, he thought it was an excellent way to describe most of those government assholes.

He yawned and covered his mouth. The Red Bull and the sweet tea had filtered through his system, and he needed to take a leak. Rather than go into Bianchi's store, he drove the truck next door to a neighboring gas station and backed the truck into a parking spot that faced The Pit Stop.

Now that darkness had fallen, the lights in the canopy above the pumps had come on, as had the lights built into the roof overhang along the side of the building. Attached to The Pit Stop store was a two-bay automatic car wash with three vacuums along the outside wall.

Slipping out of the Ram, Scott went into the gas station and used the restroom. He bought another Red Bull before retreating to the truck. As he opened the door, he glanced across the street and saw a black Cadillac CTS stop at the rear entrance to The Pit Stop's car wash.

Strange, he thought. *Why would you wash a car at night?*

He stood in the truck's open door and watched the car. The driver didn't put any money into the machine to make the wash operate, but the bay door opened. The car drove inside, and the door closed. His curiosity piqued, Scott ran across the street and crouched by the vine-covered fence that enclosed the storage lot behind The Pit Stop.

Scott then darted across the alley to the car wash and pressed himself against the rough block wall. Carefully, he peered through the garage door window. The Cadillac's trunk was open, and two men were using a hand truck to move boxes of cigarettes through a storage room door and into the Cadillac. Wishing he had the big Pentax camera, Scott withdrew his cell phone and snapped off several pictures of the car and the men. With the evidence captured, he ran across the road to the Ram and jumped in.

When the Cadillac exited the wash bay, Scott slipped the Ram's transmission into drive, crept across the road into The Pit Stop's parking lot, and, thankful that there was little traffic on the road at this time of night, followed the Cadillac. Fifty feet down the road, the car turned into a parking lot beside a large multi-bay service and sales building labeled Wilmington Motor Sales, then drove onto a flat-bed trailer attached to a white Ford dually pickup truck.

Scott slowed and turned into the parking lot of another car dealer across the street. He quickly circled around and stopped the truck so he could see the action. Grabbing the camera, he snapped pictures of the two drivers, the truck, the trailer, and the trailer's license plate. He then waited for the truck to leave so he could follow it and possibly get a glimpse of its license plate, but he doubted he'd be successful, on account of the trailer blocking the view.

A second car pulled into the lot. The driver of the Cadillac got into it, and they sped away. The truck driver fastened the Cadillac to the trailer with chains and tie-down straps, then pulled out of the parking lot. When the rig turned onto Gordon Road, Scott assumed the truck driver was on his way to I-40. Within an hour and a half, he would be on I-95, heading north to Albany.

After following the truck to I-40 and getting several pictures of what he hoped was the license plate, Scott turned off and headed for Wrightsville Beach Marina. When he was aboard *Huntress*, he found her dark and silent. He lifted his finger to punch in the alarm code but saw the red light that showed the system was active wasn't blinking.

He paused in the still night air, listening to the sounds around him. Then he heard voices, speaking in hushed tones, followed by a peal of laughter. Scott turned toward the sound and saw two men standing behind the marina's office building, facing the seawall. When one man took a puff on his cigarette, Scott saw it was Ryan.

Curious, Scott set the camera on the aft deck table and walked back up the dock, staying in the shadows as he moved along the building until he could overhear the conversation.

"Yeah, we were giving tickets out right and left on Memorial Day," Chief Gene Terry said.

"I believe it," Ryan replied. "I grew up here. Most of the guys running around on small boats don't have the required safety equipment."

"Tell me about it. We found an old guy about five miles offshore in a fifteen-foot rowboat he'd put a twenty-horse eggbeater on. He had three fishing lines out and was drunk off his ass. So, we pull up beside him and he has no clue where he is or why we stopped him. Then he reels in his lines and he's got no bait on them. I asked him what he was doing out there, and—get this—he turns to me with this very serious face, pushes up his hat and asks me, 'Son, are you married?'"

Ryan burst out laughing, and Scott chuckled to himself. He remembered getting married at eighteen as a young seaman apprentice, right out of bootcamp. His new bride, Michelle, had been his high school sweetheart, and once he'd graduated from SEAL training, he had moved her from their hometown of Casper, Wyoming, into an apartment in Little Creek, Virginia. They'd lasted three years before she moved out and filed for divorce. Scott hadn't been home for much of their marriage, and when he was there, she had gradually pushed him away. That last year had been nothing but screaming matches and hurt feelings. He understood exactly what that old man was doing in the middle of the Atlantic in a rowboat. Sometimes, a guy just needed some peace and quiet.

"What did you find out about that HIN we asked you to run?" Ryan asked.

"Stolen," Terry replied. "The owner lives in Charleston. He filed a report two weeks ago."

"I figured."

Terry clapped Ryan on the back. "And I figure you owe me another round."

"Let me lock the boat, and we'll head over to the Bluewater." Ryan turned to look right where Scott had sequestered himself in the shadows. "You coming, swab?"

Scott stepped into the light, told Ryan he could go screw himself, and then said, "Put the camera in the cabin while you're locking the boat."

Terry walked over to Scott. "Ryan said you were working some case."

"Yeah. I called it a night."

"Does it have to do with that stolen boat?"

"Partly. We caught the kids that brought the Hinckley up here, and we think they killed the couple who owned the Pilot so they could steal it."

"Shit," Terry lamented.

"You can say that again."

Once Ryan had secured the *Huntress*, the three men walked along the waterfront to the restaurant. The hostess at the Bluewater Grill seated them, and Angie quickly brought over the first round, remembering what each man liked to drink. Scott sipped his beer and watched Angie as she walked away. She reminded him of Michelle. Maybe that wasn't such a good thing. After getting out of the Navy after a six-year hitch, he'd gotten a recruiting call from Trident and he hadn't looked back. While Texas was better than Wyoming, it wasn't where he planned to spend the rest of his life. He glanced around the bar, then at Angie. Yeah, he liked North Carolina.

"Earth to Scott?" Ryan said.

"Oh, sorry," Scott replied. "I was just thinking ..."

"And staring at Angie's ass like you just got back from six months on a submarine."

Scott flipped Ryan the bird. He hadn't realized he was staring, or, at least, he hadn't *intended* to.

"She shoots down every guy who asks her out, you know," Terry said.

Scott snorted. She hadn't met the legendary Scott Gregory.

"As I was saying," Ryan continued, "my mom and dad are cooking up a feast for Thanksgiving. You guys are welcome to come. I know what it's like to be away from home on the holidays."

"You sure?" Terry asked.

"It would be an honor to have you," Ryan said.

Both men said thanks. Scott sipped his beer and stared out over the water. The last Thanksgiving dinner he'd been to in Wyoming was when he'd gone to get Michelle. His folks had divorced when he was young, and he had few memories of his father. His mother had died in a car accident when he was sixteen. She'd been drinking as usual, and ... *Dammit, stop dragging that shit up*! he scolded himself.

"You okay?" Ryan asked.

"Yeah. Just thinking, is all," Scott said, not wanting to give anything away. The Navy had been his family, and once he'd left it, the men of Trident had taken their place. Ryan was like a brother to him, even though they'd only met a year ago and had seen little of each other except when working operations together. But that was how it was. Planning and working operations together had forged a strong bond between them.

Angie brought a round of drinks to replenish the men, and she laid a hand on Scott's shoulder. "You doin' good, hon?"

He felt a wave of giddiness sweep over him, and he grinned up at her. "I'm good, Angie. Thanks for asking. But ..." Scott turned his grin to Ryan and Gene Terry, then back to her. "I'd be even better if I could get your number."

"Oh, sweetie, I don't date customers," Angie said.

Scott stood. "Then I'll never come in here again."

Angie laughed. "In that case ..." She scribbled her cell phone number on her pad, tore off the sheet, and handed it to Scott. "Call me, hon."

"Okay. You got it," Scott said, a bit *too* enthusiastically.

Angie smiled coquettishly and walked away.

Scott started to sit down, but Terry, who was sitting across the table from Scott, used his foot to shove Scott's chair out from underneath him. Scott missed the chair and tumbled onto the ground.

"What the hell was that for?" Scott demanded.

Ryan laughed while Gene Terry said, "You don't drink here anymore, remember?"

Scott stood and brushed sand off his pants. "No problem. I've got her number, so I don't need to drink with you shitbirds, anyway."

"Have fun, *hon*," Terry sneered.

"Oh, I will. My date with Angie will be *lots* of fun. By the way, Ryan, I've got some pictures I think you'll want to see."

With that, Scott turned and walked over to Angie. He told her he was leaving and that he would call her.

"I'm off on Sundays and Tuesdays," she said.

"Sounds great," Scott replied.

"I gotta get back to work. I'll see you, okay?" Angie squeezed his hand.

"You bet," Scott said, feeling the hormones rush through his body.

He went back to *Huntress*, grabbed an icy beer from the fridge, and sat down at the navigation desk. Using the boat's Wi-Fi, Scott connected the Pentax camera to his laptop and downloaded the pictures he'd taken at The Pit Stop and of the truck and trailer. Once he had them on-screen, he enlarged them and scrolled through them to see if he could spot things he hadn't seen in real time.

Ryan came aboard and leaned over his shoulder. Scott could smell the cigarette smoke on his clothes. Even though Ryan had promised Emily he would quit, he still seemed to sneak one occasionally.

"*Damn*. That's a lot of cigarettes in the back of that car," Ryan said.

"If we're serious about taking down Bianchi's network, we need to notify the ATF about the delivery."

Ryan got himself a beer from the fridge and sat on the sofa. "I think we should see what they bring back first."

Scott turned to face his friend. "Okay. What do we do until then?"

"I want you to continue to stake out Bianchi's car lot. I'll have Barry hack the delivery truck's GPS so we can track them. Once we know where they're taking the cigarettes and what they bring back, then we'll have the ATF bust the place in Albany."

"Sounds good," Scott said. "Any word about the river shack?"

"Kyle took a team up there and disarmed the grenades. They're searching the place now."

"No word on the kids?"

"Not yet." Ryan yawned. "I figure it's just a matter of time before they find them."

CHAPTER TWENTY-FIVE

Time was not on Tim Davis' side.
He had the throttle down on the Yellowfin 42 Offshore center console fishing boat. Its four Yamaha outboards rocketed the boat down the ICW as the Carteret County Marine Patrol units chased after him.

They'd caught him red-handed at a private dock while P.J. was looting a big sportfisher in Bogue Sound. Tim had thrown the throttle forward and left P.J. to fend for himself. The darkness made it difficult for him to navigate by anything other than the lights of the onshore houses and the navigational beacons in the channel. Normally, he would have put P.J. in the bow and used him to spot the shifting sandbars and grass flats as they attempted to escape, but the marine units had apprehended P.J. at the dock. As a result, Tim couldn't see where the hell he was going.

It was of little consequence, because Bogue Sound was one long bottleneck and there were limited places he could exit to the ocean. Tim wasn't as familiar with this stretch of The Ditch as he should have been, and once he passed the Marine Corps Landing Field at Guthrie Point, the ICW necked down and became one long, dredged channel among a myriad of others that wove through the grassy islands.

He watched the lights on the Emerald Isle Causeway draw closer and had a feeling that the Coast Guard would be waiting for him under the bridge. Instead of taking the main channel, he killed his running lights and veered off for Hunting Island. The channel markers took him close to shore, and he passed slowly under the bridge without incident while the stupid Puddle Pirates idled in the main channel.

When the two channels came back together just south of the bridge, Tim threw the throttle forward and rocketed away, sure the roar of his high-horsepower engines would alert everyone to his position. And he was right. No sooner had he come onto plane, the red and blue lights on the Coast Guard's boat came on and joined the chase. Farther back were the lights of the local marine units. Somewhere ahead was Bogue Inlet, the place where he'd escape into the open ocean.

Just over a mile later, he slowed the craft to forty miles per hour and carved an arc in the water as he turned hard left around Shark Tooth Island. The big boat handled like it was on rails. Tim righted the wheel and threw the throttle all the way forward. The Yellowfin was capable of sixty-seven miles per hour, a number he had seen on the GPS screen earlier in the evening, but the four engines were thirsty beasts, and the needle on the fuel gauge dropped precipitously with every nautical mile. Once he was offshore, he could slow and conserve fuel, then make a run into Brown Inlet or the New River and get fuel. Maybe he could hole up for a while and let the heat die down.

Suddenly, a wave of helplessness swept over him at just how futile his escape efforts were. There were both marine units and Coast Guard patrol boats chasing him. He glanced over his shoulder and saw flashing lights in the sky.

Great! A freaking helicopter.

Turning his attention back to the view ahead, Tim saw the channel markers to his right and edged that way. Beyond them was the vast, rolling expanse of the dark Atlantic. If the Coast Guard didn't use thermal imagery, he could shut off the engines and drift.

But that was a huge *if*. Of course they had thermal and night vision and radar. All these guys did was search for boats. This was all going terribly wrong. Had Bianchi set him up? Or was it that rat bastard Chad Yeager?

Tim bumped the throttle again, but it was already at its stop. The digital number on the GPS said sixty-five miles per hour.

I might just make it.

Then the boat stopped dead in the water.

Tim's body flew off the leaning post, slamming his chest against the steering wheel and smacking his head against the T-top tubing. His right hand had been on the throttle, and as he fell, his arm lodged between the throttle lever and the thick aluminum post of the T-top.

The radius and ulna snapped with the sound of a gunshot.

Lying on the deck, Tim stared up at the high-powered spotlight mounted on the belly of the Coast Guard's Eurocopter MH-65 Dolphin and wondered if it was the light at the end of the tunnel. As his vision blurred into unconsciousness, he reached up and touched his head.

His fingertips slick with blood, the darkness closed around him.

———

Lt. Cmdr. Brian Milestone ordered his Rapid Response

Boat to come alongside the Yellowfin center console. The fishing boat had beached itself on a sandbar near the mouth of Bogue Islet. When the nose of the rigid hull inflatable boat bumped against the port stern of the Yellowfin, Milestone climbed aboard and kneeled beside the inert driver. A pool of blood had seeped from the gash on the fugitive's forehead onto the deck, and his right arm lay at an unnatural angle.

Bile rose in Milestone's throat. He wiped his mouth with the back of his hand, not wanting to puke in front of his sailors. "Hey, Rosa! Get over here and take care of this guy."

Kelly Rosa, a health services technician assigned to Station Emerald Isle, had ridden on Milestone's command boat for an emergency such as this. The medic swung her legs over the Yellowfin's gunwale and set her kit on the deck beside the unconscious man. She immediately assessed his injuries, checked his pulse, and shone a light into his pupils. "He's got a concussion and a broken arm, but he'll live."

Rosa had another crewman from the response boat help her set the arm and apply a splint while Milestone used his handheld radio to direct the helicopter to come overhead and take the injured man.

The Dolphin dropped a litter, and the crewmen from the Rapid Response Boat loaded Tim Davis into it and signaled for the helicopter to retrieve the basket.

―――――

As the basket rose into the air, the helicopter's rotor blades whipped the surface of the water. The salt spray struck Tim in the face, causing him to regain consciousness. Not knowing where he was and why he was spinning slowly in circles frightened him, and he bucked against the restraints.

When the aircrewman pulled him into the helicopter, Tim realized he must have passed out after running his boat aground on the sandbar. Restraints bound his feet, and there was an excruciating pain radiating up his arm and through his shoulder and neck. No matter how he shifted, he couldn't get comfortable.

The crewman flashed him a thumbs-up and spoke into his radio boom mike, but Tim couldn't hear him. All he could hear was the sound of the rotors overhead. His eyes drooped, and once again, he passed out.

―――――

WHEN TIM DAVIS woke the next time, he was in a hospital room with a cast around his right arm, encasing it from his upper bicep to his fingertips. Two uniformed police officers sat in the room with him. When one noticed he was awake, the officer stepped out of the room and escorted in a man and a woman. Tim knew the man as Kyle Fowler, a deputy for the New Hanover County Sheriff's Department. He'd had several run-ins with the detective and thought he was a self-righteous prick.

"How you doing, Tim?" Kyle asked.

Tim rolled his eyes and sighed.

"That's good. Hey, listen, I've gotta read you this little card and then I'll introduce this young lady." Kyle read the Miranda Rights from a laminated card before putting it back in his pocket and turning to the woman. "This is Assistant District Attorney Karen Riker. She'd like to talk to you for a few minutes."

Tim shook his head. "I want a lawyer."

"Look, Tim," Kyle said, stepping closer to the bed. "We've got you dead to rights for fleeing and evading in a stolen boat, and we raided your shack on the river."

"Go screw yourself," Tim snarled, watching the detective's

face. This guy had nothing on him, and Tim planned to walk out of the hospital a free man.

"That's no way to talk around a lady, son," the overweight, gray-haired cop in the chair beside the bed interjected.

"Screw off, Pops," Tim growled.

"You're not helping yourself here, Tim," Kyle said. "We don't care about you, bud. We want Charles Bianchi. You give us evidence against him, and we'll kick you loose with a minimum sentence."

"Immunity," Tim stated.

Riker moved closer to the bed, keeping her arms crossed.

She don't like me at all, Tim thought. *That's okay. I could like her enough for the both of us. She's pretty.*

The detective leaned in, and Tim could smell the stale coffee on the man's breath. Kyle said, "You don't have many options here, pal. Me. I like you for ICON, but Ms. Riker reckons you'll make a good snitch."

Tim shuddered. ICON, or intensive control, was a term used by the North Carolina correctional facilities. It was basically long-term solitary confinement. Inmates saw six hours of daylight in a normal week. Tim had done two weeks in ICON for fighting with another inmate the last time he'd been to prison.

"Rest up, Mr. Davis," Ms. Riker said. "We'll move you down to Wilmington in a few days."

Tim didn't like the sound of that, but he could roll on Bianchi and walk away from this. They had said nothing about the deaths of the old couple on the Pilot. He couldn't help but wonder if they had found the rings and bracelet in his room. Suddenly, he wished they had never laid eyes on that trawler.

If questioned, he could just say they'd found the boat adrift and that he'd found the jewelry on it, but if the cops had snatched up P.J., that little bastard might just roll on him.

For now, he'd keep calm. They wanted information on Bianchi, and if it kept him out of ICON, then he had plenty of stories he was more than willing to share.

The prick detective and the hot little number headed for the door.

"Hey," Tim said as Fowler reached for the handle. They turned to look at him. "Call me a lawyer. Immunity and I'll roll."

CHAPTER TWENTY-SIX

Early the next morning, Ryan Weller spread a map of coastal North Carolina and the Atlantic Ocean across the galley island on his catamaran *Huntress*. In Henry O'Shannassy's dusty filing cabinet at the marina office, he had found a map identical to the one he had seen on Bianchi's desk. On a notepad beside him was the list of names he remembered from Bianchi's list. It hadn't taken much digging to find they were vessels owned by United Atlantic Shipping. When Scott had searched for *Star of Sumatra*, the search engine had led him straight to United Atlantic, whose listing of the shipping line's fleet included the rest of the names.

The fleet of twenty ships made routine stops along America's Eastern Seaboard and at ports across the Mediterranean, Africa, and the Middle East. Ryan opened his computer and inserted the memory stick Stellar Electronics had provided him with when the woman had downloaded Parnell's GPS unit. He opened the software included on the stick and stared at the tracks that *Skater* had left.

Ryan sighed in frustration as he tried to decipher the mess. He tried by date, but most of the tracks wandered all over the place, from Parnell's home on the ICW out into the Atlantic and back. He made trips up and down the Ditch, using the boat as one would use a car. Ryan rubbed his head and opened an Internet browser. He pulled up vesseltracker.com and searched for the ships on the list. According to the website, he needed to pay for a subscription to the tracking service to view the vessel's past routes.

Straightening, Ryan reached for his cup of coffee and sipped it while trying to decide what to do next. There *had* to be a connection between those ship tracks and whatever Parnell was doing, otherwise Bianchi wouldn't have been looking at the chart.

"You look like you're about to have a stroke," Scott said, coming into the salon and pouring coffee into a travel mug.

"Thanks."

Scott stepped over to the island and looked at the chart. "You need to overlay the ship tracks and Parnell's GPS."

"I've thought about that, too," Ryan said. "There must be something these ships have in common because Bianchi didn't have all twenty of them on the list."

"Ports of call. Crew. Routes," Scott suggested.

Ryan shook his head in frustration. "I'm gonna have to stare at a computer all day to figure this shit out, and *that* makes me go stir-crazy just *thinking* about it."

"I know Barry's been your go-to guy so far, but Ashlee could help you with this."

Ryan sipped his coffee and stared at the chart. Ashlee Williams worked for both Dark Water Research and Trident as an IT and programming specialist. She had helped Ryan with multiple missions until the parameters of his requests meant that he'd needed a hacker, and he'd leaned on Barry Thatcher for his computer support needs since. He glanced at the clock. Texas was an hour behind them, so he would need to wait a bit to call her.

"I'm headed over to the car lot," Scott said. "Are you sure we don't have something else for me to do?"

"Not right now. It's a waiting game. You ought to know all about that."

"Yeah," Scott mused. "I do. '*Hurry up and wait.*' The motto of the military."

Ryan refilled his coffee cup and topped off Scott's travel mug. The big ex-SEAL pulled on his jacket and headed out the door. Ryan watched him drive away in the Ram, then reached for his cellphone. He hit the speed dial button for Greg Olsen.

"You freezing your ass off yet?" Greg asked by way of a greeting.

"Close to it. I think it could snow at any minute."

Greg laughed. "Better you than me. How long will you be in North Carolina?"

"I've got a few things to wrap up, and I promised my parents I'd stay for Christmas."

"You do that. Spend as much time as you can with them. That's important."

Ryan could hear the catch in his friend's voice. Greg had lost both his parents when a terrorist had driven a car bomb into the Texas Governor's mansion during a fundraising luncheon. Greg's father, Allen, had run ops for the Department of Homeland Security when he was the CEO of Dark Water Research, and since Greg was a paraplegic, he had needed someone to take Allen's place. Ryan had been that person, filling the liaison role between DWR and Homeland until a Mexican cartel had placed a bounty on his head, and he'd gone into hiding. He'd worked for Greg in some capacity since, both directly employed by DWR and, later, as an independent contractor.

Greg cleared his throat. "How's Scott doing?"

"Fine," Ryan said. "Speaking of that, I need to borrow

Ashlee's expertise for a bit." He explained what he needed from her.

"Why do you think it relates to Parnell and those ship tracks?" Greg asked.

"Just a hunch. Bianchi came out the winner on Parnell's with the real estate deal, but I think there's something else there."

Greg sighed. "All right. Call her, but if I were you, I'd wait until after nine. She gets cranky if she hasn't had a shower and coffee."

"Thanks, Greg. Anything special you want in your stocking?"

"Uh, yeah, now that you mention it. I'd like the black sheep to come back to the fold."

Ryan laughed. "I'm a black sheep now?"

"*Now?* You always have been." Greg laughed. "Hey, congrats on the engagement. I need to get rolling."

"How about we do a double wedding?" Ryan asked.

"Don't curse at me, man. I'm your friend."

Ryan laughed again. After the tension of the last few days, it was good to crack jokes with one of his best friends. "I'll have Emily call Shelly."

"Don't you dare," Greg growled in warning.

Still chuckling, Ryan told Greg goodbye, hung up, and walked to the back of the marina office. He lit a cigarette and stared out across the Intracoastal. Yesterday, he'd smoked his first cigarette in months, but the actions were automatic and gratifying as he stood alone at the breakwater. He tried to clear his mind of all the clutter, letting it drift with the wind and the smoke, enjoying the quiet. There was a low, lonely moan to the breeze as it flowed around him, and it made him shiver.

An approaching Coast Guard Rapid Response Boat interrupted his thoughts, and Ryan watched it slow and come along the seawall at his feet.

Chief Gene Terry leaned out the open cabin hatch. "Hey, squid. Did you hear Station Emerald Isle caught that kid, Tim Davis, and his buddy Patrick Jefferies in Bogue Inlet?"

"No." Ryan shook his head.

"Seems Davis left his boy at the dock when the first marine units showed up. He was in a Yellowfin center con with quad Yamahas and gave them all a run for the money. If he'd gotten into the open ocean, he might have had a chance, but he hit a sandbar going out the inlet. He's in the hospital with a concussion and a broken arm."

"Glad they found him," Ryan said.

"My station commander wants to know about that HIN you asked me to run. There's a BOLO out for that boat."

Ryan stabbed out his smoke in the butt can. "You didn't see that when you were running the numbers?"

"The number wasn't flagged in the database."

"But it triggered an alert somewhere," Ryan stated.

"It did. Where's the Hinckley at?"

"Last time I saw it, it was at Bradley Creek Marina."

"Any idea who stole it?"

Ryan shook his head. "No idea who stole it, but Tim Davis brought it in. He used it to tow in a VDL Pilot called *Due South*. I think Davis and Jefferies killed the couple who were aboard it."

Terry cocked his head and adjusted his ball cap. "If that's true, then we need to open an investigation."

"The Pilot is at 117 Marine, up on the East Branch."

Chief Terry nodded. "I'll talk to my supervisor and the sheriff's department to see how we can help."

"Thanks, Chief. Have a good one."

"I gotta run. Have a better one."

"Roger that," Ryan said.

Terry ducked back into the cabin and ordered his coxswain to idle away from the seawall.

Ryan watched them go, then went back to *Huntress*. He dialed Ashlee Williams' number.

When she came on the line, she said, "Hello, *Ryan*," with as much sarcasm as she could muster.

He laughed. "Hello to you, too, Ash. How have you been?"

"I was doing well until *you* called."

Despite their adversarial conversation, the two were good friends. Ryan had used the redhead's expertise on many of his jobs, including a search for gold bars in a sunken ship. He'd been a groomsman at her wedding and considered her husband, Don, to be not only a good friend, but one of the best mechanical engineers he'd ever worked with.

"I talked to Greg," Ryan said. "He said you would help me search for some information." Ryan asked her to collate the tracks of the ships owned by United Atlantic Shipping and overlay them with the GPS tracks from John Parnell's boat.

"Shouldn't be a problem," she said. "How far back do you want me to go?"

"A year."

Ashlee groaned. "Oh, boy. I'll start this morning, but it'll take some time to figure it all out."

"You're the best, Ash."

"Why aren't you using Barry for this?" Ashlee asked. "I hear he's your go-to man these days."

"I have him doing some other stuff."

"Okay. Anything else *you* need?"

"Nope. Just get those tracks together and see how they overlap. I can take it from there."

They ended the call after a few more pleasantries, and Ryan sat down in front of his laptop. He started with a search for John Parnell and read everything he could about the man's disappearance. After that, he moved to a property search for the land that Bianchi and Parnell had been in dispute over. It turned out to be a twenty-four-hundred-acre tract of undeveloped land along the Intracoastal Waterway near Rich Inlet, between the towns of Kirkland and Hampstead. Once he had the plot number, Ryan went to the Pender County auditor's website. According to the records there, the property was still in Parnell's name.

Ryan leaned back in his chair and thought about what McClelland had told him. Parnell had signed the property over to Bianchi before disappearing. Maybe the reporter had his information wrong?

His next Internet search revealed that Bianchi had filed a master development plan with the county to build two housing subdivisions and a large marina. *How could he do that if he doesn't own the land?* Ryan wondered.

Digging further, Ryan saw that attached to the development plans was a land contract. In the fine print, it said that in the event of Parnell's death, the land would automatically be placed in a joint trust administered by Green Channel Development, LLC. Doing a quick search for the limited liability company resulted in nothing more than a post office box address in Hampstead. But it hadn't, and that made Ryan curious.

He reached for the phone and dialed Ray McClelland. "Hey, Mac, it's Ryan Weller. I spoke to you the other day about—"

"Bianchi," McClelland cut him off.

"Have you ever heard of Green Channel Development, LLC?"

"What the hell is that?"

Ryan explained what he had found through his searches.

"Sounds fishy," McClelland said. "Just like everything else associated with Bianchi."

"Did you get the scoop on the capture of Tim Davis?" Ryan asked.

"I read about it in the paper like everyone else."

"Don't be so disgruntled. Can you do me a favor and dig into this Green Channel thing?"

"I've got too much work to do. Besides, if my boss catches me looking at something related to Bianchi, he'll have my scalp—and I'm tired of being yelled at."

"I hear you. But while I have you on the phone, I forgot to ask the other day—does Parnell have any next of kin?"

"A niece in Beaumont, Texas."

Beaumont wasn't far from Dark Water Research's headquarters in Texas City. "What's her name?"

"Claire Ecclestone."

Ryan did a quick Internet search and found her address and phone number.

"You're the best, Mac. Don't worry about the Green Channel thing. I think I know how to circumvent it."

"Are you screwing with Bianchi?"

Ryan hung up without responding and pondered his next move. Then he dialed Greg Olsen again.

When the owner of DWR answered, Ryan said, "I've got a job for you."

CHAPTER TWENTY-SEVEN

Wilmington Motor Sales sprawled across three city lots and included a large showroom, multiple service bays, a body shop, and a car detailing service that used the car wash attached to The Pit Stop. Behind the main car lot was a large, fenced enclosure that Bianchi's towing company used to store repossessed and wrecked cars.

Scott Gregory had to admit that Rocky Bianchi had a good thing going for himself. He'd watched cars come and go from the car lot and the gas station for most of the morning and had moved his truck several times to keep from being noticed.

But someone had spotted him.

He'd just gotten back in the truck with a fresh Red Bull and pulled out his phone to text Ryan when a siren *whooped* behind him.

Scott watched as Mike Boostrom, the cop who'd been guarding Chad's room, got out of his cruiser and approached his truck.

"Hey, man," Scott said as he buzzed the window down. "What's going on?"

"I'm going to ask you the same thing," Boostrom said. He was in uniform, and he had his hand on his sidearm.

"I pulled over to send a text and grab a Red Bull."

Boostrom nodded suspiciously as he glanced around, keeping a close watch on his surroundings. "I've had a complaint about you loitering."

"Loitering?" Scott questioned. "I'm sitting in a parking lot."

"You've been here for the last two hours. Why?"

Scott glanced at the clock on the dashboard. Someone must have called him in.

"Look," Boostrom said, continuing to glance around. "I need to see your driver's license, registration, and insurance."

Scott handed over the paperwork.

Boostrom held up Scott's license, comparing the photo to Scott's face. "Texas, huh? You're a long way from home."

"Just visiting some friends."

"You're also a long way from the hospital." Boostrom walked back to his cruiser, got in, and closed the door.

Scott waited for the man to run the plate and his license, check the rental agreement, and do whatever else he had to do. This surveillance gig had turned into a cluster. There was no way he could sit there and monitor the car lot with the cops harassing him. In fairness, the gas station had 'no loitering' signs posted on the building and in the parking lot.

Officer Boostrom came back to the truck window ten minutes after he'd left. He handed the license and registration back to Scott and leaned his head in the window. Boostrom sniffed. "You been drinking?"

"Just Red Bull," Scott said.

"Mixed with vodka?" Boostrom asked. "Get out of the truck."

Scott knew there was no use in arguing with the man, so

he slid out of the truck and braced himself for whatever came next. At least there were plenty of witnesses.

"Arms up," Boostrom ordered, and he patted Scott down. He quickly found the concealed Springfield XD-M Elite pistol and removed it from the holster on Scott's waist.

"Concealed carry permit from Texas," Scott said. "I'm sure you saw that on my license. N.C. has reciprocity with Texas."

"I know the law," Boostrom snarled. The cop laid the handgun on the truck's hood after dropping the magazine and popping the cartridge from the chamber. He pulled Scott's hands down one at a time and clamped a pair of handcuffs around Scott's wrists, cinching them tight. Scott stood passively as Boostrom searched the truck before landing on Scott's backpack and dumping its contents on the passenger seat. He rooted through everything, then picked up the Pentax camera and scrolled through the contents. "A real sailing fan, huh?"

"I like to take pictures of boats," Scott said.

"Then what are you doing here?"

"I'm on my way to take pictures of boats." Scott turned to face the patrol car. "For the record, I, Scott Gregory, did not consent to a search of my vehicle or its contents."

Boostrom slammed the truck door closed, leaving the gear from Scott's go-bag strewn across the seat and the floorboards. He stepped menacingly close to Scott. "It's illegal to drink and drive."

"Blow me," Scott muttered.

The cop stepped intimidatingly close to Scott. "What the hell did you just say to me?"

"I said, get the breathalyzer so I can blow a perfect zero, *sir*."

Boostrom walked to his car and came back with a handheld breathalyzer. Scott blew into it as a crowd of onlookers assembled, one of whom was now videoing the encounter with his cell phone. The analyzer found zero alcohol on his breath, and Scott smiled in triumph. Boostrom unhooked him and put his cuffs back on his belt. He had Scott sign the loitering ticket and handed over a copy.

"I don't want to see you around here again, understand?" Boostrom said. "We're watching you."

"Are you telling me I can't stop here to get gas or buy a Red Bull?" Scott asked, trying hard to keep the irritation out of his voice.

"You're free to do those things, but if I get another call that you're sitting in your truck for hours on end *anywhere* near this block, I'll run you in for vagrancy."

"Fair enough," Scott said. He wanted to whip this guy's arrogant, overweight ass, but that would only get him thrown in jail and he'd be of no use to anyone there.

Boostrom got into his cruiser and pulled away, and Scott did the same in his truck. He drove straight to the rental agency and traded the Ram in for a black Chevy Camaro, not wanting Boostrom to easily spot him in the same vehicle. Driving back to Wrightsville Beach Marina, Scott thought about what Boostrom had said: "*We're watching you.*"

Who is watching me? And why?

Another thought occurred to Scott as he approached the turnoff to the marina. *If they're following me, are they following Ryan?*

Scott parked the Camaro in front of the Redix Store, a department store declaring themselves a Southern lifestyle outfitter. He went inside and looked around before purchasing a new navy-blue ball cap with a light blue fish on the front. Back outside, he walked around to where workers were building a ramp for handicap accessibility into the Gulfstream Restaurant. He made small talk with one of the construction crew while his gaze roved over the cars in the adjacent parking lot.

Scott saw no one suspicious, but that didn't mean there wasn't someone he'd missed. There were a lot of cars in various lots around the marina area, and people were constantly coming and going. The watcher could even be on a boat.

He went back to the car and climbed in before calling Ryan.

"What's up?" Ryan asked.

"I think Bianchi has people watching us. I just got a ticket for loitering at The Pit Stop and that fat ass cop Boostrom made me blow into a breathalyzer."

"Did you call a witness?" Ryan asked.

"What do you mean?"

"North Carolina law allows for the drunk driving suspect to call for a witness to the breathalyzer."

"That asshole," Scott muttered, then returned to the reason for his call. "Boostrom said they were watching us. I'm here at the marina now. I want you to drive somewhere; see if you have a tail."

"Got it. Give me ten," Ryan said, and hung up.

Scott started the Camaro and turned around, so he was facing out. Minutes later, he received a text from Ryan saying he would turn left out of the parking lot.

Ryan's gray four-door Jeep Wrangler Unlimited rolled past Scott, and he waited impatiently to see if anyone followed Ryan out of the parking lot. After a full five minutes, Scott saw no one and called Ryan. "False alarm."

"No worries," Ryan replied. "I needed to go to the hospital, anyway. They're discharging Chad."

"Maybe me getting that ticket was just a coincidence," Scott said.

Before Ryan hung up, he said, "I don't believe in coincidences."

CHAPTER TWENTY-EIGHT

Peter Uttal was a pot-bellied, slope-shouldered man with thinning white hair and a scraggly white beard. He'd worked in the Wilmington Police Department's Criminal Investigation Division for most of his career, bouncing between the Robbery, Homicide, and Narcotics divisions. He'd been on Bianchi's payroll for the last ten years and had steered many investigations away from Bianchi's nefarious dealings.

Rocky Bianchi leaned against the Riverwalk railing beside Uttal, staring across the water at the battleship and thinking Uttal looked as smarmy as ever. The man had always had a strange quality about him. Bianchi didn't know if he hated him because Uttal claimed to have an eidetic memory or if he'd just become tired of paying the man for little results. It seemed Uttal's enforcer, Mike Boostrom, was getting better results in uniform than Uttal was from behind a desk. At least he'd been able to provide Bianchi with the names of the men goading him.

"The Sheriff's Office is working on a package to give to the D.A. for Tim Davis," Uttal said. "It turns out that Kyle

Fowler is a friend of both Chad Yeager and the guy who busted into your office."

"Weller," Bianchi stated with contempt.

"Yes," Uttal agreed.

"What are we going to do about Davis?"

"*We?*" Uttal asked.

"You're up to your neck in this shit, too, *Peter.*" He said the cop's name with as much disdain as he had Weller's.

"There's not much we can do," Uttal declared.

Bianchi turned and looked down the walkway. "Can you get to Davis in jail?"

"Just him? Yes. But you're looking at squashing three people," Uttal said. "Davis and those two Jefferies idiots."

"What we need to do is entice them to keep their mouths shut." Bianchi turned and leaned his back against the railing. He used the fingertips of both hands to rub his forehead just above his eyebrows, where a headache had formed last night after he'd heard Davis was under arrest. "There's nothing that really ties me to these kids. They pay me cash for helping to run their theft ring, and Yeager supplied the boats. We can deflect it all to Yeager, make him look like the bad guy."

"Davis lawyered up last night."

"Who's he got?" Bianchi asked.

"A public defender," Uttal said. "That kid doesn't have the money for a lawyer."

"I'll make some calls and get one of my guys in there. We'll tell the cops that whatever he said before he lawyered up is inadmissible."

"He *does* have a concussion," Uttal added.

"Brilliant," Bianchi said. "He can claim that he didn't know what he was saying because of his injuries. The lawyer will clarify the story that Yeager is the ringleader, and that I had nothing to do with it."

"I stepped on his boat motor theft, but we can bring that back into play. Shows prior history of intent," Uttal said.

"Good." Bianchi nodded, feeling the tension in his head ease. "Yeager gets out of the hospital today. We snatch him and his mother and make him write a confession."

"Where do you want to stash them?"

"117 Marine. We'll keep Janice there and you take Yeager into custody."

"I'll handle it." Uttal ambled away, his hands behind his back, and Bianchi wondered how it was even possible for a vegan to have such a fat belly.

Bianchi's cell phone rang, and he pulled it out. "Yeah, Mike?"

"Two things. I just ticketed Weller's asshole buddy for loitering at The Pit Stop, and there was nothing on Parnell's GPS."

"What do you mean there's nothing on it?"

"Just that, Rocky. Weller must have had that chick at Stellar Electronics wipe the GPS's hard drive."

"Did you press her?"

"I can, but I don't think it'll help. If he had her wipe the unit, then he probably had her delete the download off her computer, too."

"There's always an electronic record, Mike. Just get over there and take her computer. Send someone now. Ongoing investigation and all that shit."

"Yes, sir. I'll go myself."

"No. Call Uttal and have him handle it," Bianchi instructed. "We need you for something else."

"Roger that," Boostrom said.

Bianchi punched off the phone and slipped it into his pocket. The fact that Weller had Parnell's GPS data and none of his guys had bothered to look at it stuck in his craw.

Someone would pay for that mistake. Yeager would take the fall for the theft ring, and Bianchi was going to find the gold that Parnell had stashed away.

And he didn't care who he had to kill in the process.

CHAPTER TWENTY-NINE

Chad Yeager didn't want to go to his mother's house, and he'd argued that fact with Ryan for the last hour. He wanted to go back to his own apartment, where he could rest without anyone fussing over him. While he didn't want Chad to be a burden to his mother, Ryan had argued for him to stay where he could keep an eye on them both. Having them split between addresses meant having to cover two places in addition to their ongoing surveillance of Bianchi's businesses.

"Scott and I will come stay with you there," Ryan said. "You'll be safe."

Janice nodded. "Ryan's right. You know you need help. Don't be so stubborn. Besides, Bianchi has made threats against both of us, and I'd rather have you with me. We stand a fighting chance together, even if you're not in the best of shape."

"Fine." Chad swung his legs off the side of the bed. His face was still a mass of bruises and bandaged cuts. It would be a while before his body healed from the external and internal injuries. He would need help to dress, to change his bandages, and to do routine chores around the house, so it was better if he wasn't alone in his apartment.

And they had Bianchi to worry about.

Ryan had grave concerns about Chad's safety. The loan shark had his claws deep in Chad's flesh, and they still had a long road ahead of them to take Bianchi down. He didn't want Bianchi's goons snooping around Janice's place and causing more damage. He wanted Bianchi worried, and he hoped that the arrest of Tim Davis and Patrick Jefferies had put the entrepreneur on his heels.

The nurse came into the room with Chad's discharge instructions and prescriptions. He signed all the paperwork and gingerly stood. He'd already dressed in sweatpants and a T-shirt. Janice placed a jacket over his shoulders, and Ryan, Janice, and Chad walked out of the room.

It didn't bother Ryan one bit to be leaving the hospital behind. He hated the smell and the sounds. At least he hadn't been the patient, forced to endure the poking and prodding of the medical staff or to eat the horrible food. He'd done enough of that for one lifetime.

Ryan got them into the Jeep and headed for Janice's place. It had been years since he'd been to the Yeager family home, but muscle memory took over and he automatically maneuvered through the streets to her place off Beasley Road, in an older section of town. Ryan remembered playing in the backyard with Chad and Kyle and exploring the woods across the street that bordered a branch of Hewletts Creek, back before his father and other contractors had developed the area.

Both boys and Kyle Fowler had helped on the construction sites and earned money to fund their dream of buying a boat. Once Ryan had started working at the marina for Henry, they'd no longer needed to buy a boat because they could use one of Henry's rentals. Ryan had eventually used the money he'd saved to buy his first sailboat; a Sabre 36 he'd called *Sweet T*.

He glanced in the Jeep's rearview mirror at Chad's pained face and glimpsed a black sedan following them. Ryan mentally cursed. His minder was back. Not wanting to heighten Janice's stress levels any further, Ryan drove on, keeping his mouth shut.

At the house, Janice unlocked the door, and Chad went inside. Ryan remained outside, hanging around the Jeep. He texted Scott to tell him he'd been followed. Scott responded that he'd received word from Barry that the tow truck would be back in town tonight from Albany, and Scott planned to be at the drop.

Ryan went inside and settled on the couch beside Chad.

"I don't have much to fix for you boys," Janice called from the kitchen. "I need to go to the store."

"Give me a list and I'll go," Ryan volunteered.

"No, honey. I'll do it." Janice came into the living room, carrying her purse. "Anything special you boys want?"

"You know what I like, Ma," Chad replied.

"What about you, Ryan?"

"I'm good," he said. "I'll go with you."

"I'll be okay, hon. I need to get out of the house. I'm just going to the Lowes Foods around the corner. I'll see you in a bit."

And with that, she left. The two men heard her car start, and Ryan walked over to the window to peer out from behind the curtain. The black sedan peeled away from the curb, following Janice's car.

"Are you okay by yourself?" Ryan asked.

"I'm good," Chad groaned as he stretched out on the couch and reached for the TV remote.

"I'll be back in a few minutes."

Chad waved the remote. "Knock yourself out."

Ryan ran outside and jumped into the Jeep. He revved the engine through each shift as he raced to catch up to Janice and the black sedan. He had an awful feeling in the pit of his stomach that something bad was about to happen.

The drive was just shy of a mile. He circled the grocery store parking lot, searching for her car, but he didn't see it anywhere. Ryan punched in Chad's number. As soon as Chad answered, Ryan barked, "Your mom said she was going to Lowes on Pine Grove Drive, right?"

"Yeah, I guess so. Why?"

Over the phone's speaker, Ryan heard pounding on Chad's door. Then someone screamed, *"Police. Open up!"* A second later, Ryan listened to the sounds of a door exploding inward and police clearing the house and arresting Chad.

He punched the *End* button on the phone and pounded the steering wheel. *What the hell just happened?*

Ryan continued to search for Janice. A wave of relief washed over him when he saw her car. Then he saw the driver's door was wide open. Fear clutched his insides like an icy hand.

Sliding the Jeep to a stop, he jumped out and ran over to Janice's vehicle. The engine was still running, and her purse was still on the seat.

Shit!

He scanned the lot again for any signs of Janice being dragged away against her will, but he saw nothing untoward. Out of options, Ryan called Kyle Fowler.

"What's up, Ryan?" the detective asked.

"The cops just arrested Chad. And I just found Janice's car with the door open and the engine running in the parking lot at Lowes Foods. I think someone snatched her."

"Slow down," Kyle said. "Go step by step."

Ryan explained everything, from being followed from the

hospital to sensing something was about to happen to Janice. He hadn't expected the police raid at all.

"Stay where you are," Kyle said. "I'm on my way. I'll also call Wilmington P.D. and have them come to you. Don't touch anything!"

Ryan was leaning against the Jeep, smoking a cigarette, when the cops charged into the parking lot. There were three cars in total: two black and white Dodge Chargers, lights flashing and sirens blaring, and one plain black Charger. He'd stowed his pistol in the Jeep's locked console and steeled himself for the litany of questions the cops would undoubtedly pepper him with.

A white-haired man in a light gray suit introduced himself as Detective Uttal. He glanced quickly into Janice's car, then spent the next twenty minutes grilling Ryan about what he'd seen. Ryan kept his temper in check, despite the slow pace in which the cops seemed to move. In fact, he saw two of them come out of the store carrying doughnuts and coffee. He took a deep breath to calm his nerves.

"Are you okay, Mister Weller?" Uttal asked.

"I'm angry that my friend has just been arrested and now his mother has disappeared."

Uttal had a notepad and pen in hand. "What friend are you referring to?"

"Chad Yeager. I was on the phone with him when you guys busted down his door."

"Good to know." Uttal made a note.

"What about Janice?" Ryan gestured toward the car.

"Maybe she was distraught over her son's arrest and wandered off."

"Bullshit," Ryan snapped.

"Easy, Mister Weller. She hasn't been gone for twenty-four hours, which is the minimum time we require before you can file a missing person report."

"What about the CCTV footage from the store or witness reports? Your guys are standing around doing nothing."

"You've watched too much television," the detective commented.

"Am I free to go?"

"Free as a bird." Uttal fluttered his hand.

Ryan got in the Jeep and drove back to Janice's house. The cops had left it in disarray, having busted the door and frame of the unlocked front door and searched the house. Pulling out his phone, Ryan scanned the street for the black sedan. He called his father and asked him to rush a crew over to Janice's place to fix the door.

David Weller let out a long sigh. "All right, Ryan. I'll get some guys over there this evening."

"Thanks, Dad."

"Are you okay, son?"

"I'm fine, Dad. I'm just pissed."

"Don't do anything rash."

"Trust me, Dad. I'm not the one you need to worry about."

CHAPTER THIRTY

It shouldn't have surprised Ryan how quickly he'd fallen back into old habits. When he opened the pack of cigarettes he'd purchased yesterday, he saw he'd already smoked half of them. He muttered a curse about his lack of willpower, then sparked one up as he sat on the front stoop of Janice Yeager's home, waiting for the repair crew to arrive.

Ryan pulled out his phone and sent a quick text to Emily to let her know he was thinking about her. He smiled when she responded immediately that school was boring, and she was ready to get back to him and *Huntress*.

About to put his phone back in his pocket, it began vibrating in his hand and he almost dropped it. Feeling chagrined about being startled by the phone, he punched the *Answer* button and said, "What's up, Ashlee?"

"I retrieved the tracks of all the ships belonging to United Atlantic Shipping for the last six months. As you can imagine, it was a complete jumble, but lucky for you, I am *excellent* at my job."

"That's why I called you, Ash."

"Do I get the same going rate as Barry?"

"He told me he worked on a sliding scale," Ryan said.

"And you're at the top end."

"Have you been talking to him?"

Ashlee giggled. "Actually, yes. He helped me out a bit."

"Well?"

"United Atlantic is based in Norfolk, Virginia, so everything comes and goes from there. I focused on the ships on your list: *Mary Russell*, *Star of Sumatra*, *Ariana*, *Torrie Lynn*, and *Carrie Jane*. All of them made ports of call in Charleston, Savannah, and Jacksonville before heading across to Africa. The only port they have in common over there is Abidjan in Côte d'Ivoire. On their way back, they made port at the same places in the States before returning to Norfolk."

"The Ivory Coast," Ryan muttered.

"Have you been there?" Ashlee asked, knowing Ryan had been around the world as a Navy EOD tech.

"No, but I went to Djibouti one time. That *sucked*."

Ashlee giggled again. "You said ja booty."

Ryan laughed with her. Bringing Ashlee back on topic, he asked, "What's special about those ships?"

"I had Barry hack United Atlantic Shipping to get me the records. Besides visiting the same ports, only four men captained those vessels. I discovered that once a month, a ship captained by a man named Roger Hammersley made that run. He brought his ship in closer to Frying Pan Shoals than any other captain, and Parnell's tracks cross over Hammersley's. I sent you expanded maps and overlays in an email."

"Got an address for Captain Hammersley?"

"I do, but you won't be able to talk to him."

"Why? Is he at sea?"

"No. He's dead. The police report says he was killed in a botched robbery."

Ryan kicked the ground, raising a tiny cloud of dust. "I'm striking out all over the place."

A white pickup truck with a ladder rack mounted in the bad and a Weller Construction sign on the door pulled into the driveway, and David Weller climbed out.

"Hey, Ash, I need to go," Ryan said.

"Call me if you need anything else."

"Thanks. You know I will." He hung up as she was saying something about the sliding pay scale. "Hey, Dad. I didn't expect you."

"All my crews were busy, and I knew you were waiting. Let's look at the damage."

They found the jamb had splintered at the striker plate, and the area around the doorknob had shattered on impact with the police battering ram.

"We'll need to install a new door and frame," David said. "For now, let's screw it shut and we can go out the back door. Do you have a key to the place?"

"No," Ryan said, "but I'll check the fake rock in the back garden where she used to keep a key."

Ryan found the key right where he'd remembered. When he walked into the house, David had the front door closed, and he was shooting long screws in at an angle through the door into the frame with an impact driver.

"I found the key."

"Good." David handed Ryan the driver and a handful of screws.

Ryan put two in the top where his shorter father had trouble reaching and squatted to put two in the bottom.

"Why did the police arrest Chad?" David asked.

"I don't know." The impact driver's chatter made it hard to talk. When the last screw was in, Ryan stood. "Janice is missing, too."

"Maybe she went to the station."

"I don't think so. Yesterday, I noticed a car was following me, and I saw it again outside here when I brought Chad and Janice back from the hospital. When she left for the store, the car followed her. By the time I got there, she was gone. They snatched her right out of the parking lot, leaving the car door open and the engine running."

"That sounds serious, son."

"It is. Chad knows some bad people. I think Rocky Bianchi is tied up in all of this."

David Weller stepped closer to his son. He sniffed, and his nose wrinkled in disdain at the stench of cigarette smoke. He'd never liked smokers and had made it known to Ryan on multiple occasions that a smoker was a one-handed worker. If Ryan or any of the crew wanted to smoke, they had to do so on their breaks, not during working hours. Emily had told everyone that Ryan had quit to help keep him on the straight and narrow, but it was plain from his father's face that the smoking was the least of his worries. Ryan felt like a little boy about to receive his punishment.

The elder Weller backed away and crossed his arms. His gaze bore into his son, who looked away. "I've had my own run-ins with Rocky Bianchi, and he's not a man you want to tangle with."

Ryan's investigative mind switched into gear. "What kind of problems did you have?"

"We were under contract to repair his apartments. I was hoping to expand our business model, but things quickly went sour because Bianchi had done little maintenance on the units and he needed to do a lot of work to bring them up to code. Over the course of a year, I persuaded him to do some work, but it wasn't enough, and the housing inspectors started making the rounds. He blamed me for getting notices to repair, but he ordered the work done, anyway. We had it all in writing, and I kept all the change orders. He kept making the minimum payments, and after a year, I couldn't carry the load anymore, so I demanded he make the back payments before we did any more work. He dropped us as his contractor, and I sued him. I won, of course, but it wasn't worth it."

"Why?"

"The lawyers got their chunk, and suddenly our construction sites were getting shut down for the smallest violation. It cost me a ton of money, and it was always the same inspector, so I complained to the city and they investigated him. Turned out he was taking bribes, but they couldn't pin down who from. They fired him, but I know ..." David shook his head. "I know Bianchi was behind it."

"Bianchi is a bully, Dad. He's neck-deep in some shady shit."

"Language, son."

"Bianchi's like a black cloud over this city, Dad. But, tonight, I'm hoping that will change. I've got reason to believe he's involved in cigarette smuggling to Albany. I'm hoping to get a look at what he brings back tonight."

"How do you know that?" David asked quizzically.

"Well, sir, Scott and I have been watching Bianchi because he's got his hooks in Chad and won't let go."

"Chad needs to work out his own problems."

Ryan shook his head. "He needs help."

"I love you, son, but you can't save him every time he's in trouble."

"You don't understand, Dad. This is what I do for a living. I help people like Chad. You told me one time that you didn't want to know what I was doing other than working as a commercial diver. Well, I'm going to spell it out for you. When I went to DWR, I worked for Homeland Security, and I've been helping them ever since. Remember that ship the Navy blew up in the Florida Straits? I led the team that boarded it. And Emily? She gunned down the terrorist leader and saved my team's bacon."

David remained silent as he seemed to ponder his son's confession.

"Look, Dad, you were the one who put me on this path. I watched you help a lot of people over the years, even if it was just a few bucks for a meal or free work around their home. You told me that service should be a daily part of our lives. I joined the Navy for that reason, and now I'm doing this. Service above one's self, right?"

David nodded. "I also told you that family comes first. What about Emily?"

"She's an insurance investigator. Her job can be just as dangerous as mine, and we work together to solve cases."

David shouldered his tool belt. "You make an excellent team, son," he conceded. "Take care of her."

"Yes, sir."

"Ryan, I love you and I'm proud of you. Just be safe." David clapped Ryan on the shoulder, then walked to his truck.

Standing in the side yard, Ryan watched his father drive away. It felt like a weight had been lifted from his shoulders by telling his father about his work. At the same time, he had a lump in his throat from hearing his dad tell him he was proud of him. When Ryan and his siblings were growing up, their father had always made it a point to tell them he loved them and that he was proud of them, but it had been a long time since Ryan had heard him say those words in person. Ryan had tried hard to make his own way in life, to separate himself from the construction business, but he'd always craved the approval of his father.

As Ryan turned back toward the house, Kyle Fowler pulled his red 1997 Ford F-250 to a stop outside Janice Yeager's home and got out. He wore jeans, black combat boots, a polo shirt, and a brown windbreaker with the word 'Sheriff' printed across the back in bold yellow letters.

"Detective," Ryan said as Kyle walked up.

"Give me one of those coffin nails."

Ryan shook out two cigarettes, and both men lit up.

"How're things at home?" Ryan asked.

"Tim Davis lawyered up," Kyle responded.

"Smart, but surprising. Who's paying the bill?"

"I don't know," Kyle said with a sigh.

"It should be a slam dunk case for you guys."

"As long as they don't dig too deep into the tip we received. Technically, you were breaking and entering."

"I thought the point of the anonymous tip line was just that," Ryan said.

"It is, and I'll keep you as a confidential informant. How's Emily doing?"

Ryan shrugged. "Safe from all this bullshit."

"I saw your buddy got a ticket for loitering at The Pit Stop. What's that about?"

"You'll have to ask him," Ryan said.

"Don't play me for a fool, Ry. We both know you're yanking Bianchi's chain."

Ryan took a draw from his smoke and thought about how things were going to go down. He needed help to bust the cigarette smuggling ring. It was a federal crime to traffic contraband cigarettes, and a conspiracy to defraud the government by not paying tax on the contraband. "Know anyone in the ATF?"

"Yeah. Why?"

"Bianchi is smuggling cigarettes from The Pit Stop to a store in Albany, New York. They take them up in a car on a flatbed wrecker."

"Why doesn't that surprise me?"

"The tow truck is coming back tonight. Scott will be in place near Bianchi's car lot to see what they bring back."

"Drugs. Cash. People," Kyle suggested. He dropped his cigarette butt and ground it into the sandy soil with the toe of his boot. "I'd like to be wherever Scott is tonight."

"Okay. I'll put you two together."

"Thanks. I'll call a friend of mine in the ATF. He works locally, but he can put some guys on the place in Albany."

Ryan called Scott and told him to meet Kyle at a used appliance place down the street from The Pit Stop.

Kyle checked his watch. "I need to go. I have to swing by the house."

"See you," Ryan said as Kyle got in his car.

The noose around Bianchi's neck was tightening, but Ryan still didn't know exactly how John Parnell fit into the scheme of things. There was only one way to find out, and that was to keep digging.

CHAPTER THIRTY-ONE

Scott Gregory nosed the Chevrolet Camaro into a parking space in front of the used appliance store just down the street from The Pit Stop.

He had been careful since leaving the department store by the marina, driving aimlessly through the streets and sitting in a little café near downtown Wilmington. He could have easily passed the time by sampling the many locally brewed craft beers, but he drank coffee to stay alert. Someone was tailing him and Ryan, and he needed to know he was clean before heading to his rendezvous with Detective Kyle Fowler. After leaving the café, he'd bunked down in a motel room to get some sleep.

Now, it was just after five p.m., and the city streets were dark and congested with traffic. Kyle got out of his truck and jumped into the Camaro. He put a large duffle on the backseat that Scott naturally assumed contained Kyle's kit in case things went sideways. Scott had a similar duffle of his own back there.

Pointing to the GPS tracker on his phone, Scott said,

"The tow truck is coming off I-40 right now. It shouldn't be long before it gets here."

"Where do we need to be?" Kyle asked.

"If they unload in the same place they loaded, the body shop building."

"Okay. Pull around to the car lot across the street."

They waited twenty minutes for the truck to arrive. Both men snapped away with their digital cameras as the tow truck driver pulled in beside the body shop and unloaded a newer model Honda Accord. No sooner had the truck driver gotten the car off the trailer than a man came out of the body shop, hopped into the Honda, and drove away.

"Let's go," urged Kyle.

Scott had to wait for cross traffic to pass before he could pull out and follow the Honda. Kyle had it in his sights and gave Scott directions as they gave chase.

The Honda's driver crossed town to Independence Mall, parked, and went into a Chinese restaurant.

"I've got a tracker we can put on the car," Scott offered.

"Where's it at?"

Scott dug a tracker out of his bag and handed it to Kyle, who walked over to the Honda and discreetly fixed its magnet to the car's undercarriage.

When Kyle got back to the Camaro, Scott pointed to a man exiting the restaurant. "There's our guy."

The man walked right past the Honda and drove away in a different car.

"What's going on?" Scott said.

"It's an old drug runner trick," Kyle explained. "They drop the keys on the table of the guy who brought the money, and the money guy takes the drugs. There's no parking lot meets, and it lessens the chances of being seen."

"Okay. Do we follow the money car, or do we go with the Honda?"

"The Honda."

The two men slid down in the seats of the Camaro and waited for the next man to arrive. An hour later, a woman with long red hair came out of the restaurant and got into the Honda. Scott reached for the key to start the engine.

"Wait," Kyle said as he snapped off several pictures of the new driver. "We've got the tracker installed. Let's hang back."

Scott gave the Honda a nice lead, then pulled out after it, slowly trailing the blinking dot on his phone.

"Where did you get that tracking device?" Kyle asked.

"Do you really want to know?"

"Yes," the detective replied.

"I work for a company called Trident."

"The PMC?"

It was Scott's turn to say yes. The company had tried to keep a low profile, but the takedown of the terrorist ship in the Florida Straits had brought the PMC to national prominence, even though both Ryan and Greg had done their utmost to keep them out of the news.

"That explains a few things," Kyle said.

Scott had no clue what he was talking about, so he just kept his mouth shut and drove the car. The Honda turned onto a road that led to Portwatch Industrial Park along the Cape Fear River. The narrow two-lane street ran through a suburban housing development, then darkened considerably as they entered a heavily wooded area. Scott slowed at a curve in the road and waited as the dot on his map stopped in what looked like a storage lot.

"Douse the lights and pull into the drive up ahead," Kyle ordered.

Scott did as he was told, and both men got out of the car, careful not to slam the doors. They walked to the chain-link fence, quickly scaled it, and hid behind several semi-trailers. Kyle snapped photos of the Honda, which sat in front of what looked like a mobile home the lot owner had turned into an office. Two men came outside and shook hands with the redheaded woman.

Scott watched through binoculars as a white-haired man and the cop, Mike Boostrom, opened the trunk. They began unpacking large plastic cases from the trunk. Once all the cases were out, they carried them into the office.

With Scott in his wake, Kyle circled through the trees, campers, and semi-trailers to get closer to the office. Through a window, they could clearly see the men unloading what Scott assumed were kilos of cocaine, based on their packaging and the white contents. The white-haired man slit open a package and snorted some powder off the end of his knife, which confirmed it.

All the while, Kyle was busy snapping pictures. The woman handed over a satchel, and the white-haired man counted out packets of money before handing the satchel to Boostrom. The overweight cop carried it outside and placed it in the rear of a black Dodge Charger before he returned to the office.

Turning to Scott, Kyle whispered, "You got a gun?"

Scott nodded.

"Okay. These guys are committing a felony. I'm officially asking for your help. If you accept, you'll have the same authority to arrest and prevent escape as I do as a Deputy Sheriff."

"I'm with you." Scott reached for his pistol as Kyle set his camera down and pulled out his own gun. They walked straight to the door and pushed it open. Kyle brought his gun up and shouted for everyone to freeze. "I'm a detective with the NHCSO. Hands in the air. You're all under arrest."

The white-haired man chuckled. "Easy, Fowler. You know who we are."

"Yeah, I do know you, Uttal. Get your hands up," Kyle

ordered again. To Scott, he said, "Start cuffing people." He handed over a set of cuffs and gestured to Uttal. "Start with him."

Scott cuffed the white-haired man and patted him down, finding a pistol and a set of cuffs. He moved to Boostrom and cuffed him, clamping the cuffs as tight as he could before removing the cop's gun and cuffs. Then Scott used Boostrom's handcuffs on the redhead.

"You're making a big mistake, Fowler," the older man stated. "We're undercover. Working a drugs case."

"We'll sort it all out soon enough," Kyle said. He pulled out his phone and dialed Dispatch, ordering backup and a supervisor.

Ten minutes later, the storage lot was ablaze with flashing red and blue lights. Sheriff's department and police patrol cars sat haphazardly around the office in a semi-circle.

Scott stepped back from the scene and watched as Kyle Fowler explained the scenario to the Sheriff and the police chief and showed them the pictures of Peter Uttal and Mike Boostrom unloading and snorting cocaine before accepting the payoff. Uttal maintained his innocence when questioned by the chief and the Sheriff. The chief confirmed he was unaware of any undercover investigation being led by Uttal or Boostrom.

Until they could sort everything out, the two department heads agreed to kick Uttal and Boostrom loose under their own recognizance. The NHCSO would hold the woman for forty-eight hours, even though Uttal vouched for her as his confidential informant.

Kyle walked over to where Scott leaned against the hood of a patrol car, watching with disinterest as he sipped a cup of coffee someone had handed him. The detective had a cell phone to his ear and told the person on the other end to be safe, then pocketed the phone.

"That was my buddy at the ATF," Kyle said. "He deployed assets to a warehouse in Albany and scooped up the car dealer. They found half a million cigarettes and the Cadillac you photographed. The paperwork from Bianchi's car lot was still in the glove box."

"No one said criminals were smart."

"It's always the cover-up that gets you," Kyle replied.

CHAPTER THIRTY-TWO

After leaving Chad's house, Ryan stopped at a restaurant for dinner. While he was eating, he received a phone call from Greg, saying his visit to John Parnell's niece, Claire Ecclestone, had gone well. Even though Bianchi had filed plans with the county to build his new subdivision, he'd failed to make a payment of twenty-five thousand dollars to Claire. Bianchi had called her to assure her the payment was on its way and that he just needed a couple more days to get the money together. According to the real estate contract, this was a violation that allowed Claire to void it, and Greg had made her an all-cash offer. Claire had jumped at the chance to get rid of the real estate without having to accept structured payments over the next ten years.

With the contract in hand, Greg had wired the cash into Claire's account and forwarded the paperwork to an attorney in Burgaw, North Carolina, the Pender County seat, allowing Blue Shores Management, an investment holding company that Ryan owned, to take possession. They had successfully stolen the property out from under Bianchi.

With a digital copy of the paperwork on his phone, Ryan

drove across town to the Foxy Lady. He saw the waitress from the last time he and Scott had been in the bar. For some unknown reason, Ryan was glad he'd kept Scott occupied enough that he hadn't had time to come back and question her. He doubted she knew anything about Bianchi's business other than to collect her tips and paycheck. After Ryan tipped her another twenty-dollar bill, she told Ryan that Bianchi was in his office, and she told the new guard at the base of the stairs to allow Ryan to go up.

Ryan knocked on the loan shark's office door and went in when Bianchi shouted with annoyance that the door was open. Bianchi's face twisted into a mask of rage at the sight of Ryan in his office once again.

"What the hell do you want?" Bianchi demanded.

"I'd like to show you something. Can I email it to you?" Ryan asked.

"I don't have time for your bullshit," Bianchi fumed.

"I think you'll want to see this. It concerns John Parnell's property. It seems you missed a payment to Claire Ecclestone."

Bianchi's head snapped up. "What did you say?"

"Since you violated the contract, she signed an all-cash offer this afternoon. My attorney will file the paperwork first thing tomorrow morning at the Pender County Courthouse."

"You *son of a bitch*," Bianchi growled.

Ryan sat in a chair across the desk from Bianchi. "What's your email address?"

Bianchi recited it to him. A moment later, his computer dinged with an incoming message. He used the mouse to open the attached documents, skimmed them, and sat back in the chair. Tapping the desk with his index finger, Bianchi asked, "What do you want?"

"I told you that already," Ryan said.

"Okay. I'll let Chad go. Are you happy?"

"No."

"Why not?"

"Because your goons snatched his mother off the street. Where is she?"

Bianchi smiled and leaned forward, placing his forearms on the desk. Ryan felt a knot tighten in his gut.

"It looks like I have something you want, and you have something I want."

Ryan hadn't planned to use the land as a bargaining chip. He'd only come here to let Bianchi know he had gained control of his land. It was a clue for what was to come for the loan shark and his businesses. He let the silence stretch between them to see what Bianchi had to say.

"Let's do even swaps," Bianchi suggested. "The land for Chad and his business."

"And for Janice?"

"Scuba diving skills," Bianchi replied.

"What does diving have to do with this?"

"Parnell left something out in the ocean that belongs to me. Now that you have Parnell's GPS tracks, you can bring it back, and when you do, I'll give you the Yeager woman."

"Is that what you're doing with the chart? Searching for whatever is missing?"

"Very astute, Weller. Find it and call me." Bianchi flipped a business card across the table. With a sneer, he added, "You're a fighter like your old man."

The thought of being in cahoots with Rocky Bianchi sickened Ryan, but the life of a woman he considered a second mother hung in the balance. The noose around Bianchi had tightened as Ryan pressured his businesses from all sides, and Bianchi was clutching at whatever he could to keep himself afloat. Janice Yeager was his life preserver, and Ryan his new servant.

"Let's see your chart," Ryan said.

Bianchi spread it across the desk, but it told Ryan little.

Looking up from the chart, Ryan said, "You and I both know that Tim Davis is going to roll on you, so what's the point of all this?"

Bianchi chuckled. "Don't be so sure of that. Your friend, Chad, is the one in jail, not me."

Ryan wanted to gloat that he knew about the cigarette smuggling operation, but he had to let things play out tonight to see where everyone stood. The ATF would hopefully indict Bianchi on federal charges, and local authorities would press charges for masterminding Davis' theft ring. If Bianchi was committing fraud in one area of his business, Ryan felt sure that fraud existed in all the rest.

As Ryan stared at the chart and the vast expanse of blue Atlantic Ocean it depicted, the task at hand seemed hopeless. The last two times Ryan had salvaged things from the ocean, he'd known where to look. But in this case ...

Come on, Ashlee. Find me something in those ship tracks.

Bianchi rolled up the chart. "We both have work to do. Take this with you, and call me when you have my property."

"What exactly am I looking for?"

"A steel strongbox about one-foot square."

"What's inside?"

"Janice Yeager's life."

Ryan and Bianchi stared at each other for a long moment.

"How do you know the box is in the water?" Ryan asked.

"The ship captain Parnell worked with dropped it along his course for Parnell to receive. They had some kind of code, so Parnell would know where to find it. It's now your job to crack it and save Janice Yeager." Bianchi tapped his expensive-looking chronograph watch. "Times ticking, Weller."

With one last furious glare at Bianchi, Ryan spun and went down the stairs and out to the Jeep. He navigated his way out of the narrow downtown streets before heading across town. In the rearview mirror, he saw the black sedan fall into line behind him, and a plan slowly formed in his mind.

He grabbed his phone and saw it wasn't quite eleven o'clock yet. Kyle and Scott were tailing the tow truck, and Chad was in jail. If he could get his hands on the person tailing him, then maybe he could find out where they were holding Janice.

Driving slowly through the darkened streets, he ensured the black sedan stayed close. As he crossed the C. Heide Trask Bridge into Wrightsville Beach, the plan crystalized. Old Causeway Drive doubled back toward the bridge, passing under it to the parking lot for the Wrightsville Beach Boat Ramp. If Ryan turned left, he would go to the marina where *Huntress* waited patiently in her slip. But he went straight, following the road under the bridge, shut off his lights, and pulled onto a dirt path along the bridge abutments. Between the concrete pillars and the bushes, the man tailing Ryan missed the turnoff and continued past him into the parking lot. Ryan slipped out of the Jeep and watched as the man circled the lot and then sped onto the road.

As part of his plan, he needed to make his minder think he'd just lost track of the Jeep, so Ryan parked it behind the marina's boat storage racks and sent a quick text to Scott, telling him to call him on his way back to Wrightsville Beach.

Aboard *Huntress*, Ryan spread out the map Bianchi had given to him, then opened his laptop. While he'd been downtown, Ashlee Williams had emailed him several maps. The first showed United Atlantic's ship tracks. The second detailed Parnell's GPS tracks overlaid on that map. It wasn't hard to see where those lines intersected, but there were a lot of crossings. Ashlee had narrowed it down to certain days when Capt. Hammersley had piloted his ships closer to the North Carolina coast. Unfortunately, Parnell's GPS continu ally overwrote the data, which left only one recent track where Parnell's boat had intersected with the route of Hammersley's vessel. But Parnell had set waypoints in the GPS, and Ashlee had marked each of those on the map.

Ryan discounted all the data points that were deeper than one-hundred-and-thirty feet, feeling that Parnell wouldn't want to go that deep to retrieve whatever Hammersley had dropped. That left about a dozen places. Next, he placed those points on the map illustrated with the ship tracks, narrowing the field to eight places he would need to search.

He had his starting point.

His next order of business was to find a dive boat and start searching. The dive season off the Carolina coast typically ended in late October because of cooler temperatures and rougher seas. The Gulf Stream brought warm water up from the Caribbean, keeping temperatures moderate, but Ryan knew he'd need a dry suit if he planned to do repetitive dives.

He was wrapping up his maps when his phone pinged. It was Scott, letting him know Kyle had tried to arrest Boostrom and Uttal for possession of cocaine with intent to distribute and receiving payments from a drug dealer. The police chief had allowed the two cops to go free, pending investigation, and Scott was on his way back to the boat.

Ryan rolled his eyes and sighed through puffed-up cheeks. It shouldn't have surprised him that Bianchi was working with dirty cops. He called Scott and told him to watch his six for a tail. If someone did have him under surveillance, then it would provide a perfect opportunity for a snatch operation.

Grabbing a sweatshirt and a jacket, Ryan pulled them on and stepped off the boat, walking casually along the waterfront to the Bluewater Grill. He said hello to Angie and had a beer before going out the side entrance and walking along the docks toward the bridge.

He called Scott. "Anything?"

"Got a tail."

Ryan explained what he wanted Scott to do and ended the call. The wind moaned through the bridge abutments, and Ryan shivered. He rubbed his hands together and shoved them in his pockets. It was unseasonably cold, and the meteorologists were calling for frost.

Another ten minutes passed before Ryan saw headlights on Old Causeway Road. They swept across the ICW and over the concrete pilings before cutting out, and the Camaro pulled into the same spot that Ryan had recently parked his Jeep.

Then they waited.

The Camaro idled softly in the still night, a cloud of exhaust hanging in the air above the tailpipe. A car crept around the corner, its headlights off. As it slipped under the bridge, Scott backed out of his spot. The driver of the follow car must have suspected a trap because he mashed the accelerator.

There was a tremendous crash as the Camaro's rear end slammed into the other vehicle's front fender. Scott kept the pedal down, sliding the other car sideways and jamming the hood against an abutment. Ryan leaped from his hiding spot, his gun drawn, and ran over to the car.

When he grabbed the door handle, he found it locked. The driver was slumped over the wheel, his head lolling to one side. With no need for the gun, Ryan holstered it, then smashed the window with the glass breaker on the end of his tactical folding knife. He checked the driver's pulse. It was strong, and the man was breathing.

Scott pulled the Camaro forward, then drove off while Ryan stayed with the unconscious man. He only had to wait about five minutes before he heard a boat motor start. Two minutes later, Scott pulled a flat-bottom center console skiff under the bridge and nosed it up to the beach where Ryan waited. Both men horsed the unconscious driver from his vehicle and carried him to the boat, dumping him unceremoniously in the bow before zip-tying his hands behind his back. Ryan then drove the wrecked car around to the boat ramp parking lot before jogging back to where Scott waited.

Jumping aboard, Ryan took the wheel and backed the skiff away from the beach. He turned north, fighting the strong currents as they made the two-mile run to Mason Inlet. Once they turned into the narrow channel with its shifting sandbars, Scott held the spotlight on the water. A half-mile in, Ryan stuck the boat's bow into the sand, and they carried their prisoner off the boat.

"Does this ever bother you?" Ryan asked.

"What?" Scott grunted.

"The torture."

"Never fazed me. It's part of the job."

After dropping their man on the sand, Scott bent and retrieved the unconscious man's wallet. He handed Ryan the driver's license. Shining his flashlight on it, Ryan read, "Jamal Lewis."

As they waited for Jamal to come around, Ryan shoved his hands in his pockets and glanced around. To the south were the lights of Shell Island Resort, marking the end of Wrightsville Beach, and to the north were lights of the high-rise condos on Figure Eight Island. Ryan had been here many times in his youth, drinking beer on the sandbars and partying with Chad and Kyle and the host of other boaters who came to play in the sun. He remembered bringing Sara Sherman, his then-girlfriend, there on the night they'd lost their virginity. The stars had been bright, and the night warm. If he stood still enough, he could still hear her laughter.

"Yo, Ryan. He's awake. Let's get to it," urged Scott.

Ryan came out of his trance and took a deep breath. *This guy might know where Janice Yeager is.*

And they needed to find her. *Now.*

JAMAL LEWIS DIDN'T KNOW where Janice Yeager was being held. He was a foot soldier for a local gang, hired to follow and report on Scott's movements. Ryan and Scott left him on the sandbar in Mason Inlet and drove the boat back to Wrightsville Beach Marina. Ryan filled Scott in on Bianchi's demand that he find the strongbox Hammersley had dropped from his ship. When they reached *Huntress*, the two men pored over the charts, and Scott printed out the two emails from Ashlee, illustrating the track overlays.

The only thing Ryan and Scott could agree on was going to bed. It had been a long night for both of them, and each yawned multiple times as they talked about the charts and Parnell's tracks. They headed for bed, but as Ryan lay in the dark with his hands behind his head, he had trouble falling asleep. He thought about how Janice must have been feeling and tried to determine where Bianchi would have stashed her. What would happen if he couldn't find Parnell's box? Would Bianchi really hurt Janice?

Ryan steeled his mind, pushing that thought away, because he knew the answer. He had to find the box and deliver it to Bianchi before the ticking clock wound down.

CHAPTER THIRTY-THREE

Despite his lack of sleep, Ryan was up early. He used his key to open the marina store and made a pot of coffee. He was sitting in Henry O'Shannassy's office when the old man arrived, his rolled-up charts on the chair beside him. Henry poured himself a mug of the dark brew and sat behind his desk.

"I know that look. What's troublin' ya, lad?"

"I need to borrow a boat that I can dive from."

Henry nodded. "It'll be rough out there."

Ryan leaned forward. "I don't have a choice."

The old man sipped his coffee. "Want to tell me about it?"

"Not really."

Henry narrowed his eyes and fixed Ryan with one of his infamous disappointed looks that could coax anyone into spilling their guts. "Give me the scuttlebutt."

With a sigh, Ryan recounted the abduction of Janice Yeager and his meeting with Bianchi. What should have been a gloat fest over purchasing Parnell's property had turned to being strong-armed into a search and recovery operation.

Henry began moving things around on his desk to clear a spot in the middle. "Show me the charts."

Ryan unrolled them on the desk and watched Henry, the old man's reading glasses slipping down his nose as he leaned over.

"How sure are you sure about these locations?" Henry asked.

"We overlaid Parnell's tracks on United Atlantic's ship tracks," Ryan stated. "Plus, the tech pulled these coordinates from Parnell's GPS."

"It looks like the ships run the contiguous zone line," Henry pointed out. "And most of your drop points are along it."

Ryan had noticed that, too, and had looked at what that line might be. The 1982 U.N. Convention on the Law of the Sea had established the limits of a nation's maritime boundaries, defining the contiguous zone as a band of water extending up to twenty-four nautical miles from the shoreline, within which a state could exert limited control to prevent or punish infringements of its customs, fiscal, immigration or sanitary laws and regulations.

In 1999, the U.S. had extended their standard twelve-mile territorial waters to the twenty-four-mile nautical limit allowed by law. The new contiguous line followed the coastal topography, meaning it curved inward from Frying Pan Shoals at the bottom of Onslow Bay, then circled out around Cape Lookout at the top.

"Somewhere along that line is a one-foot-by-one-foot steel box," Ryan said.

"Still a large search area," Henry mused.

"Bianchi told me that Parnell and the ship captain had a system to determine the drop point."

Henry scratched his chin before lifting his coffee mug to his lips. Both men stood silently and stared at the chart.

"There's little doubt," Henry stated. "Ya need to find the key."

"By extrapolating the data, I've narrowed it down to here." Ryan pointed to a yellow weather buoy labeled '217' that lay due east of the contiguous line.

"You might see some right whales while you're out there," Henry said. "They run this time of year."

"Now we've circled back to the dive boat."

"Well, the fella across the Ditch is closed for the season, but he might run ya out if the pay is right."

"Don't you have a boat I could use?"

"No, I don't. You're gonna want something with a cabin to get out of the weather."

Ryan mulled it over. "What about one of the local fishing charters? Do they take divers?"

"A couple of them do, but you know how some of those guys are. They don't want no tanks bangin' around their decks, dingin' up the gel coat. Have you talked to Greg? Does he have any crews operating in the area?"

"I did. There's nothing close."

Henry picked up the phone receiver and dialed a number. "Hi, Jed, it's Henry. Are you looking for a charter?" He ran a hand through his thick black hair, then glanced at Ryan. "Two days at least. You'll be about twenty-five miles offshore." Henry nodded. "Good. I'll send 'em over."

Ryan waited while the two men exchanged more pleasantries and then Henry hung up.

"Jed Elliott is over at Motts Channel. You might remember him. He used to keep his boat here back when you were pumping gas for me."

"Why'd he move?" Ryan asked.

"You know fishermen. They're some of the cheapest bastards on earth."

Ryan smiled. "Sailors are worse. If you don't believe me, just ask me."

Henry chuckled. "Cheapest lot I've ever seen."

The two men shook hands, and Ryan walked out of the office. He still had a few errands to run. While he had purchased dive gear to replace what had burned up on *Windseeker* and Greg had returned his commercial kit, including his dry suit and Kirby Morgan helmet, Ryan needed a diving rig for Scott.

Back aboard *Huntress*, Ryan found Scott awake and eating breakfast. He had two eggs, toast, and bacon on a plate in front of him and a cup of coffee by his hand. Ryan quickly fixed himself a similar plate and sat down beside his friend. "We need to do some diving. Do you have any kit with you?"

Scott shook his head and munched on a strip of bacon.

"I was afraid of that. I'll call Greg because the shops around here won't have what we need or won't be able to get it quick enough for us."

"You expect me to dive with you?" asked Scott.

"Buddies, remember?" Ryan extended both index fingers and brought them together in scuba diver sign language to indicate they should stick together.

Scott snorted. "Since when do you need a buddy?"

"At least back me up if you don't want to get wet."

Scott sighed. "I may be a highly trained Navy SEAL, but I prefer to keep my feet dry nowadays."

"Scratch you off the Caribbean list."

"*What?*"

"No dive. No list."

Scott screwed up his face in disgust. "Fine. I'll show you how it's done."

Ryan dialed Greg's number and listened to it ring. It went to voicemail, and he redialed the number. He kept dialing it until Greg answered in disgust. "What do you want, Weller? Can't a guy get any peace?"

"Did I wake you?" Ryan asked sweetly.

"Stick a sock in it."

"Well, good morning to you, too."

"*What* do *you* want?" Greg growled again.

"Any crews in my area?" Ryan asked.

"Not since you asked yesterday. What time is it?"

"Seven here."

"You know we're an hour behind you, right?" Greg snapped.

"I need dive gear. Scott and I are going after sunken treasure, and a woman's life hangs in the balance."

"I'm going to buy you your very own salvage boat, how about that? Then you can stop harassing me and you can earn your keep."

"Cool. All I need right now is a couple of rEvo rebreathers, spare tanks, Scott's dive kit, and a dry suit for him. Oh—and a metal detector."

"Anything else, *princess*?"

"What kind of boat are you buying me?" Ryan grinned at Scott, who was shaking his head.

Greg hung up without another word.

Ryan put his phone down and poured another cup of coffee. "We need the gear before we can dive, but let's go look at Jed's boat anyway. Then we need to visit Chad. Maybe he can shed some light on where they took his mom."

The two men cleaned up the breakfast dishes and drove down the street to Motts Channel Marina. They found Jed Elliott puttering around his thirty-eight-foot Evans Boats Traditional Chesapeake Bay deadrise, *Heaven Born*. The commercial vessel had a flybridge and the bridge roof covered most of the cockpit. Jed had rigged the deadrise to accommodate divers by installing benches and tank racks down both sides of the cockpit. The boat also had twin fishing outriggers and a large swim platform with a big aluminum ladder. It looked like Elliott was ready for whatever his customers wanted to do.

Capt. Elliott was a thick-set man with a ruddy complexion. He wore a black watch cap, a camouflage waterman's coat, grubby jeans, and white rubber boats. Ryan vaguely remembered the man as he introduced himself and Scott.

"You worked the pumps at Henry's place, yeah?" Elliott asked.

"Sure did," Ryan said.

"I got a thing for faces."

"I need to hire you for a few days. Henry said you'd be okay with that," Ryan said.

"Yeah. We goin' after the tuna?" Elliott asked.

"Nothing like that," Ryan said. "We're going diving."

Elliott shook his head. "Bad weather for that."

"I don't have a choice. We'll be ready to go tomorrow morning."

"I'll be ready," Jed Elliott said. "And I can guarantee it won't be real fun."

Ryan and Scott said their goodbyes and drove across town to the police station to see Chad. The cops brought him to an interview room and only allowed Ryan in to see him. Chad told him they were charging him with being the mastermind of Tim Davis' theft ring.

"I need a lawyer," Chad said.

"We'll find one," Ryan told him. "What about bail?"

"The judge denied it because of my priors, and he said I was a flight risk."

"Did you offer to testify against Bianchi?"

"I've kept my mouth shut," Chad said.

"Good. Got an attorney you like?"

"No." Chad snorted. "Does *anyone* like attorneys? They can rot in hell, for all I care."

"I get the sentiment, but you *need* to care."

Chad fiddled with his handcuffs. "Yeah, I know, but this is *bullshit*, Ryan. They're reopening the boat motor theft, too."

Ryan glanced down at Chad's bruised knuckles. "You punching the wall or other people?"

"Gotta let them know I ain't layin' down, bro."

"Just watch yourself. Don't give the cops any more reason to hold you."

The door opened, and a uniform leaned in. "Time to go back to your cell, Yeager."

Chad stood and shook his head in disgust. "Get me a lawyer, and get me out of here."

The officer led Chad away, and Ryan walked out of the station. Standing on the sidewalk in front of the Wilmington Police Headquarters, Ryan wondered who he should call to help Chad. Then he remembered Ray McClelland. He pulled out his phone and dialed the reporter's number.

When McClelland answered, Ryan said, "Mac, Ryan Weller. I want to trade information with you."

"Yeah?"

"Corrupt cops on Bianchi's payroll for the name of a talented attorney."

"No shit?"

"And I've got pictures," Ryan declared.

"Shuckin' Shack. Twenty minutes."

"No. We've had people following us all week. Do you know where Luck's Tavern is?"

"Sure do."

"Meet us there in an hour."

"You got it," McClelland said, and he hung up.

Ryan got in the Jeep with Scott and pulled away from the

police station. They spent the next thirty minutes driving around Wilmington, watching for tails. When they didn't see any, Scott rolled under the Jeep and found a GPS tracker attached to the frame. He removed it and placed it on another car.

They drove to the bar along the Northeast Cape Fear River, but instead of pulling into the Luck's Tavern parking lot, they went to the boat ramp on the other side of the street and watched the passing traffic. After ten minutes, they had seen nothing suspicious, so Ryan drove across the road and backed the Jeep into a spot under a tree. If someone was following them, they hadn't seen them.

McClelland was waiting for them at a table inside, a dark brew in front of him. Scott and Ryan placed their orders, and Ryan handed over the Pentax camera so McClelland could scroll through the pictures.

The reporter let out a low whistle. "And you guys saw all this?"

"Scott did," Ryan replied.

"I'll be damned. Uttal *and* Boostrom."

"Keep it down," Scott hissed.

McClelland glanced around the half-empty tavern, then fished a business card out of his pocket. "Call her. Best attorney I know."

"Nicky Pence," Ryan said. "I thought she worked at the Latimer House."

"Be careful with that one," McClelland said. "She's a shark."

"Because she's a woman or because she's a lawyer?" Scott asked.

McClelland chuckled but didn't answer, turning his attention back to the camera.

The server brought their food and drinks, and the men tucked in while Scott told McClelland about the cigarette smuggling and seeing Uttal and Boostrom with the cocaine.

The reporter scribbled notes on a small pad, then forwarded pictures from the camera and Scott's cell phone to his email.

McClelland had been so engrossed in the story and eager to get it to print that he left without finishing his beer or his lunch.

As Ryan and Scott lingered over their hamburgers and sodas, Ryan's phone chimed with an incoming text. He checked the message and smiled. "Our plane has finally come in."

CHAPTER THIRTY-FOUR

When Ryan and Scott stepped aboard Jed Elliott's deadrise the next morning, they carried large boxes of dive gear, spare gas bottles for the rebreathers, and a cooler full of drinks and sandwiches. They also had a third diver with them. Greg Olsen had flown in with the gear and would act as a standby diver, but what he had brought with him would be of greater help than a paraplegic struggling in the ocean's current with his meager hand paddles.

As Elliott got *Heaven Born*'s engines started and headed for Masonboro Inlet, the men rigged the Marine Magnetics SeaSPY2, a towable magnetometer, on its fifty-foot cable to the deadrise's right outrigger. Once the SeaSPY2 was connected to Greg's laptop computer, they uncrated an underwater drone. It had powerful lights, a video camera, and a gripper arm. Ryan doubted it could pick up the heavy box they were searching for, but they could use the drone to rig a lift bag to the box without ever having to get in the water.

That would be nice, Ryan thought. While the water was warmer than the breeze that buffeted them, Ryan wasn't looking forward to the dive. He'd tucked himself into a waterman's parka and pulled the hood over his head. The wind was straight out of the east and the waves were three-footers that seemed to break right on top of one another, making the ride wet and rough.

"You're gonna get a lot of interference on that magnetometer," Elliott said. "Lotta wrecks and scrap metal scattered around the seabed."

"I know," Ryan said. He was grateful Henry had given him Elliott's number. The deadrise handled the waves well, but it was the enclosed cabin he appreciated the most. It kept all of them out of the spray and gave Greg plenty of places to hold on to as the boat pitched and rolled through the swells. "We'll start by weather buoy two-seventeen and go from there."

"That's a forty-five-mile run from the mouth of the inlet. You sure your friend can handle that?" Elliott asked with a nod toward Greg.

"He's been through worse," Ryan replied.

Jed Elliott nodded and lit a cigarette.

"What's *Heaven Born* mean?" Ryan asked the captain.

"Sun Tzu. *'One who changes his tactics and wins is a heaven-born captain.'* I try to remember that when the fish ain't biting. You know?"

Ryan nodded. A change in tactics would be good for him, as well. He had to figure out how to make an end run around Bianchi to save Janice and get Chad out of jail. Once they had the box Bianchi wanted, Ryan would have the high ground. From there, he might have a clearer view of the battlefield.

The going was indeed rough, with the wind and waves increasing as they made their way farther offshore. By the time they reached the buoy, the waves were four to six feet in height and the wind was gusting to twenty knots.

Jed Elliott did his best to mitigate the bouncing, but he couldn't reduce all of it.

Holding onto the overhead railing, Ryan bent close to

Greg, who had transferred to the settee and wedged himself into a corner. "Can we deploy the magnetometer?"

"I don't know. This is the roughest weather we've tried to use it in."

"We're out here," Scott said. "Let's get it done."

Ryan and Scott donned their undergarments and dry suits before stepping out of the cabin. Not only would the dry suits keep them dry, but they would also act as exposure suits if they went overboard. While they unreeled the SeaSPY2 unit and its cable, Elliott kept them pointed into the waves. When the unit was overboard, the captain turned the boat to run along the contiguous zone line. The waves battered the side of the boat, washing over the stern rails into the cockpit. With the full scope of cable out, the outrigger bent precariously under the strain.

After twenty minutes of beating northeast, Ryan stuck his head in the door. "Anything?"

"Nada," Greg said, staring at the magnetometer's waterfall display on his laptop screen.

"What's your recommendation, Captain?" Ryan asked.

"Let's go to the beach. This is only going to get worse."

"Roger that. Point us upwind, and we'll reel in the fish."

Ryan closed the door and held on as the boat swung through the waves, the bow lifting and the boat rolling dangerously to port. Once things settled down, the two men quickly retrieved the SeaSpy2 and re-entered the cabin for the ride home.

"It'll be snotty for the next couple of days," Elliott said. "We got high pressure offshore and a cold front coming in from the west."

"That's not a good combination," Ryan said.

"What's the hurry in finding whatever you're looking for, anyway?" the captain asked.

"All I can tell you is that there's a time limit on it," Ryan answered. He dug out a sandwich from the cooler and chewed it slowly while staring out the water-streaked window. They couldn't do anything in this horrible weather, and while he'd dove in worse conditions, he wasn't looking forward to getting in the water. It would be hand-in-front-of-face visibility, making the search for the box even harder.

Just when it looked like things couldn't get any more complicated, Ryan's phone rang.

He pulled it out and glanced around, not expecting them to be in cell range. "What's up, Kyle?"

"Good news, Ryan. The ATF has filed federal charges against Bianchi for the cigarette smuggling, and the woman the police took into custody last night had multiple outstanding warrants, so they won't be kicking her loose anytime soon."

"That *is* good news."

"The bad news is that Bianchi is in the wind."

Ryan turned to look at Scott, who was sitting beside Greg to help keep him from moving about.

"He must have gotten word about the arrest warrants," Kyle continued.

"Probably," Ryan replied stoically.

"Look, Ryan, I told my Captain about your theory that Bianchi kidnapped Janice. We've put out a BOLO, but that's all he'll authorize because we have no proof."

"Okay. Thanks, Kyle." Ryan ended the call.

Greg looked up at his friend. "You okay? You look white as a ghost."

"A touch of the *mal de mar*?" Elliott asked with a grin.

Greg laughed. "If Ryan gets seasick, it's time to panic."

"Just some unsettling news," Ryan replied. He shook out a cigarette from his pack and lit it before stepping into the cockpit. Pressing his back to the bulkhead, Ryan stayed out of the spray to smoke. Elliot had to keep the power on in the following seas, fighting the mounting waves as they headed for port.

How was he going to find Janice now? They hadn't found the box, and Bianchi had disappeared. Why hadn't he expected this? Once he knew Bianchi had taken Janice, he should have called Kyle and told him to back off the Feds, but he hadn't, believing he had time to get the box and rescue the woman before the federal indictments came crashing down. What a fool he'd been.

There was nothing he could do until they got back to Wrightsville Beach, but then what? The weather would be snotty for days, if not a full week, which meant that diving would be dangerous at best. What they needed was to figure out exactly where Capt. Hammersley had dropped the box.

By the time they arrived back at the dock, all of them were sore and tired. While Ryan and Scott carried gear to the Jeep, Greg helped Capt. Elliott spray the salt from the deadrise. Afterward, they took the old captain over to the Bluewater Grill to treat him to a cold beer and a hot meal.

Scott started after them, but Ryan held up his hand. "You swore never to go there again. Remember?"

With a roll of his eyes, Scott stalked back to *Huntress*.

When the glasses were empty and the plates had been cleared away, Jim Elliott told Ryan to call him when he was ready to dive again, then walked out of the restaurant. Ryan paid the tab and walked with Greg back to *Huntress*.

"What did Kyle say?" Scott asked when the three men reconvened in the salon.

Ryan poured himself a cup of coffee from the pot Scott had brewed and relayed what the detective had told him.

"That's not good," Scott said.

"Where would he keep her?" Greg asked. "Maybe we can get the police to search his properties."

"Kyle said that without proof that Bianchi took her, the cops won't do anything more about it than the BOLO."

"Do you have a list of Bianchi's properties?" Greg asked.

"I think so," Ryan said. "Barry put one together." He opened his phone and scrolled through his email exchanges with Barry. There was a list, but Ryan knew it was incomplete. He dialed the hacker's number.

"What?" Barry answered in exasperation.

"Two things," Ryan said. "I need a list of all of Bianchi's businesses, and I want you to find his phone."

"I'll put the list together while Carmen works on the phone," Barry said and hung up.

The call ended before Ryan could say more. He set the phone down and finished his cup of coffee. Then he grabbed his phone and called Bianchi, but the message said the number he'd dialed was no longer in service. "No answer." Turning to Scott, Ryan said, "Let's roll. We're going to search Parnell's place and find that map key."

"It'll be dark in a couple of hours," Greg said.

"Then there's no time to waste," Ryan answered.

CHAPTER THIRTY-FIVE

On the way to the Jeep, Greg said, "Drop me at a rental agency so I can get a car. I'll take Bianchi's property list and drive around and see if I can spot something."

Ryan chuckled. "You don't want to drive Scott's smashed-up Camaro?"

"I'd like something less conspicuous. Besides, I need a vehicle I can mount my portable hand controls on." Looking at Scott, Greg said, "I hope you got the extra insurance."

Scott grinned. "It's not an option when I'm around you two clowns."

"Ain't that the truth," Greg said, staring hard at Ryan.

Ignoring their attempts at lightheartedness, Ryan said, "Come on. We're wasting time."

Ryan drove to the airport and dropped Greg off at the car rental agency, then went north of I-40 before turning east on the outer belt, joining Route 17 on the northeast side of the city. Three miles later, he downshifted and slowed, pulling into a narrow drive that disappeared into the trees. The Jeep swayed as it crawled along the sandy road, dipping into bumps and ruts. They passed long rows of mature, purposely planted trees, and about a mile down the drive, Ryan turned to the left at a fork in the road.

Ryan increased his speed as they wound through the heavily forested land. Eventually, they came to a house situated on a small peninsula. It could have been an island if not for the narrow neck of land used for the driveway. A long dock extended from the rear of the house over marshland to a T-shaped dock with an empty boat lift. The Craftsman-style home had a fresh coat of white paint and new hurricane windows. Beside it was a two-car garage with an outer staircase leading to a loft above.

"This place is in the boonies," Scott stated. "I see why Parnell refused to sell."

"Thinking of buying property now?" Ryan asked. "I'll make you a good deal."

A wistful look crossed Scott's face. "I could hunt and fish on my own property and never have to leave."

"It's not the Caribbean," Ryan said.

"No, but it could be paradise."

Ryan snorted. "Let's see if we can find some clues."

The two men headed for the house. They found the door unlocked and let themselves in. Someone had beaten them to the punch and ransacked the house.

The two men poked among the open drawers, cabinets, and closets, seeing nothing of value in their search to find Parnell's code. Ryan suspected the house's previous visitors had been after the same thing. They walked to the end of the dock and stood, watching the wind play across the water. Small sand and scrub islands—created when the U.S. Army Corps of Engineers had dredged the ICW canal in the early 1900s—provided breakwaters for the spit of land the house sat on.

Scott was right: this place was close to paradise. *If* Ryan was inclined to stay in North Carolina.

After making their way back to the house, they went around to the garage. The walk-in door was wide open. Inside, Ryan turned in a circle. Thieves had stripped the garage, taking the shovels, rakes, and hoes from their hooks, the toolboxes from the workbench, and the pegboard was devoid of any hand tools that had once hung there, as evidenced by the many vacant hooks and metal loops. They'd had plenty of time to work in the isolated house.

The two men mounted the steps to the second level, which turned out to be a loft-style apartment that Parnell used as an office. Again, the door was also unlocked, this time done so by the thieves breaking out a pane of the six-light window in the door. Both men stepped inside and looked around the office. The desk lay on its side, and the filing cabinet drawers stood open with their contents scattered across the floor. The bookshelves under the gable window were empty.

It saddened Ryan to see the condition the thieves—or whoever had rifled through the house and garage—had left them in. He righted the desk and checked under the drawers and shelves, then pushed around the files on the floor with his foot. Bianchi's guys had been thorough, but Ryan knew they hadn't found what they'd come for, otherwise he wouldn't be in a hostage negotiation.

Scott picked up a pair of binoculars that had been kicked under the desk and stood by the window, glassing the woods.

"What are you doing?" Ryan asked.

"Looking for deer." Scott paused in his sweep back and forth. "And there's Parnell's deer stand. Have a look."

Ryan took the binoculars and scanned the trees to where Scott pointed. "To the right of that big live oak with all the Spanish moss on it."

"Got it." Ryan focused on the permanent deer stand that was like a little hut on stilts, painted green and brown to help camouflage it. "Rangefinder in these binos says half a mile out."

"Looks like a good place to bag some bucks," Scott said.

Ryan put the binoculars on the bookshelf. "Let's check it out."

The two men walked downstairs. Ryan consulted his phone before getting in the Jeep. The satellite map view showed the hunting stand in the center of what looked like a wagon wheel, with paths leading out like the spokes. One spoke led past a pond to a tidal creek.

They drove back to the fork in the road, following it to the right. Keeping the map he'd just looked at in his head, Ryan drove past several two-track trails that branched off the main line and turned onto a broader track. This one led them straight to the deer stand.

The two men got out and walked to the base of the stand. Parnell had constructed it using old utility poles for the support legs, and it reminded Ryan of a miniature fire lookout tower. He scaled the ladder built on the side of a pole and climbed through the entry hole at the top. The stand was ten-feet-by-ten-feet, with window coverings that folded up and hooked onto the overhanging roof. Parnell had equipped the room with several chairs and a small propane stove for heat and cooking.

Scott pulled himself up through the trapdoor and stood at the railing. "I love this place."

"Clearly, so did Parnell," Ryan said. He opened a cabinet that hung on the wall beside the stove. It contained several bottles of liquor, a few cans of beef stew, jugs of water, two bowls, and several spoons. Ryan moved things around, and when he replaced the last can on the bottom shelf, he dropped it in frustration. It made it a hollow *thunk*.

Ryan glanced at Scott, but he was busy glassing the surrounding trees for deer, focusing on the patch of corn near a salt block. No matter which window the hunter looked out, he could see a path leading away from the stand. The narrow alleys made perfect shooting lanes for when a deer stepped out of the woods. It would make a great defensive position, as well.

Turning his attention back to the cabinet, Ryan leaned down to inspect the bottom. At a quick glance, there was nothing extraordinary about it, but on closer examination, Ryan saw what looked like a false bottom. He started tapping the sides and bottom of the cabinet, looking for an access point to the hidden compartment.

After five minutes of searching, he was about to give up when Scott suggested he try pushing up on the bottom panel. Ryan did so, and the latch clicked. The bottom dropped down to reveal a Glock 17 pistol and a handheld Garmin GPS unit nestled in black foam.

Scott pulled out the pistol, dropped the magazine, and racked the slide to eject the cartridge in the pipe. He inspected the gun quickly and put it back together while Ryan turned on the Garmin.

"I heard you like to hand out party favors," Scott said.

Ryan snorted. "You've been talking to Chuck."

"Yep. That's a nice Browning he has. I think I'll consider this Glock as *my* bonus."

"Enjoy," Ryan said. He had once found a Browning in a sunken sailboat, and when the owner had refused to take it back, Ryan had given it to Chuck Newland, one of DWR's pilots, for helping him with the job.

The Garmin powered up, and Ryan scrolled to the stored waypoints. There was only one, and it was on a tiny island not far from them.

"The mystery deepens ..." Scott said when Ryan showed him the GPS.

"We need a boat."

Ryan and Scott climbed down from the tree stand and walked back to the Jeep. While Ryan wanted to get going, Scott didn't seem to be in any hurry to leave, ambling along, peering into the trees, and scuffing the toe of his boot at piles of fallen leaves that had accumulated on the side of the path. Ryan jumped into the driver's seat. He glanced up at the tree branches as a powerful gust of wind rattled them. The wind moaned through an opening in the Jeep's top, sending a chill down Ryan's spine and reminding him why he didn't like winter.

Scott eventually joined Ryan in the Jeep. "Enjoy your walk, Robert Frost?"

"What?" Scott asked.

"You know, the poem '*The Road Not Taken*.' Two paths diverge in a wood, blah, blah, blah."

The corner of Scott's mouth turned up. "Two *roads* diverged in a yellow wood, And I was sorry I could not travel both."

"And it made all the difference, huh?" Ryan twisted the ignition key.

"Would you like me to recite '*The Ocean*' by Nathaniel Hawthorne?"

"I know a sea shanty myself. There once was a man from Nantucket ..."

"*You* can suck it," Scott said. "Those poems helped me when I was going through Hell Week."

Ryan continued down the narrow two-track lane as there was no place for him to turn around. The road bent to the right at another intersection and he kept going until the road petered out on another narrow peninsula. It looked like someone had been launching and retrieving small boats from the sandy ramp.

"What now, Captains Courageous?" Scott chided.

Ryan stared out the window at the still waters. Despite

the high winds that wrecked the ocean's surface, the protected inland waters were smooth as glass. Beyond the small barrier islands, the wind chopped the surface of the ICW, but it was nowhere near as bad as what they'd experienced earlier that day in the Atlantic.

Pointing out the window to his left, Ryan said, "The GPS says the coordinates are down there, on this side of the barrier islands."

"Want to paddle over there now?"

Ryan gave Scott a questioning look.

"There's a canoe hidden in the weeds back in the tree line."

"Might as well," Ryan said. "The weather's not going to get any better, and by the time we drive back to Wrightsville, get a boat, and get back up here, it'll be dark."

"Then let's go find some treasure," Scott said.

CHAPTER THIRTY-SIX

The black Chevy Tahoe reminded Greg Olsen of something the FBI or one of the other alphabet agencies would drive. It was also the most practical vehicle the rental agency had to offer because it was easy to equip with his hand controls. Greg quickly clamped them to the brake and gas pedals before looping the nylon strap over the steering column. He threw his legs into the footwell, then levered himself into the driver's seat. Next, he removed the wheels from his chair, tossed them into the back seat, then pulled the chair frame across his body and set it on the passenger seat.

He took a moment to catch his breath, wishing he had a beer. Leaning his head against the headrest, he closed his eyes. He had come to Wilmington because he'd needed to get away from Texas City or else Shelly was going to give him another job to do, and he wanted to help Ryan. He felt guilty over not seeing his best friend in a while because he had been preoccupied with prepping the bid to build a new shipping port in Bluefields, Nicaragua. DWR had won several contracts, but they wouldn't start for another year. Regardless, he was glad the preliminary project was finished, and he was ready to take Shelly away on a long vacation. Maybe even for good.

In the brief span of time his private military contracting business, Trident, had been operating, Greg had already received several offers to sell the business, and he was considering it. The business of private wars financed by the U.S. government had taken a downturn. That said, Trident still had plenty of work, and he enjoyed having his hand in the business of war. It made him feel useful, even though he couldn't deploy with his men.

It still galled him that the faceless terrorist bomber the U.S. military had nicknamed Nightcrawler had ambushed his Navy EOD team in Afghanistan and shattered his back with an IED. Greg had bled and cried in that dirt. He had cried himself to sleep many nights afterward, and for a long while, he'd refused to eat as a coping mechanism. Then he'd turned to alcohol to dull his senses. The VA classified him as an alcoholic, but then again, Greg figured every prior and active-duty service member could probably qualify under their strict guidelines, unless they were teetotalers. He remembered Ryan coming to visit him at the hospital and shoving him into the pool when Greg had slapped the cigarette lighter from Ryan's hand because the little bastard had been annoying him. Everyone had annoyed him back then. But being upended into the pool had been the catalyst that had gotten him off his ass and back to reality.

His father had added an elevator to DWR's headquarters and had put Greg to work, planning for him to take over the company's reins. That day had come sooner than anyone had expected when a terrorist had detonated a car bomb on the steps of the Texas Governor's mansion, killing Greg's mother and father and a bunch of other people who had been attending a fundraiser there.

Greg punched the Tahoe's steering wheel. Part of the reason he'd started Trident was to avenge his father and mother—and himself. He'd made it a pet project to hunt down Nightcrawler, but all the leads had evaporated. The man was just as much of a ghost now as he was back when Greg's team had been hunting him in the deserts and mountains of Afghanistan. The sneaky little Ali Baba must have jumped on his magic carpet and fled to Pakistan, because everyone under the sun knew those jokers were aiding and abetting Al-Qaeda and the Taliban. Hell, they'd been hiding Bin Laden for years. Why not a lowly bomb maker?

Greg felt his heart rate rise as he thought about that day. Shit, he needed a drink. He tried to calm himself with the usual breathing and visualization techniques, but he needed to feel the burn of tequila sliding down his throat.

No! he told himself. He wasn't weak. He could deal with his addiction and keep his promises to himself and to Shelly. Everything was under control.

Picking up his phone, Greg found the first address on the Bianchi property list and put it in his map application. He followed the route to an office building near the airport, then he crisscrossed town, looking for a place Bianchi could use to hold Janice Yeager.

Greg was in and out of the Tahoe multiple times, wheeling into buildings, asking questions, and checking properties, but no one had seen the woman in the photo he showed them. He was feeling low when he saw a drive-thru near one of Bianchi's partner businesses. Without giving it much thought, he pulled in and ordered a Mountain Dew, then saw a bottle of tequila sitting on a nearby shelf. He told the clerk to hand him the bottle of Patrón Silver. As he drove away, his mouth was salivating for a taste of the liquor, and he promised himself he would only have a taste.

After pulling into the lot of the next-to-last place on the

list, Greg decided he deserved a reward for his arduous work. His shoulders ached from getting in and out of the vehicle, and he'd knocked his leg open on the door and the wound had bled through his pants. Yeah, the tequila would taste wonderful.

Uncorking the bottle, he took a long swig. Greg closed his eyes as the liquor burned down his throat and warmth spread through his stomach. Sweet Mary, it tasted good. Then he took a second drink. He stared at the crime scene tape around the storage office where Kyle Fowler and Scott Gregory had busted the dirty cops snorting cocaine. Screw those guys.

The third drink went down even smoother than the last two. Greg was on the verge of giving up. They were tilting at windmills to believe that Bianchi would have sequestered Janice at one of his businesses. He decided to look at the last property, another warehouse near the river. At least he could tell Ryan he had done his best. Greg recapped the tequila and tucked the bottle under the passenger seat, then swallowed some soda.

It was dark by the time Greg arrived at the last property, and the business had long closed for the day. A storm was brewing, and the inevitable boom of thunder and streaks of lightning rolled across the night sky. A flash of lightning illuminated the dark storefront, giving Greg a glimpse of the inside of the empty furniture store.

Greg called it quits for the day and headed for a hotel near Wrightsville Beach Marina. He wanted a hot shower and cold tequila. After that, he could decide what to do next in this Quixotic mission. As he drove across the city, he called Ryan but got no answer. He didn't leave a message.

Before going into the hotel, he opened the email Ryan had forwarded to him and dialed the number for Barry Thatcher that was included within it. He'd only spoken to

Thatcher once, preferring to use his in-house computer specialists to do his dirty work.

"Hello?" Barry answered tentatively.

Greg introduced himself and told him he was helping Ryan with the hunt for Janice Yeager. Barry quickly brought Greg up to speed on the work he was doing to track down more properties. He had found several that Bianchi owned jointly, but none were likely candidates for keeping a kidnapped woman.

"Call me if you find him," Greg told him. "Ryan is busy with something else."

Barry agreed, and Greg ended the call. He got out of the SUV and grabbed his overnight bag. The wind was still up, carrying the storm with it, and the night had a bone-jarring chill to it that made Greg shiver in his jacket. Ever since his injury, his body had been slow to regulate his temperature. He typically wore a long sleeve shirt and a light jacket most of the year. Now he wished he had an extra sweatshirt.

Inside, he checked into his room, turned on the television, and stripped down to take a shower. While he liked to hit the gym and his upper body looked great, his legs had atrophied to just skin and bone. He took a long pull from the tequila bottle, wishing like crazy that he could just get up and walk. How many problems would that solve in his life?

He decided to forgo the shower and just get drunk instead.

CHAPTER THIRTY-SEVEN

Evening was rapidly approaching as Ryan and Scott slipped the green nineteen-foot-long Old Town canoe into the water. Scott got in the front, and Ryan took the rear seat. Together, they pushed through the shallow water toward the island indicated by the GPS unit Ryan had found in a secret compartment in John Parnell's deer stand.

They hugged the small barrier islands where the water was deeper and skirted around another long, narrow island between the barriers and the mainland. The wind swept across the little beaches, trying to push the canoe off their set course and blasting them with sand. Another eighty yards and they arrived at their destination, which was an island no more than a hundred feet across. Dwarf palmettos, red cedars, silverling trees, and sea oats grew thick on the tiny clump of sand.

When the front of the canoe ground into the sand, Scott hopped out and dragged it up on the beach. Ryan climbed out and turned in a semi-circle, looking for the best way through the scrub while dialing in on the location indicated on the GPS screen.

"You can see the guy's house from here. Why launch from where we did?" Scott asked.

"Because he doesn't want anyone to find whatever he'd buried out here."

Scott snorted. "Then he shouldn't have put it on a GPS unit."

Ryan started through palms, turning sideways so they wouldn't catch on his clothes or cut his exposed skin. Fifteen paces in, he stopped, and Scott fought through the fronds and branches to stand beside him.

"The GPS says right here, but this thing probably has a deviation of ten or fifteen feet," Ryan said.

Scott clicked on the tactical flashlight he'd plucked from his backpack and shined it along the ground, the cone of light illuminating the sandy soil and dead grasses. Ryan clicked on his own high-powered LED light.

"Search grids," Ryan stated. "Straight to the other side of the island. Then we take one step out and turn around."

The men crossed the island and moved away from each other by one step. They kept their heads down and swept their lights back and forth across the ground.

"Got a spot," Scott said.

Ryan marked where he'd left off by digging the toe of his shoe into the ground, then walked over to where Scott squatted beside the twisted trunk of a salt-spray-stunted silverling. He was using a chunk of driftwood to dig a hole. After five minutes of scratching at the ground, Scott had dug a decent hole, but they'd found nothing.

Scott stood and kicked the loose dirt back into the hole. "We need a metal detector."

Ryan stepped back to where he'd scuffed the ground and resumed his search. It was fully dark now, and scrambling around in the brush would be even more difficult than it was in broad daylight. Far out over the ocean, thunder rumbled, and the smell of rain was heavy in the air. Squatting in the small clearing, Ryan swept the beam of his light across the ground as he turned slowly in a circle. Halfway around, his beam fell on a shallow depression in the sand. He pointed to it, and Scott went to work with his makeshift shovel.

Moments later, his shovel struck something hard. The two men crouched over the hole, digging with their hands. Their fingertips brushed metal at the same time, and they shared a quick glance, grinning like little boys playing pirates.

They had found buried treasure.

Quickly, they excavated the site, hefted two military surplus ammunition cans out of the ground, unsnapped the lid catches, and pulled them open.

Scott's contained twenty boxes of nine-millimeter hollow points, another Glock 17 with spare magazines, and an emergency survival kit.

Ryan's box held four plastic containers. He pulled each out and held it up to the light. They were all filled with little gold nuggets. Tucked in at the bottom of the ammo can was a sheet of paper inside a zip seal bag. Training the light on it, Ryan read a list of coordinates. He tried to remember the numbers from earlier in the day when they'd been searching the ocean floor near Buoy 217, but a lot had happened between then and now, and he drew a blank.

Even if they couldn't find the box Parnell had lost, they could bargain for Janice with the gold in the ammo can.

"Let's pack up and get out of here before it starts raining," Scott suggested after a low boom of thunder rolled in the distance.

The two men closed the cans, keeping the page of coordinates, and reburied them before going to the canoe. Ryan took the front seat where he could better judge the water and guide them back to the Jeep, while Scott steered from the rear.

They were almost to their landing when Ryan's phone rang. He dug it out of his pocket and, still holding the light for Scott to see by, put it to his ear.

"What's up, Greg?" he asked.

CHAPTER THIRTY-EIGHT

The clear liquid in the tequila bottle was a quarter gone, and Greg Olsen had a pleasant buzz going when his phone rang. Rolling into a seated position on the bed, he answered with a slurred, "Yellow."

"Greg, it's Barry. I found a property that Bianchi owns through a third party. It's an old boatyard called 117 Marine."

"I'll get to it tomorrow," Greg said, reaching for the bottle of Patrón.

"Here's the thing. Bianchi hid his car in the bushes by the marina office."

Greg grunted and didn't bother to listen to any more of what Barry had to say. He started pulling on his clothes as fast as he could, laying on the bed and rolling back and forth to get his pants over his hips and fastened. He then transferred into his chair and put on his shoes, followed by a T-shirt, a hooded sweatshirt, and a jacket. He wheeled out of the room while shoving his SIG Sauer P320 pistol and spare magazines into his cross-draw holster.

By the time he'd gotten into the Tahoe, he'd killed thirty minutes. He started the vehicle and dialed Ryan's number.

The phone rang through the Bluetooth system while Greg jerked the transmission into drive, backing out of the handicap parking space and silently begging Ryan to answer.

When he did, Greg said, "Bianchi is at 117 Marine. Do you know where that is?"

"Yeah. I know it well. We'll head there now."

"Where are you?" Greg dropped the transmission into drive and mashed the accelerator.

"I'm in a canoe with Scott who thinks he can steer."

Greg really wanted to know why Ryan and Scott were canoeing in the dark, and he couldn't let go of an opportunity to take a shot across their bow. "When you two lovebirds get done fooling around, get to 117 Marine."

"Got it," Ryan said, then followed up with, "Hey, Greg? Let us handle this."

"Just get there, Ryan. And bring your sweetheart Scott. He might be useful."

"We're on the way." Ryan's voice hardened. "Seriously, Greg, let us handle it."

Greg ended the call. His mouth was dry, and his hands were sweaty. It had been a long time since he'd ridden into battle. Despite the booze, his head had cleared, but he knew he wouldn't pass a sobriety test. He gunned the motor and swerved out of the parking lot, following the directions on his phone. It would take him less than ten minutes to get to the marina, and he wondered whether he should call Ryan's friend Kyle for support. *Nah, I'll let Ryan get the first crack at the bastard—if I don't get him first.*

He skirted much of the slower traffic by taking I-40, then jumped off at the Castle Hayne exit and crossed the Northeast Cape Fear River. Less than a mile later, Greg pulled the Tahoe onto the dirt access road along the blacktop and coasted to a stop by the gate in the chain-link fence.

The phone rang as he was trying to decide how to get past

the chain and padlock that kept the gate closed. He punched the *Answer* button. "Yeah, Barry?"

"I found another satellite to give me real-time data, but it's really hard to see because its dark and there aren't many lights around the boatyard. So, I was thinking about switching again when I realized the satellite had thermal capabilities."

"Get to it, Barry," Greg snapped.

"So, anyway, when I switched to thermal, I saw two people walking from the office to a boat. It looks like a man and a woman, and the woman has her hands behind her back."

Greg threw the transmission into gear, shoved the hand control for the gas to the floor, and backed the SUV up about twenty feet. He changed gears and floored the gas again. The big Tahoe leaped forward and slammed into the gate, busting it wide open, but one gate caught in the front wheel well and wrapped chain-link around the tire, bringing the Tahoe to a screeching stop.

Throwing open the door, Greg put together his wheelchair and dropped into it. He double-checked that there was a round in the chamber of the SIG, then jammed the gun back into his holster. Greg pushed himself around the rear of the Tahoe, his wheels cutting twin tracks through the hard sand.

The problem with having to use his hands to push was that he could hold neither his gun nor his flashlight in them. Historically, he had solved the light issue by using a headlamp, but they were rarely as powerful as a handheld tactical light. The gun was another matter altogether, and he could only solve that problem by stopping to draw. Wheeling one-handed while wielding the gun in the other was an exercise best performed on a smooth surface, and this boatyard was anything but that.

Greg leaned back slightly. The front wheels just skimmed the ground, so they wouldn't fall into a rut and pitch him from the chair. Several times, he had to ride a wheelie to get over minor obstacles, thankful there was just enough light spilling from the security lamp mounted on a pole near the office that he could see the road ahead. All the while, he visualized seeing Bianchi and quick drawing on him. Stop, pull up the jacket with his left hand, and draw with his right. It was something he had practiced many times on the range.

Greg had had enough sense to look at the overhead view of the place before charging in, but that was about it. He was charging into this blind. He stopped pushing and stretched his arms. His stomach muscles ached from being clenched during his extended wheelies, and his arms were sore from the vigorous exercise. He wondered if he could even shoot straight with the way his hands were shaking. Regardless, he pushed on, fighting the soft sand.

A man came out of the office and crossed the path to a boat.

Assuming it was Bianchi, Greg veered off the road between two large sportfishing boats, wanting to approach from the blindside of the compound, and not straight up the gut. The ancient wooden hulls of the offshore battlewagons dwarfed him as he weaved around the metal stanchions, concrete blocks, and rotten logs used to keep the boats upright. The ground was softer here and choked with weeds. He fought through and turned to wheel along the back side of the boats.

Lightning sizzled across the sky, illuminating the bare prop shafts, rotten hulls, and the log that lay in Greg's way. He had to go around it, and the only way to do that was to go deeper into the boatyard. Ten minutes later, he had skirted the office and found himself on the far side of the canal. From his observation post, he could see Bianchi loading bags onto a pilothouse trawler.

He raised his gun and braced his hands on an overturned rowboat. The three glowing dots of photoluminescent paint on his pistol's sights automatically aligned on the center mass of Charles "Rocky" Bianchi.

Time to enter the ring, tough guy.

CHAPTER THIRTY-NINE

The Jeep Wrangler bounced and rocked as Ryan Weller kept the gas pedal pinned to the floor. From the canoe landing along the ICW to the blacktop of Route 117 was two miles of forest trails. Ryan followed his entry route in reverse, shot across the empty northbound lanes of U.S. Route 17, and headed south.

As he turned onto the Wilmington Bypass, Ryan pressed the phone's *Speed Dial* button for Kyle Fowler. When the deputy detective came on the line, Ryan explained their mission. Kyle hung up as soon as Ryan told him Bianchi was at 117 Marine.

Halfway through their twenty-minute drive, Kyle called back to say that deputies were en route, and that Ryan was to wait for them.

"I repeat, Ryan—you are to *wait* for the deputies. I'm on my way right now."

Ryan bumped the *End* button and glanced at Scott, who shrugged. Neither man was going to wait around for law enforcement when there was so much at stake.

As they passed over the Northeast Cape Fear River, a

jagged bolt of lightning illuminated the Jeep's interior. Ryan saw that Scott had pulled out his Springfield pistol, and was ready to go as soon as they came to a stop.

Ryan swung the Jeep onto the dirt access road and came to a stop behind a scuffed Chevrolet Tahoe that had rammed the marina's gates and sat with its front tire wrapped in the chain-link fence.

Ryan slid out of the Jeep with one singular thought: *Find Janice*.

The first fat drop of rain hit his hand, and when Ryan looked down, he saw that his Walther PPQ M2 had appeared there. He didn't remember drawing it as he'd exited the Jeep. That one simple act scared him and yet invigorated him at the same time. He was hunting again; hunting a man that found weakness to be an unworthy trait and who used those who were poor and afraid to do his bidding. A man who preyed on the helplessness of others. Now he was Ryan's prey.

A dark prey.

Ryan eased around the Tahoe, seeing the rental sticker on the rear window and the portable hand controls mounted to the gas and brake pedals. Greg Olsen had gotten there ahead of him. He wanted to call out for Greg, but that would give away his position. As Ryan and Scott stood there, ready to move into the lot, Ryan strained his ears for sounds that might tip him off as to where Bianchi, Janice, or Greg were.

"We split up," Ryan instructed Scott. "Look for Greg and get him out of here."

"If you find Bianchi, call me," Scott said.

"You do the same," Ryan replied, even though he knew he never would. Bianchi was his and he would make that bastard pay for the pain he had caused, not only to Chad and Janice but to all the others he'd screwed over in his short miserable life.

The rain fell harder now, pattering off Ryan's Columbia

jacket and slicking down the outer surface. A gust of wind moaned through the boat hulls and the trees. Old boats lined both sides of a center road that Ryan knew led to the small canal and a dock at the rear of the property. There was everything from giant wooden cabin cruisers to overturned rowboats, and all around them, weeds sprouted from the ground and shrubs cloaked the fence lines.

Ryan and Scott slowly walked along the road, each man keeping a close watch on his side, sweeping the muzzles of their firearms and the beams of their tactical lights along the tiny isles between the boats.

It was Scott who spotted the wheelchair tracks in the mud along the edge of the road. The indentations veered off to the right between two large sportfishing crafts held in place by wooden blocks and steel posts. Beyond them was the rest of the yard; acres of unattended boats that Ryan feared they'd have to search individually. He motioned for Scott to follow Greg's tracks while he stayed on the road.

The rain drummed down now, drenching Ryan to the skin, soaking his clothing and making him shiver. He doubted Scott was faring any better, and what about Greg? Had he gotten stuck in the mud? What had made him leave the road?

What the hell were you thinking, Greg? Why are you even out here?

The answer matched the reason Ryan was there. Someone needed to bring Bianchi to justice and a woman's life hung in the balance.

Refocusing on the task at hand, Ryan kept moving, sweeping the beam of his light along the ghostly boat hulls, relics from the past ready to be cut into scrap. As he neared the old brick house the boatyard owner had converted to an office, Ryan paused. It was a typical Carolina brick ranch, probably built in the fifties during the post-war boom. This one had what looked to be an oversized carport attached to the front of the garage with a Rover 42 cabin cruiser under it. Ryan recognized the distinct lines from when his father had owned a similar boat.

He went to the front door and checked the knob. Locked. After using the butt of his pistol to smash the side light, Ryan reached through the shattered glass to unlock the door. It was as dark as a tomb inside with the blinds pulled. The smell of turpentine, paint, and mold hung heavy in the air.

Ryan swept his light over several desks in what had once been the living room. The kitchen sink had dirty dishes and ramen packets on the counter by a microwave. He made his way deeper into the house, sweeping the light from side to side, vanquishing the darkness to the corners and letting it return as he moved away.

A chill swept over him as he recalled the last time that he'd searched darkened rooms such as these. It had been at an abandoned hospital in Mexico. Now, instead of pentagrams and candles on the floors to summon evil spirits, there were just old desks, stacks of musty papers, cigarette butts, and empty beer cans.

Where are you, Janice?

He entered the last bedroom.

Outside, a motor coughed as it tried to turn over, and Ryan spun toward the sound. His light swept across the room in a broad arch, and he saw a woman sitting in a chair in the corner of the room.

On instinct, he trained his gun on her. "Put your hands up!"

She didn't move.

Advancing toward the unflinching woman, he ordered her to put her hands up again, this time adding, "Or I'll shoot."

Still, she didn't move. Then he realized there was a gag over her mouth, and someone had bound her arms and legs to the chair. Ryan kept his gun and light trained on her, but as he drew closer, he realized the woman was actually a lifelike mannequin. The boat motor now ran smoothly as Ryan studied the figure in the chair. Was it a trap?

Then a pistol barked outside.

Ryan ran out of the house into the pouring rain. The security light broke the darkness. Rounding the corner of the house at full sprint, he recognized the VDL Pilot 44 that was backing out of the slip. Another gunshot shattered the night, a tongue of flame reaching out from the trees crowding the canal's opposite bank.

"He's on the boat!" Ryan heard Greg Olsen shout.

Ryan tried to increase his speed, lifting his knees in a full speed sprint toward the retreating trawler. The boat driver threw the throttle forward, the propeller thrashing against the water, trying to pull the heavy steel boat back toward the river. At the end of the dock, Ryan leaped into the air, throwing himself toward the polished stainless-steel safety railing surrounding the Pilot's bow.

His hands latched around the narrow tube, but he could feel them slipping as his feet dragged through the water, threatening to tear him away. With all his strength, Ryan squeezed the railing and did a pull-up. His head and shoulders cleared the deck.

A jagged bolt of lightning suddenly lit Rocky Bianchi's maniacal face in near-daylight brilliance. In that brief instant, Ryan's mind registered the gun in Bianchi's hand, and he let himself drop back below the deck. His right hand slipped off the railing and his legs sprawled behind him, churning in the wake as the boat continued backward.

Two more gunshots rippled the night air. A clap of thunder boomed so loud above them that Ryan felt his body shake. The suddenness of it almost made him let go of the boat, but if he let go now, he might never get another chance to save Janice.

The stern of the boat struck something with enough force to jar Ryan loose. As he fell into the water, he grabbed at the loose end of the bow line, but it slid through his wet fingers as he dropped deep into the inky, cold blackness. Above him, the boat's engine revved as it labored forward.

Ryan's feet sank into the silty river bottom. He pushed off, launching himself toward the surface, extending his arms to protect his head from the boat above. Kicking with all his might, he broke the surface of the shallow canal and saw the Pilot headed straight for him.

As it passed, Ryan grabbed the bow line he had knocked off moments earlier. Then the Pilot reversed course again, backing into the river. Ryan wrapped his hand around the rope to keep from slipping off. The chilly water flowed around him, making his body shiver and his fingers cramp.

He *could not* let go.

The Pilot slowed as Bianchi threw the drive into neutral, then into forward. With the boat headed downriver, it increased in speed, pulling Ryan tight to the hull. He fought to keep his head above water, but the wake foamed off the bow, right into his face. Each time he wanted to breathe, he had to tuck his face into his shoulder and open his mouth like a freestyle swimmer. His right arm felt like it was being pulled from its socket, his muscles shredding off the bone. He got his left hand on the rope, pulling himself forward to ease the pressure on his right hand. Slowly, he forced his body to move.

Shifting his mind to a place of numbness, beyond the aches and pains and the cold, Ryan Weller clawed his way along the rope. He couldn't stop now. He couldn't let go. Ryan knew he couldn't do anything but climb that damned rope and face Bianchi.

Fortunately, the loan shark hadn't taken in the fenders, and Ryan's hand closed around the one closest to him. He pulled himself up and grasped the bottom rail of the safety railing. Ryan levered his leg onto the deck and hung there, taking the weight off his hands and shoulders in a moment of sheer relief. Then he rolled himself onto the deck, levered himself up to his hands and knees, and, finally, let the bow line fall from his hand.

Ryan found himself amidships. He crawled aft along the raised cabin to where the pilothouse window had shattered from Bianchi's gunshots. The rain poured off him, dripping from his head and his clothes. His wet garments clung to his skin, and his muscles trembled from the cold and the effort he'd exerted to pull himself onto the boat. More thunder boomed as the sky flashed, illuminating snatches of the dark shoreline, the white deck of the boat, and the rain that pounded the swirling waters below.

Unsure if Bianchi knew he was there, Ryan drew himself into a crouch and pulled out his pistol. Again, the night air sizzled with electricity, making the hairs on his arms stand up. Standing swiftly, he aimed through the window.

There was no one at the wheel.

The pilothouse was empty.

CHAPTER FORTY

Inching toward the back deck, Ryan saw the aft steering station was also unmanned, and the cabin door stood open. Cautiously, he entered, sweeping his gun back and forth, clearing the space like the military had taught him all those years ago during a close quarter combat course. To his left was a wraparound settee and table. Ahead was the pilot's seat and controls and a spiral staircase that led down to the lower cabin. He tried to remember the layout from when he and Emily had last been aboard.

With a glance at the controls, Ryan determined the boat was making three knots down the river. He had firsthand knowledge of how the river twisted and turned, and he thought the boat would ground. Flooding often changed the river's flow, depositing new sandbars, and hiding new snags that wouldn't appear on the navigation software. That didn't matter right now. He had more pressing concerns.

Ryan started down the steps, feeling his way into the dark cabin. He was halfway down when his legs were swept out from under him. Falling backward, Ryan smacked his shoulder against the railing and dropped his gun as he slid down the steps. Before he could gather his feet beneath him, pain exploded through his body and all the air left his lungs in an audible *whoosh* as he took a kick to the ribs. Ryan lay on the deck, gasping for breath like a dying fish and clutching his chest with his arms.

Bianchi laughed, looming over him with a club in his hand. "I knew you'd come, Weller. Where's my gold?"

The air seemed to return to Ryan's lungs in tiny increments, like he was breathing through a straw. Each breath was raspy, seeming to fill the cabin, and the only thing that drowned it out was the boom of the thunder.

He wanted to answer, but he had no breath to do so.

In a flash of lightning, Ryan saw Bianchi raise his club. As the man swung down, Ryan lashed his foot out, connecting with Bianchi's ankle. The loan shark stumbled, dropping his club as he fell against the galley cabinets.

Ryan scrambled to his hands and knees; a feral animal trapped by a man who had seized a knife from the sink. He snarled, anger and adrenaline flushing through him. He disregarded the pain of his injured ribs and his frigid body. There was nothing but the fight.

One of them was leaving this boat in a pine box, and it was not going to be him.

Bianchi crouched into a boxing stance. He'd reversed the knife in his hand so the blade ran along his forearm. He lunged forward, raising the knife to stab downward.

Ryan's training kicked in. The long hours of practicing Krav Maga during his time in the Navy paid off as he automatically lifted his left forearm to block Bianchi's knife hand, and he tried to punch Bianchi in the face at the same time. But the man obstructed Ryan's blow. Instinctively, Ryan turned his left hand and grabbed his opponent's wrist, shoving it back, controlling the knife. As he did so, he kicked Bianchi in the balls. When the man doubled over, Ryan brought his right knee up, smashing it into Bianchi's face—once, twice, then a third time for good measure.

The knife fell from the loan shark's grasp, and Ryan kicked it away. In a bright flash of lightning, Ryan saw his Walther on the deck and snatched it up. Another flashbulb popped outside, providing a Kodak snapshot of Bianchi sprawled on the floor, his face busted and bleeding. Ryan stumbled to the stairs, finding the light switch and flipping it on. The cabin flooded with the soft glow of the LEDs.

Ryan left Bianchi on the floor and went in search of Janice. The first place he looked was in the aft bunk room, but she wasn't there, so he went forward to the V-berth stateroom. She lay on the bed, still in her jeans and sweatshirt, with her arms bound behind her back and her legs tied together. Jamming his pistol into his back pocket, Ryan sliced through the ropes with his folding knife, and she pulled the gag from around her mouth. Janice kneeled on the bed and wrapped her arms around her adopted son.

He felt her tense as he comforted her. Then her hand jerked the Walther from his back pocket, and the gun thundered in the tiny enclosure.

Ryan turned to see Bianchi standing in the doorway, staring down at the hole in his chest. His face was a mass of blood and snot from his broken nose. Blood from the gunshot wound flowed freely down his chest, soaking his shirt. Slowly, the knife he held slipped from his grasp.

Rocky Bianchi sank to his knees then toppled face-first onto the cabin sole.

Janice dropped the gun, and it clattered to the deck. Ryan left it where it lay and helped Janice out of the cabin and up to the pilothouse. He set her behind the table and went back below to search the galley for something to drink. In a fridge, he found a bottle of water and a bottle of Jack Daniels. He carried both upstairs and set them on the table, then he stepped to the wheel and examined the controls. Bianchi had set the autopilot to take them down the river and out to sea.

Bringing the throttle back caused the autopilot to shut off, and Ryan made a slow turn in the channel. Once he had the Pilot headed back upriver, he threw the throttle forward, racing through the alligator-infested waters toward the dock at 117 Marine.

The VHF radio crackled before a voice called out, "*Due South, Due South, Due South*, this is New Hanover County Sheriff's Deputy Kyle Fowler. Heave to and shut off your engine."

Ryan snatched the mic off the holder. "Kyle, this is Ryan. I'm on *Due South*. We're on our way back to 117 Marine."

"Copy that. Are you okay?"

"Yeah, we're good. I found Janice, and we have Bianchi aboard."

"Roger that. We'll be waiting for you."

Seven minutes later, Ryan maneuvered the VDL Pilot 44 alongside the dock at 117 Marine. The whole place was lit with portable floodlights and the strobing reds, blues and yellows mounted on the assembled patrol cars and ambulances.

Kyle Fowler and Scott Gregory stood beside Greg Olsen on the dock. Scott grabbed the Pilot's bow line from where it still trailed over the side of the boat, and Kyle secured the stern line to the dock cleat.

Ryan leaned out the window. "You boys know where I can get a good cup of coffee?"

"Not around here," Greg replied.

"Find two cups because Janice and I are freezing."

Kyle stepped aboard and entered the pilothouse. Janice

Yeager had the bottle of water clutched in one hand and had the other locked around the neck of the open bottle of Jack. She took a long, hard swig of whiskey as she stared vacantly into space. She had just killed the man who had taken her hostage and Ryan knew she would need time to process everything she was feeling. He sat down beside her and pulled out his cigarettes, but they were waterlogged, so he tossed them onto the table.

"I could use one of those," Janice muttered.

Kyle stepped outside and shouted for someone to give him their cigarettes and lighter. A deputy handed over his pack, and Kyle passed them to Ryan.

"Where's Bianchi?" Kyle asked after Ryan and Janice had both lit up.

"Down below. He's dead," Ryan said, leaning back and letting out a cloud of smoke.

Kyle nodded solemnly and went down the steps. He came up a few minutes later and walked off the boat. Within minutes, a paramedic was sitting beside Janice, and several deputies had gone below to photograph and analyze the murder scene.

"Who shot him?" Kyle asked.

"I did," Janice volunteered. "He was about to stab Ryan in the back, so I grabbed his gun and shot him."

"Is that what your story is?" he asked Ryan.

"Yep."

"Okay. Go get cleaned up, then go to the station," he told Ryan. Turning to Janice, he added, "We're transporting you to the hospital for a full check-up."

"Where's Chad?" she asked.

"He's in jail," Kyle informed her. "The police arrested him while Bianchi's people were kidnapping you."

Janice put her face in her hands and sobbed softly. Ryan wrapped his arm around her shoulders. "Scott will go with you to the hospital. You get checked out, and I'll take you to see Chad tomorrow," he promised.

The paramedic escorted Janice to an ambulance with Ryan following behind her. He told Scott to go with her, and he walked to the gate where he'd left the Jeep. Someone had removed the fencing from the Tahoe's wheel and parked it out of the way. He started the Jeep's engine and cranked the heat to high.

As he drove back to Wrightsville Beach Marina, he tried to figure out all the angles. How was he going to get Chad out of jail? With Bianchi dead, was there any way to refute the story Tim Davis was telling about Chad being the mastermind of the theft ring? Ryan couldn't protect Chad from everything, especially if the prosecutor went digging around in Chad's past. From his time working with Emily, Ryan knew it was a felony to defraud an insurance agency, and that meant jail time.

He sighed through puffed-up cheeks. By the time he got to the marina, his clothes had partially dried, but he was still shivering despite the full force of the heater blasting in his face. He ran onto *Huntress* and quickly shed his clothes, then he stepped into the shower and turned the water to scalding hot.

When he stepped out, he saw he'd missed a call from Kyle.

He dialed the detective's number.

Kyle answered with a curt, "Fowler."

"What's up?" Ryan asked.

"They're keeping Janice overnight for observation, but everything seems to be fine."

"That's good."

"I thought you'd want to know, WPD is kicking Chad loose. Turns out he wasn't the only one supplying boats to Davis and the Jefferies. The owner of 117 Marine was doing it as well, and he was parting out stolen boats for Bianchi. The guy kept a lot of paper, and he's singing like a bird in the springtime."

"That's good news," Ryan said.

"Yeah, but Chad's not in the clear for everything, buddy."

CHAPTER FORTY-ONE

One month later

The metal detector in Ryan's right hand was clicking like crazy as he approached the steel box half-buried in the mud and sand. The day they'd tried to dive in a driving storm, they'd been in the wrong location because their data points had been incomplete. But with the coordinates taken from Parnell's buried ammo cans, they had been able to pinpoint the exact location where Capt. Hammersley had dropped his cargo of smuggled African gold.

Ryan swam to the box, reflexively checking the computers hooked to his rebreather. He could have used the ROV, but where was the fun in that? Scott swam up beside Ryan, and together they used two ratchet straps to form a web around their prize.

Scott deployed his surface marker buoy and a few minutes later, the dive boat was overhead, driven by Greg Olsen, his girlfriend Shelly Hughes beside him. They were on board

Skater, the Judge 34 Express that had once belonged to John Parnell. Ryan had scooped it up for pennies on the dollar from the insurance company, and Cape Fear Dive and Salvage had repaired the hole in the hull. There wasn't a single blemish in the gel coat.

The dive had been quick, taking less than fifteen minutes from the time they'd gone over the side of the boat to when they'd found the box. A rope dropped through the water column to them, and Ryan tied it to the box, making sure it wouldn't fall out of the straps before the two men ascended the line.

Once aboard *Skater*, Emily Hunt helped them shed their dive gear and stow it in the boat's custom racks. Ryan and Scott hauled the box aboard, and the custom sportfisher headed for the dock at what was now Ryan's new house on the Intracoastal Waterway.

Scott and Greg had stayed in North Carolina to wait out the weather to dive. Shelly had joined them two days ago so they could all celebrate Christmas together. It was good to have the gang together again. In two days, Mango and Jennifer Hulsey, Ryan's former dive partner and his wife, would arrive to join the festivities.

As Greg ran them back to Rich Inlet and navigated into Green Channel, Ryan leaned against the gunwale and watched the scenery pass by. During the summer months, boaters would line the many sandbars and beaches, picnicking, sunbathing, and visiting with family and friends. He remembered doing it himself with his own family and with Chad and Kyle when they'd had access to a boat. The secluded beaches were perfect for drinking beer and getting laid.

Emily stepped beside him and rubbed his shoulder. "A penny for your thoughts?"

Ryan smiled. "I was just reliving old memories."

"You love it here," she stated.

"In the summer."

"It would be a great place to raise kids. And they'd get to see their grandparents."

Ryan's eyebrows rose. *Now* she was talking about kids.

The sudden stoppage of the boat put an end to their conversation. Ryan glanced over the side at the sandbar Greg had driven them into.

"What the hell, Greg? I just had this thing fixed," Ryan chided.

"Sorry, man. The sun got in my eyes and I missed the channel marker."

"Oh, yeah," Scott joined in the ribbing. "The *sun* got in your eyes."

"Shut up and push us off," Greg growled.

Ryan and Scott pulled on their dry suits again, jumped overboard, and pushed the boat off the sandbar. With the boat floating again, they climbed aboard, and Greg drove them up to the dock at what used to be John Parnell's place. They unloaded the boat, raised it up on the lift so it was out of the water, and sprayed it down with fresh water.

It took both Ryan and Scott to carry the steel box to the house. They went up the access ramp that Ryan and his father had constructed for Greg and set the box on the living room floor. Everyone was eager to see what was inside, but Ryan made them wait while he and Scott changed from their dry suits into regular clothes.

When they came back into the living room, Greg and Mango had already removed the straps off the box, and Greg motioned for them to hurry. Ryan and Scott unclasped the waterproof top and detached it before they dumped the contents onto a plastic sheet laid over the rug.

The gold nuggets sparkled in the sunlight.

Greg let out a low whistle. Emily crouched beside her

fiancé and ran her hand through the pile. "How much is here?"

"We'll have to weigh it to be sure," Ryan said, feeling gold fever himself.

There was a knock on the front door, and Shelly walked over to answer it while Emily, Ryan, and Scott scrambled to put the gold back in the box. When they had the lid on, Ryan shoved the box under the coffee table as Scott wadded up the plastic.

The knock came again. Shelly glanced over her shoulder to see that they'd cleaned everything up before opening the door. Kyle Fowler walked in with Chad Yeager in tow. Ryan gave Chad a hug and bumped fists with Kyle before he grabbed cold beers from the fridge and handed them out to the two newcomers. True to McClelland's word, Nicky Pence was a shark who lobbied the judge and the D.A. for Chad to receive a lighter sentence because he was under duress from Bianchi. They had agreed and sentenced him to twenty days in jail and two years of probation.

Chad cleared his throat after a swallow of beer. "I know it's been a while, but I wanted to thank you all again for helping my mom, both for rescuing her from Bianchi and for helping her while I was in jail. I'm going to be moving back in with her for the time being. It's best for both of us."

"That's great to hear," Ryan said.

"And thanks for fixing her front door."

"It was the least we could do," Ryan said.

"Well, you did a lot more than that and we both know it." Chad said. "I don't know how I can ever repay you."

"That's what friends do, buddy," Ryan stated.

Kyle kicked the box under the coffee table. "What's in there?"

"Nothing you need to worry about, *Detective*," Ryan said.

Kyle frowned. "Is that what Parnell was smuggling?"

"Plausible deniability," Scott said. "Just forget you ever saw that box."

"Let's take a walk," Ryan said to Kyle. "I want to talk to you about something."

"That box?"

Chuckling, Ryan shook his head. "You're like a dog with a bone, Kyle."

The two men walked outside and down the dock, then mounted the steps to the upper deck, which also acted as a roof over the boat lift. A cool wind blew over the marshland, bringing with it the smell of the ocean. A boat passed them, speeding down the ICW, leaving a wide, foaming wake.

"What's going on?" Kyle asked.

"I just wanted to ask you if you'd be my caretaker here."

Kyle shook his head. "I can't move my family out here. Cheryl won't make that drive out to the blacktop every day."

Ryan nodded. "I know you and Cheryl have been having problems. She told Emily about things after we had dinner at your house the other night."

Kyle shook his head. "I told you not to worry about me."

"But I do. I want you to be happy, and I know how much you love your wife and kids. You should patch things up with Cheryl."

"I'm trying, Ryan."

"Just know the offer stands. You're welcome here anytime."

"Can I hunt your deer?"

Ryan smiled. "You're more than welcome, but you might have to fight Scott for them."

"What's in the box?" Kyle asked again.

Ryan leaned against the railing and shoved his hands in his coat pockets. He wished he had a cigarette, but he was back on the wagon since Emily had returned from Florida. "Parnell was working with a cargo ship captain to smuggle gold from

Africa. As near as I can figure, Bianchi was the fence, using his pawnshop to move it."

"So that box is full of gold?"

When Ryan didn't answer, Kyle said, "You know you have to report that, right?"

"Report what?" Ryan smiled innocently.

"How are you going to get rid of it?" Kyle demanded.

"Why? Do you want a cut?"

Exasperated, Kyle said, "No. I don't want a cut of smuggled gold. But you need to do the right thing, Ryan."

"Well, Kyle, here's the deal. I found that box on the bottom of the ocean floor, and according to the laws of salvage, I get to keep what I find. Can I sell it easily? Probably not. But it's a rainy-day fund."

Kyle shook his head. "Yeah, you found it, but that doesn't make it right."

"It is what it is, Kyle."

The detective nodded. "You always liked to live dangerously. I think that's what you love about Chad. He gets away with all the shit we always wanted to do but never had the stomach for."

"He's paying for it now," Ryan said.

"Yeah, he is." Kyle stared out across the water. "Every time we rode up and down The Ditch, I would check this place out and wonder what it looked like inside and who lived here."

"It could be you. You can have the house or the loft above the garage."

"I'll keep an eye on the place, but I doubt I'll move in. When are you leaving?"

"After Christmas," Ryan said. "Mom and Dad are sailing down to Florida with me and Em. You want to come?"

"I'd love to, but I have my hands full here," Kyle said.

The two men walked back to the house, where Ryan gave Kyle a spare key.

"Come on, Chad," Kyle said. "I need to get back to the house."

"Don't forget," Ryan said as the two men got into the truck. "You're supposed to be here on Christmas Eve."

Both gave him a thumbs-up.

As Ryan stood at the window watching Kyle's Ford drive away, Emily linked her arm in his, and said, "You're a good friend, Ryan Weller."

As the F-250's taillights faded into the trees, he said, "I try. But it takes one to know one."

EPILOGUE

Christmas Eve was clear and cool, with the temperature hovering in the mid-fifties. Ryan leaned against the dock railing, smoking cigars with Scott, Greg, Mango Hulsey, Kyle Fowler, Chad Yeager, Henry O'Shannassy, and Gene Terry, the Coast Guard chief. Ryan's parents and siblings were in the house with the other women and children. He expected his sister, Trisha, to come out and smoke a cigar before his brother ever would, and his father had declined one of the Montecristos.

The ever-present breeze carried away the smoke as the men chatted about Bianchi's death and the arrest of several corrupt police officers for their involvement in drug smuggling. Ryan had given a full—*anonymous*—account to Ray McClelland, and the reporter had broken multiple stories about Charles Bianchi and his crooked chain of businesses.

Once they'd finished their cigars, the men retreated to a house filled with laughter and noisy kids. Emily and Shelly had set up a Christmas tree and found decorations that Parnell had stored in the garage. Under it were presents for the kids, and they clamored for Uncle Ryan to please let them open them. He relented and settled in beside Emily to watch them tear the pretty wrapping paper to shreds and triumphantly hold aloft their new treasures.

Even Kyle's kids had gifts that Ryan had bought from a list that Cheryl had supplied him. She gave Ryan a warm smile when Stevie pulled out a new pack of Lego, but she frowned when her thirteen-year-old unwrapped a pocketknife that hadn't been on the list. Ryan shrugged and returned John and Stevie's high-fives with a grin. Every boy needed a pocketknife, especially one who would spend as much time wandering the woods and waterways as he knew John would. He was like his dad, a straight arrow with an adventurous streak. Kyle had already brought his kids out to sit in the deer stand, and John had shot a nice six-point buck last Saturday.

Kyle ruffled John's hair. "You can skin your next buck with that thing."

The grin of joy on John's face was more than enough of a gift for Ryan.

Ryan saw Greg sneak out the front door and roll down the dock. He glanced over at Shelly, who shrugged and nodded sideways, telling Ryan to follow him.

After grabbing a bottle of tequila, he walked to the end of the dock. "Sort of reminds me of your place on Tiki Island."

"There's no view of Galveston here."

"You doing okay?" Ryan asked.

"Just family stuff. It's hard this time of year."

"I'm sorry, man. It's got to be tough," Ryan said. He didn't want to even contemplate losing his parents. "How's your sister?"

"She's good. Handles everything with stoicism and puts on a happy face for her husband and kids."

"Sounds like she's a chip off the old block. Cliff called me yesterday. He wanted to make sure you were doing all right."

Greg sighed. "Leave it to Grandpa to check up on me."

"What else is bugging you?" Ryan prodded.

After a long pull from the bottle, Greg flipped the hood of his sweatshirt over his head. "Part of the reason I haven't gotten married is because not everything works like it's supposed to. I can't have kids."

"Because of your injury?"

Greg nodded. "Nothing works. I can't feel anything from the waist down. I talked to a doctor. He said we'd have to do in vitro fertilization, and if that doesn't work, find a sperm donor. I think every time I looked at the kid, I would know it wasn't mine."

Ryan had no clue what to say to his friend. This was one of the few times Greg had really opened up about his injury and how it affected his life. "Have you talked to Shelly about it?"

"Some. We skirt the issue and talk about work."

"She's stuck with you this long, buddy. Maybe it's time to have a serious conversation about it."

"Probably," Greg said with resignation.

In a sing-song voice to lighten the mood, Ryan said, "Double beach wedding in Florida."

Greg held up his middle finger.

Ryan took his gesture to mean the conversation about family was over. "So, what about work?"

Greg shrugged. "I'm over it."

"Over what?"

"The whole thing. I'm thinking about selling Trident to Academi. They made me a nice offer. I think they want my government contracts more than anything."

"What about Scott, and Jinks, and all the other people you've hired?"

"I don't know. The thing has taken on a life of its own, and it's a grind having to be on-call twenty-four hours a day. That's why I hired a CEO for Dark Water."

"So do the same thing with Trident."

Greg shrugged. "Truthfully, I thought I could put boots on the ground in Afghanistan and track down Nightcrawler. But all the contracts I keep getting are for Africa. No one will talk to me about Nightcrawler because I don't have the right clearances or they just don't know what happened to him, blah, blah, blah. The usual CIA doublespeak."

Ryan rubbed his forehead. He hadn't known Greg was secretly hunting the bomber who had ambushed them in the desert and put Greg in a wheelchair, but it shouldn't have surprised him. "Maybe he bugged out and quit the game."

Greg snorted. "Guys like that don't just quit the jihad."

"He's probably moved on to greener pastures since we're drawing down the troops over there."

"Wherever he's at, he's dug in deep," Greg said.

Ryan stared across the tidal basin, watching the beachgrass and sea oats sway in the wind. He vividly remembered Greg's hoarse whisper of not being able to feel his legs and having to carry him across the open battlefield to a more protected area. He still dreamed about his hands being slicked with Greg's blood. Yeah, he'd like to see Nightcrawler with a bullet in his head, too. Nightcrawler had been one of the most prolific bomb makers during U.S. operations in Afghanistan, but he hadn't been operational since he'd coordinated the ambush on Greg's team as they'd traveled to dispose of a weapons cache.

"Hopefully, he's six feet under and he never pokes his head up again," Ryan said, then stood. "Come on, man. Let's go inside. It's bleedin' cold out here."

"I'll be along in a few minutes."

"No. Come on. You don't need to be alone out here, nursing that bottle."

Greg then held the bottle up in a toast. "Merry Christmas, Mom and Dad." Then he took a deep swig.

Ryan sat back down beside his friend and took the bottle. After his own swig, he raised it. "To our fallen brothers and sisters."

"Amen, brother."

The two men sat in the cold, passing the bottle back and forth, watching the clouds scurry across the sky and the water lap against the shore.

"So, I bought a boat," Greg said, breaking the silence.

"You do owe me one," Ryan said.

"It's a one-hundred-and-eighty-five-foot Damen Yachting YS-5009. It's one of their new class of ship designed to haul water toys. I'm having Lauderdale Marine Center in Fort Lauderdale do a bunch of retrofitting to make it a state-of-the-art salvage vessel. It will have elevators and other accessibility stuff so I can get around on it. I want to get back on the water with you."

Ryan was torn. He had planned to set sail with Emily and make a life together, but Greg was offering him a tempting alternative. Stuffing his hands into his pockets, he said, "Emily and I are headed to Fort Lauderdale."

"I know." Greg smiled. "I want you to supervise the retrofit. Lauderdale Marine has a berth for *Huntress*. It's free, so you'll have more money to throw away on your wedding."

"I think I need to have a discussion with Shelly ...."

Greg held up a finger. "Don't you dare."

With a smile, Ryan put his arm around his friend's shoulder and raised the bottle of tequila. "To the future."

ABOUT THE AUTHOR

Evan Graver is the author of the Ryan Weller Thriller Series. Before becoming a write, he worked in construction, as a security guard, a motorcycle and car technician, a property manager, and in the scuba industry. He served in the U.S. Navy as an aviation electronics technician until they medically retired him following a motorcycle accident which left him paralyzed. He found other avenues of adventure: riding ATVs, downhill skiing, skydiving, and bungee jumping. His passions are scuba diving and writing. He lives in Hollywood, Florida, with his wife and son.

WHATS NEXT :

If you liked *Dark Prey* or any of Evan's other books, please leave him a review on Amazon.

If you would like to receive a *free* Ryan Weller Thriller Short Story, please visit www.evangraver.com and sign up for Evan's newsletter. You can learn more about Evan, his writing, and his characters.

Made in the USA
Monee, IL
15 April 2021